THE ABYSS BETWEEN

SARA GHERASIM

ELYSIAN

THE ABYSS BETWEEN

Sara Gherasim

The Holy Bible, English Standard Version. ESV® Text Edition: 2016. Copyright © 2001 by Crossway Bibles, a publishing ministry of Good News Publishers.

ISBN: 979-8-9896262-5-0 (softcover)
ISBN: 979-8-9896262-6-7 (hardcover)
ISBN: 979-8-9896262-7-4 (ebook)

Library of Congress Control Number: 2025920353
Print information available on the last page
Elysian Publishing rev. Date: 12/13/2025

For all the people who don't think they can;
know that with Jesus, all things are possible.

Hebrews 13:2

Table of Contents

I

ALL HAIL

This was the day that I was going to die. After countless missions, hundreds of attacks, and endless dances evading death, it was finally here.

It had been over fifty days since I embarked on this voyage to Rome from Jaffa, and three since the storm began. The tumultuous sea claimed us as her enemy and was trying to do anything in her power to bring us down. The deck filled with water and was emptied just as quickly through the holes along the base of the floor. The ancient rigging held quite well, considering the conditions, but that wasn't something that gave me much comfort. We were in death's hold, just waiting for the final blow to strike. One strong wave and the ship could be overturned, leaving us all to fend for ourselves in the raging sea.

There were over a hundred people on this vessel, crew members and regular passengers alike. We were all spread about on the ship, but once the skies turned dark and the waves grew, the sailors made us board underneath, grumbling that we would be in their way if we didn't. I, for one, was quite content to be below, not being able to see what was going on. In most cases, I did like to be in control; but deep down I knew that there was nothing that I could do to solve this bad weather. The only thing being above deck would accomplish is heightening my anxiety of death.

So instead, I chose the company of the people down below. Their whispers alone would not have been heard over the roar of the sea or the creaking of the wooden boat, but as they joined together, each sending prayers to their own gods, the cabin hummed like a beehive. All were praying their prayers, all except me and this other girl beside me, both of us secure along the edge of the ship. I hadn't spoken to anyone since taking port at Jaffa, but I feared that if I didn't talk to someone soon, I would give in to my own horrors.

"Tell me, what's your secret to your clear calmness? I don't think I've heard a sound out of you since this storm started."

She chuckled, brushing her head covering and braided brown hair over her shoulder. "I don't know if it's a secret. But I put my trust in Adonai in heaven that whatever He wills will happen, so why should I worry about it."

"I see," I noted. "Do you think Adonai might give us a break from this? Otherwise, I just might be having a second taste of my earlier meal."

She laughed again, pulling her knees into her chest.

"I'm Rivka," I turned.

"My name is Sariel," she gave a nod with a sweet smile to accompany it. "Where are you traveling from?"

I pursed my lips, giving a tight smile, wondering how she might react if I told her the truth. That I was traveling from two thousand years in the future and that I had only come to this time because my partner in the Mossad, Thana, had betrayed me, sided with our enemies and left me to die in a cave.

"Jerusalem."

"I take it you were there for Passover?"

"Yes."

"I heard there was quite a commotion there this year."

She was right. Rather than just having a simple Passover celebration, Yeshua, the teacher from Galilee, was crucified. I would know, I was there, there for everything. The guilt afterwards gnawed at me, the fact that everything I tried in order to stop it had failed.

"What takes you to Rome?" Sariel spoke again.

The water interrupted, slapping aggressively against the side of the ship, knocking the boat slightly sideways. Screams filled the cabin, some of the people sliding against the wood floor. Sariel and I held tighter to the rope that was nailed to the wall, keeping us secure in this spot. I didn't normally give into fear, I was an assassin after all. But this… this was different. There was absolutely nothing I could do to control it. I couldn't go and kill the water, I couldn't bribe the thundering rain, all I could do was sit and wait. Sit, wait, and hope that this murderous sea would not drag us down as her next victim. Pulling myself forward, I had to keep my mind occupied.

"A man," I answered, giving a queasy smile. Not just any man—Evander, a Tribune in the Roman army. We had met when he saved me from a ferocious lion in the desert and kept running into each other after that. Just before he left to return to Rome, he told me about his feelings for me and asked me to accompany him. I hesitated, leaving me to miss his ship and find my own way to Rome, thus relying on the hope that I would even be able to locate him in the current largest city on earth, let alone empire.

"Ahh," the corners of her lips turned upward. "Your husband or…?"

"No," I replied, "but there is some interest there."

"That really is wonderful," she nodded, her sincerity seeming real. "What tribe is he from?"

Hesitating, I debated if a lie would be better, but didn't see what the harm was in the truth. Besides, before I had time to fully process the situation, the ship crashed against another wave, some water spilling in from the door flaps to the deck.

"He's actually a Roman," I said, tight-lipped, fingers locked firmly around the rope. "Much to every Jews chagrin."

She nodded, briefly, before adjusting herself against the wall. "While it might be an unpopular opinion, I believe we are all God's children, Jew and Gentile alike. Even Romans."

3

I was caught off guard by her progressive thinking and could tell that she was being genuine in the fact. An odd response for this era, but one I was grateful for.

"Anyways, he doesn't know I'm coming. I'm planning on surprising him."

"Alone? With no escort?"

I paused, trying to come up with an answer, but she interrupted. "I understand, I myself am traveling alone. Improper, but not unheard of," she rested her hand on my shoulder, giving it a small squeeze. "Just make sure that if someone asks you, you are traveling with someone, and they are not far off—for your own protection."

"Thank you for the advice," I said sincerely, not wanting to make any slip ups. For all my weeks being stuck in this time, I kept failing to keep in mind how peculiar it was for my traveling alone and things of that nature.

"Do you know where to find him once we dock?" Sariel asked.

"No, not exactly. I know his father's trade, so I suppose I'll just start there. It can't be that difficult to find him."

"Once you do find him, what will you do if he doesn't react well to your surprise?"

The thought had briefly crossed my mind at the start of the journey, but I pushed it away almost as soon as it entered. He asked me to go with him to Jerusalem and not enough time had passed in order for him to change his mind. Granted, the entire trip from Jerusalem to Rome would take about three months, but there would only be a day or two that didn't overlap for us in Rome. Moreover, I know the connection that we have. It's stronger than just a passing whim.

"He will react well. Honestly, I think—no, *know*—he will be happy to see me."

4

"Then I'm glad to hear it and pray that Adonai will go with you in your journey," Sariel said prayerfully, hazel eyes soft.

"And you?" I countered politely. "What takes you to Rome?"

"I'm going to visit a friend. She is having some trouble in her life, even if she cannot admit to it, so I am going to assist her in any way that I can."

"That's very kind of you. Do you mind if I ask what kind of trouble?" I questioned, trying my best to keep my mind occupied.

Sariel paused, seeming to choose her words carefully. "It's a delicate situation. She is struggling with her faith and a person from her past who hurt her gravely is stirring up trouble once again. I'm going to offer words of encouragement and to help her in any other need that arises."

"Well, you seem to be a very good encourager. I'm sure she'll be overjoyed at your company."

"From your lips to Adonai's ears," she breathed, readjusting her grip on the rope. My hand throbbed from holding the rough rope so tightly and for so long. It bothered me, but not enough to make me want to let go. Sariel took breaks here and there as we spoke, waiting to grab hold when she felt the uneasiness of the waves.

I opened my mouth to ask her another question, but something else happened. My stomach turned, feeling the ship move up on a tall wave. I braced myself for the inevitable impact of us coming back down, unknowingly gripping Sariel's hand tightly. As soon as the thought finished, the act transpired, sending the people into chaotic screams. I clenched my teeth hard to keep myself from calling out, the sound of crying children percolated my ears, sending the hairs on my neck up. It all happened in a matter of seconds, but the waiting made it feel like an eternity. Eternity was brought to an end and the ship leaned forward once again, crashing into the water before finally becoming horizontal.

The smell of urine was strong, people being unable to control their fear or their bladders. I was not so far gone as that, but the terror was still there.

"These poor people," Sariel muttered softly under her breath, looking with compassion on the fearful crowd.

Looking back at them, I felt Sariel's own compassion and the people's anxiety. Their prayerful hums grew louder, the collaboration of different gods' names became mixed in the fray. But never did I expect the voice of a quiet girl to join the mix.

"All of you!" Sariel called out, trying to grab their attention, but none paid her any heed, continuing to pray to their own gods. "All of you!" she yelled louder this time, holding the rope to help try and keep her balance as she stood. The people quieted at the sight; their minds momentarily distracted.

"Do not be afraid! The Lord is with us and will protect us in our journey! Have no fear!"

The people quietly hesitated, but hope began to fill their eyes, taking in Sariel's words of comfort.

Seeing that she had their attention, she continued. "We will pray to The Lord, God of Israel, and He will see us safely to Rome!"

Many nodded their heads in agreement, each ceasing their prayers to their false idols and turning their words into imploration before Adonai. It was peculiar, seeing people of all different races bowing their heads at the behest of this Jewish woman, urging them to follow the true God. Whether it was out of fear for their lives or seeing that their prayers to their own gods were left wanting, it made no difference, they all sent up their new prayers.

What was even more unexpected is what happened moments after. Like a mother quieting their child, the seas calmed as well, the ship slowly taking its place back to the horizontal.

"Praise Adonai, He has heard our prayers! Let us give Him thanks!" Sariel exclaimed, reclaiming her seat as she sent words of thanksgiving to God, hands raised. The hum filled the cabin once again, but each with their own words of thankfulness to the God who saved them.

I let out my own sigh of relief, glad to be done with the experience. Once everyone finished their hail of praise, Sariel turned her attention back to me, letting out a deep breath.

"I think your friend will be in very good hands indeed," I looked at her in bewilderment, never seeing something quite like it before.

<hr />

After that, Sariel and I spent much of our time together for the rest of the journey. We took comfort in each other's company, two women traveling alone. I especially liked her because she didn't press me for any information. Anything that I didn't want to speak of, like my family situation and what not, she would let go and not think anything of it. It was refreshing. She herself wasn't an overly talkative person, but I gathered that she had great morals, was calm, delicate, and the true model of a good Jewish girl. It almost made me a little envious, being so strong in... well, everything.

Throughout the journey, we focused on another challenge—learning ancient Greek. The thought hadn't originally occurred to me that most of the languages spoken in Rome would be ones that I didn't understand. Granted, when speaking with Evander in Jerusalem, he spoke the tongue of my nation, leaving me with general ease. But now, if I was to be self-sufficient, I would have to add another language to my collection.

Sariel had mentioned how her father had taught her ancient Greek—although, I suppose for her it would just be considered Greek. From what I could gather, unlike many men of the time, her father believed that women were precious as God's creation and wanted to give his daughters the best chance out in the world. It worked out well for me, considering I was fluent in Modern Greek, giving me a base; but ancient Greek was fairly different. Difficult would probably be a simple word to describe it, the grammar specifically. But we practiced and learned for the remaining leg of our journey.

Every day that we practiced, I was reminded of one simple fact, not that I forgot it often—I'm from the future. With each incorrect sentence I spoke, it was like a flashing sign before my eyes, a constant alarm.

Attached to the reminder were questions and a constant struggle of whether I should tell Evander the truth. How would this affect us? Affect him? Would it? Would it be a benefit or a hindrance? My only conclusion, whether it was a wise one or not, was to only tell him if it ever came up naturally. I was betting on the fact that it wouldn't.

Either way, I'm quite the expert on keeping secrets.

———————— ❖ ————————

"We're docking in Portus! Make ready!" the captain called out to everyone on the deck.

The sun was just beginning to rise, making its appearance slowly over the docks. I took a long, quiet breath as I looked onto the port, seeing just how busy Rome was going to be like. If the hustle and bustle of Portus was this crazy, I could only imagine the magnificence of the city with the greatest power. Vendors were all along the shore while crew members loaded and unloaded their heavy cargo from the ships. People weaved through the crowds, looking for their ships to board.

Sariel gave my shoulder a quick squeeze before moving past me and walking down the planked walkway, her covered hair swinging between her shoulder blades. Sucking in the salty air, I gathered any feeling of skepticism and followed her lead.

The thick wood still bent as we walked down, giving small bounces, but it only gave me more determination.

I was here. Evander was here. We were about to start our lives together.

Reaching the bottom, I followed Sariel to the other side of the docks. Our shoulders rubbed against men's sweaty arms and stiff tunics. The sun hadn't reached its midday heat, but the aroma of a full day's work already seemed to be in the sky. Finding a calm corner, we secured our bags on our shoulders. We had determined that we were going to travel to Rome together, and while Sariel may not know much about Rome, she knew enough about the ancient world that the knowledge would be useful for me.

We discussed the possibility of hiring someone to take us in a cart of some form but decided against it. Since we had docked early in the morning, if we left now, we could probably make it to Rome before the sun set, maybe even a few hours before, leaving me with enough time to find Evander. But before our journey continued, there was something I would have to do. Not wanting to divulge too much information to my new friend, I explained that it would be in our best interest to divide and conquer; as they say, when in Rome, do as the Romans. She would purchase the supplies needed for the road while I would search for Evander at the docks, as well as getting directions and other important information. With his family in the ship business, this would be my best chance for finding a lead, even if they were war ships and potentially not even docked. Moreover, it gave me a chance to practice my ancient Greek.

Going from front to front, I asked about Evander and his family, but the information gathered was almost futile. The grimy men confirmed that his father's boats would dock here, but that they hadn't seen Evander or his father. When I asked them to point out their spot or ship, they would either ignore me, tell me to stop bothering them, or worse, begin asking deeper questions. For most, I couldn't help shake the feeling that they were withholding information out of indifference, but what was there to do that could force them to talk? I wasn't going to bribe them, not yet anyways, because I had enough information to track him to Rome. This would have just been the easier route had they been compliant. True romance needs its challenges, that's how you know you earned it. That thought gave me hope.

Pushing past the last of the ruffians in the tight space, I found Sariel making her last purchase. She had bought grapes, nuts, and water from the vendors on the dock. They were grossly overpriced, but Sariel and I split the cost, agreeing that it was needed.

"Ready?" she asked, her few bags already secured against her shoulders.

Giving one last look at the ships, I gave a single nod, turning and taking my real first steps towards Evander.

The terrain to Rome wasn't too difficult, a path was clearly marked leading us to the capital of the world. Even so, the odd rock found its way into my sandal a time or two. Thoughts of stories I had heard about Rome and its people kept coming, making it hard to believe that I was living in the reality of it. Most of our training, mainly military training, in fact, had been based on the knowledge of Roman tactics. Seeing it in the original flesh would be a surreal experience.

Sariel and I kept silent on the walk, each concentrated on our destination. When we did speak, it was polite comments to travelers walking the road with us, exchanging greetings. Sweat trickled down my brow as the sun rose, bringing its warmth. Using an extra cloth I had to wipe it away, I squinted into the dusty distance, thinking of the coming events.

My mind contemplated the different ways our reunion would play out. Would Evander be stunned, too overwhelmed to speak? Would he shout in excitement, twirling me in the air? Or would it be a soft embrace, his arms holding me tight as he buried his face in my neck? On and on, my thoughts raced. Frankly, I had never imagined myself in a relationship, always putting my career and the safety of my nation first. But with Evander... it was different.

Moving quickly, we made better time than I had even expected. Sariel may look small, but her shorter legs kept up with my quick pace, having us arrive in Rome just after noon.

Looking at the stone homes placed along the city's edge, I bit my lip. The speed of my heart began to increase, exhilaration and nerves bubbling inside. Sariel and I placed our bags on the ground and sat beside them, dust rising as we gave ourselves a moment of rest and re-energize.

Letting the cool liquid dribble down my throat from my leather canteen, I let out a sigh in satisfaction, wiping the corner of my mouth with my thumb. Sariel did the same, scooping a little extra into her hand before dabbing it across her rosy cheeks. That's when my eyes caught something peeking from beneath her veil, tangled in her hair. Reaching over, I plucked out a bird's feather, its creamy white fluff soft against my fingers.

"How'd that get in there?" I laughed, earning a chuckle from Sariel.

After we both finished the last of our water and food, she rose, her long braided hair swaying from side to side, now feather free.

"Thank you for coming with me this far," I said to her, pulling myself up. "It was nice to have a friend on this long road."

"Rivka, I'm blessed to have met you," she exclaimed, pulling my hands into her own, giving them a soft shake. "I pray all goes well with Evander and that the Lord will guide your steps."

"Thank you, Sariel. And I hope everything with your friends turns out alright," I countered, wanting to leave her with a nice word as well.

"Lord willing," she gave a soft squeeze before letting go, picking up her small pack from the ground and adjusting the linen around her shoulder. "If you need anything at all, Rivka, you'll find me near the temple of Minerva. That's where I'm staying while in Rome."

"Thank you again," I said simply once more.

Her soft smile was her reply as she made her way into the road, her blue linen dress countering against the stone walls and road. I watched her, realizing that the next part and final leg of my own journey was beginning.

Sariel stopped, looking back at me one last time, giving a small wave. I raised my hand, wishing her well before she turned and walked into the crowd that was forming in the city streets. I watched until her small figure completely disappeared. Giving another of many deep, shaky breaths, I looked into the unknown. I pulled my bag firmly against my shoulder, my fingers turning white from my grip.

"I'm coming, Evander."

II

PAX ROMANA

Rome was nothing like I had been imagining for months. I had been here before, several times in fact, both for mission and pleasure alike. But as I looked at it now, I knew that everything was completely different. The homes and buildings were all made of stone and some form of mud, lining up the streets that led into the city. From the edge, I couldn't even see the Colosseum; the staple of Rome, the staple of Italy, a guide for the weary traveler. Instead, I saw apartments and villas lining up the streets. At least, I assumed they were apartments. The cobblestone ground could hardly be seen between the foot traffic and street performers. Small crowds circled around acrobats in action, men with knives doing daring tricks while coins were tossed at them.

Purposeful, I adjusted the leather belt around my waist and began to walk into the city. The variety of people all along the roads made it a near tight fit as I made my way inwards. Women and men were being carried around on daybeds, covered with thin linen as their slaves worked heavily to take them to their destination. I caught glimpses of their faces as the breeze blew against the curtains, their ornate clothing and hair hard to miss.

I had given myself some time to think before I made my way into the city of how I was going to locate Evander. First, I would go into the center of the city, the marketplace, and work my way outwards. All kinds of people could be found there, both low and high, so that would be the most productive place to start. After that, I would leave it up to Adonai, as Sariel would put it, and just hope that I wouldn't have to go much farther than that.

It didn't take me too long to reach my destination—the entrance to the forum. Pulling my focus from the roaring noise escaping the plaza and my damp hair sticking to the top of my neck, I walked forward into the hubbub of the plaza. Hundreds upon hundreds of people were walking to and fro, some behind vendor carts with their sellable goods. Fruits, grain, jewelry, material, animals, and a host of other items decorated the tables. People huddled under the several canopies that hung over the tables, providing shade to the vendors, their things, and their customers.

My ears went in and out as I heard dozens of languages being spoken. From Greek to Aramaic to words that sounded awfully similar to Spanish and German. But my attention was really caught when two people began to haggle over what seemed to be a sack of grain. It wasn't the haggling that piqued my interest, but in what language they were doing it in. Here, in the market of Rome, were two men having a conversation in Latin — a sound I never expected to hear beyond the walls of a classroom or Catholic church in modern day. Though Latin hasn't been used as a conversational language for over a thousand years, its rhythm and structure were familiar to me. Being fluent in more than ten languages, I could catch the general sense of their words, though the pronunciation and phrasing carried an unmistakable echo of another age.

Rubbing my clammy palms together, I knew I had to get to work if I was ever going to find Evander. The best thing that I could do would be to just start asking. My eyes went from person to person in the market, looking at who might best know. They landed on a larger woman in front of an olive stand who was lifting a basket onto the table.

"Excuse me," I asked, walking up to her.

"What do you want, girl?" she said roughly, turning towards me as she pulled her slipping shawl over her shoulder.

14

Her abruptness caught me slightly off guard, but I continued. "Do you know where I could find a Tribune of Rome? His name is Evander."

"Am I to know every leader of Rome," the old woman scoffed. "Get away from here, you're blocking the way for customers!" she pushed past me roughly, moving me to the side.

Irked, I opened my mouth. "Do you treat all your customers this way?"

"Did you buy something?" she raised her gray eyebrow.

"Well… not yet," I set my jaw as I reached into my bag, grabbing some coins and smacking them down onto the table, taking a handful of olives.

"Thank you for your business," she said nicely, a forced grin on her face.

"And the information?"

"Never heard of him," she snipped. "Next!"

Being pushed aside by the growing crowd behind me, I watched as she had no problem with customers, even with her sour disposition. Huffing, I dropped the olives into my bag, letting the interaction roll past me and moved onto the next person, changing my strategy.

"Excuse me, do you know the Marcellus family? Their business has to do with the making of ships?"

The short, fat man paused, looking at me through his small eyes. "Of course, everyone knows them."

I smiled, delighted that I found someone. "Do you know where I could find them? Specifically, their son?"

He gave a dubious smirk, scoffing into the air. "Of course you'd be looking for him," he trailed before he too pushed past me.

"Wait!" I tried calling after him, but he waved his hand dismissively before pressing forward.

My delight was quickly replaced with discouragement, making me turn my face back into the abounding crowd. The people seemed to understand my Greek clearly enough, meaning that their rudeness might just be the way the people of this city were. Clenching my fists in determination, I knew that I at least was on the right track and couldn't let two grouchy people hinder my resolve. For the next hour, I went from person to person, asking about Evander and his family, but the people of Rome all seemed fixed on keeping the information from me. They were either too busy to hear what I had to say, not thinking I was worth their precious time, or were skeptical of me as a foreigner. For all they knew, I was a paying customer. In fact, in some instances, I did buy some of their goods, but none offered up any information, just as with the first woman. Reaching the other end of the marketplace, I rubbed the back of my neck, feeling some tendrils of my bunned hair against my fingers.

"You're looking for the Marcellus family?" a young voice said behind me.

Turning, my eyes landing on a teenage boy, dark pieces of hair framing his face. "Yes, I am."

"I know where they are, I can take you to them."

Studying him for a moment, hesitance crept into my senses. I wanted to believe him, but something seemed off.

"Alright," I responded slowly.

"For a price," he interjected rapidly, making his intentions known.

At this point, no one seemed as if they would relent any information. This boy, at least, was somewhat willing to help as long as he got something in return. Pursing my lips, I scanned the area, ensuring that this boy was acting alone. I'd have to take my chances if I had any hopes of finding Evander in this ever-growing city.

"How much?"

Placing a hand on his leather belt, he responded. "Seven denarii."

It wasn't cheap, a single one was a day's wage. At least, that's what Sariel had mentioned once on the boat. One of the things we had discussed was the currency system in Rome, which bode well for me now.

"A little steep, don't you think?" I haggled.

"That's my price, take it or leave it. But you'll only have the gods help to find this family you're looking for."

I looked at his tan face, my skepticism growing, but what other choice did I have than to follow him. I couldn't go and knock on every door in Rome. Well, maybe I could, but that would be both ridiculous and exhausting.

I exhaled sharply, resigned. "Fine," I stepped forward. "Take me to them."

"Payment first," he insisted, his eyes casually looking around the market.

My shoulders tensed. "I'll pay you when we find them."

"Woman, I—"

"Take it or leave it," I said acerbically. If he was telling the truth, only then would he get his money. If he was lying or planning a trick, I'd give him seven seconds to breathe before ripping out his lying tongue. Besides, I didn't have quite that much, but I'm sure Evander would help once we found him.

He clenched and unclenched his jaw, watching me for a moment before finally speaking. "Agreed. Come this way," he turned and started making his way through the crowd. He moved fast, like a rat, weaving between the horde of people. The average person might have had trouble following, but not me. He couldn't lose me even if he tried, especially now.

We went on that way for several minutes, the boy checking every few moments to see if I was still behind him, before he finally reached an alleyway, and turned into it.

"We walk up this way for a little and then we'll be almost to their home," he said, waiting for me as I walked near him.

Nodding in response, I followed him up the road, my sandals slapping against it. My eyes looked back from the road to the boy as we trekked. He couldn't be more than sixteen or seventeen, but I suppose in this day and age he would practically be considered a man. His scrawny bones and baggy tunic would suggest otherwise, even though he was about a head taller than me. Was it fair to call him a boy? Before I could even answer my own question, he stopped in front of me, turning and blocking me from moving forward.

"What—" I began before I realized what was going on. The cold pointed steel grazed my covered stomach, its threat imminent. Glancing down at his knife, my jaw set.

"So that's how it's going to be, hmm," I noted softly.

"Give me your valuables and I'll let you go on your way," he demanded firmly, his mouth set.

I blinked slowly, tightening my jaw.

"Quickly!" he insisted, pressing his blade closer towards my stomach, hoping to remind me of his weapon and that he wasn't afraid to use it.

But he was afraid. His eyes darted back and forth as he waited for me to give him all the money I had, a slight tremor was also noticeable on the blade.

I tucked a tendril of hair that had escaped from beneath my head covering behind my ear before moving my hand near my money satchel in my bag. The boy's eyes watched me as I slowly moved it down. But instead of going for the money, my fingers locked on his wrist, slamming it down against my knee to loosen the knife from his grasp before spinning him around, holding his arm high on his back, his face pressing against the stone wall. He gave a cry out in pain before biting his lip and closing his eyes, his nostrils flaring.

"Want to tell me where I can find them now?" I whispered by his ear, the smell of his sweat filling my nose.

He said nothing, just giving a small whimper from my toughened grasp.

"I guess you want to do this the hard way," I mumbled to him, pulling his arm higher and placing my knee at the base of his spine, applying pressure.

"Okay, okay, stop!" he cried, his whimpers growing louder. "I don't know where they live—"

I put more pressure.

"But! Wait! But I know where the family business is!"

"Where?" I said firmly, not releasing my hold.

"At the Portus! Outside the city!"

My heart dropped. Had I missed them?

"You're lying," I said through clenched teeth. I knew it was true, but I needed to press him for more information.

"I'm not!" he yelled, "I swear it to all the gods! Someone in their family is always there"

"And if their ships aren't docked?"

"There's always someone there! If not one of them directly, they have a foreman!

Holding my grip a little longer, I waited to see if he would tell me anything else, other than what I had already known. But the blundering fool truly didn't seem to know.

Pressing my knee further into his spine, I put my lips close to his ear, whispering in a warm breath. "If I find out that you lied to me or withheld any information from me, I will find you when you least expect it and feed your bones to the dogs. Is that understood?"

He shook as I said the words but gave a small nod. I held him for one moment longer, making sure my threat had stuck. It seemed to have, as a putrid aroma filled my nostrils. Looking down, I saw the liquid trickling down his leg. Rolling my eyes in disgust, I stepped back and let the boy go free. He didn't waste a second to look back as he ran away, leaving a small puddle and his knife behind.

Bending down beside the urine, I picked up the weapon, studying its excellent craftsmanship. Clearly it had been stolen, the handle was made of gold with adornments carved into it. The grooves fit like a glove in my hand as I twisted it slowly from side to side. The blade was no longer than my palm to index finger, making it a perfect size. Why he still had it and didn't sell it, I wasn't sure. Maybe he just hadn't had a chance yet or was too dense to know how. I kept my eyes on it for another moment before I opened the leather flap of my bag and placed the weapon inside, looking at my surroundings. If this is what the people of Rome were like, who knew when I might need it.

Bringing my mind back to the present, I tried to retrace the steps we had made to go back to the marketplace and start my search all over again. I couldn't help but dwell on the fact as I made my way back that I might have missed Evander while in Portus. When we were there, I stopped at every dock and talked to every person I saw, asking about him and his family and not a single person gave me any information about their whereabouts, only that their ships would dock there. If they were there, I would have seen them, right?

The thought nagged at me until my feet took me into another crowd. Had I made it back to the marketplace? I looked around, but it looked slightly different than before. Instead of fruit stands and their vendors, there seemed to be another form of sale going on here.

The wind blew out of my lungs as it dawned on me what I was seeing. There were stacks and stacks of stands with hundreds of people standing on top of them, all of different races. Some were chained, others had only a tablet hanging from their necks with writing on it. Slowly, I began to make my way through this new type of marketplace.

The slaves looked at me from their downcast positions, making sure the slave trader didn't see. One unfortunate person

20

wasn't as skillful as she thought, no more than ten, before she was hit in the head with the butt of a thick whip.

"I told you not to look at them, you impudent girl!" the man loudly whispered to the pale girl. The tablet around her neck had "Gaul" written on it along with the girl's measurements and experience. My eyes couldn't leave her, even for her sake. The resemblance wasn't particularly similar, but she reminded me of Tamara, remorse covering me. I had left her in good hands, knowing that Chava and *Safta* would look after her like one of their own. But I would never forget the look that little girl gave me before the word "sold" rang through the air.

I watched as an elderly woman waited for the girl as she lay in her daybed, another slave girl fanning her. The slave master grabbed the girl by her arm, took the tablet off her head and dragged her towards the woman. They exchanged goods before the woman went on her way, the young girl following behind. I watched until they disappeared into the crowd, my throat caught.

I had to get out of here.

Shoving past the crowd, I slipped back into the alleyways.

My mind warped as I walked around the city. Some places were clear areas of where the poor and needy resided and others had wealth written all over them, marble steps leading up to their guarded villas. I stopped people who were walking past if they knew of Evander or his family, but again, they gave me no information or only what I already knew.

I tried to push back the thoughts of despair and the fear of never finding him. For all I know, his boat could've sunk on his journey over here—ours almost had, why should his be any different? Still, that wouldn't answer the question of why I wasn't even able to find his family. There were only three possible solutions as to why that was. One, I remembered his family name wrong. Two, I was asking for the wrong class of people. Or three, he had lied to me, and I was just a plain old fool. But that couldn't be, as the names were known here…

The evening sun glistened in the sky as I walked near what seemed to be a political establishment of some kind. There were still a slew of people around, either making their way into it or just walking on the road, like me. Adjacent was a small fountain. Taking a moment, I splashed the cool liquid onto my warm face, eyelids fluttering as the driblets fell off my eyelashes. Rinsing my hands and back of my neck, I used the bottom of my head covering to wipe away the remaining water, now revived. As the water of the fountain stilled, I peered at the reflection looking back at me. My dark hair was now tucked neatly under the scarf, cheeks rosy, eyebrows remarkably trim. Pursing my ruddy lips, I pulled myself together, reminding myself of who I was and my purpose.

I couldn't lose hope. I would search until nightfall, and if I still hadn't found him, I would find myself accommodations. Maybe I could even go and find Sariel. She did say that she was near the Temple of Minerva. Compelling myself forward, I began my task again.

As I pondered the thought over the next half hour, I realized that I was back at a different temple near the marketplace. Walking up a couple of the steps, I could see the vendors still there. Sighing, I sat on the temple steps, taking a small rest before I continued my pursuit. Drinking some water from my pouch, my eyes bounced from person to person, their Roman style still somewhat bizarre to me. They all seemed to have either unique headdresses, elaborate hairstyles, or clothing options that were ostentatious. All except for two men. They alone seemed to be in simple white tunics, their hair normally styled—while, granted, it was the women who wore the excessive hairstyles. I watched their backs for a moment, curious what made them the calm in a sea of crazy. Then they turned towards each other, engaging in conversation.

My heart raced, throat tightened, and my breath caught. The veil of blindness was lifted off my eyes.

There he was.

There was Evander.

He looked different here. Maybe it was the Roman leisure wear he wore, the milky material reflecting against his tan skin, giving him a sense of vulnerability. As if he was no longer a Roman Tribune in charge, but rather just an average citizen, here for the day-to-day tasks.

Mustering my courage, I rose slowly from the steps. Silence surrounded me as my feet rapped against stone, steadily lowering me to the ground. My tongue stuck to the roof of my mouth, dry and scratchy like sand, despite the water I had just sipped. With olive hands outstretched, I pushed my way through the stiff crowd, eyes never leaving his broad shoulders. Bodies smacked against me as I moved closer, but I hardly felt them.

What was he going to say?

As the one thought circled my mind, he calmly began to move forward, lengthening the distance between me and him. The concept that I could lose him again brought me back, ears vibrating with sound.

Detaching my tongue from its perch, I let out a raspy cry, "Evander!"

Still, he moved forward, his head downcast.

The animals of the market bleated while vendors exhibited their goods, drowning my hoarse voice into the void.

Trying to muster all the liquid I could, I gave a hard swallow and tried one more time before I would lose him to the crowd. "Evander!"

Abruptly, his head perked up but still faced the opposite direction. He paused only a mere few seconds, but it was enough for me to shorten the space between us. The knots in my stomach tightened with each step I took closer. Weaving through the people, ignoring the smell of body odor mixed with spices—my eyes were locked on him.

I called one last time and he stopped, head scanning to find the voice that was naming him. The man he was with continued on while Evander analyzed, providing me enough time to seal the gap, giving a final push.

Now there was nothing between me and him. Time seemed to halt, silent and unmoving. Standing directly behind him, all the words I had prepared floated out of my mind. My mouth hung slightly open as I tried to regain them, but to no avail. Instead, giving a last swallow, I lifted my hand, tapping it against his shoulder.

He turned, an annoyed expression on his face.

"Yes?" he asked. But as he realized who I was, his eyes widened and a new expression took over.

For being one who doesn't express her emotion, I stepped out of my comfort zone for the sheer fact of my overwhelming sense of joy. You know you really miss someone when you crave something as simple as the sound of their voice.

Without hesitation, my arms wrapped around him, and I buried my face in the curve of his neck, a sense of peace washing over me like warm light.

It was like I was lost, and he was the map home.

He must have been in shock, because his arms laid numb at his side, his body tensing. I only had a moment to observe it before he finally wrapped his arms securely around me, his hand gripping my tunic.

A shaky breath escaped my lips.

He pulled back, hands on my shoulders as he searched my eyes. His were filled with happiness and disbelief.

But as quickly as that look came, it left.

Instead of the warm, semi-romantic dialogue that I was expecting, an awkward, almost embarrassed, one was given.

"Rivka, what are you doing here?"

At first, I thought it must be a joke, but I saw no humor in his eyes.

"What do you mean? I'm here for you."

His lips pursed, body tensing once again as he said nothing.

I slowly took one of his hands off my shoulder. "Are you... are you not happy that I came?"

People knocked into us as they walked, pressing me closer to him. Hand on his chest, I pushed myself back.

"No... Yes... It's not that. I..." he fumbled over his words, his eyes wandered rapidly around the crowd, as if he was looking to see if anyone had seen our hug.

"Evander?" I asked, unsure of what else to say. Thankfully a somewhat welcome distraction to this strained exchange came. The man who he was speaking to prior to our reunion came into my sight, laying a hand on Evander's shoulder while he looked at me, clearing his throat.

Turning, Evander seemed to become even more uncomfortable. "Sir, this is, uh," Evander stammered as he looked from me to the man. "This is Rivka, a woman I met during my time in Jerusalem."

Vague.

Giving a small smile, I nodded politely to the man, curious as to who he was.

"Rivka," Evander stammered again, "this is my father."

III

HONEYED DATES

"Your father?"

Being caught off guard was the simplest way to explain my feelings, even though I shouldn't have been. The thought had occurred to me, obviously, that Evander would be in Rome with his family. After all, this was their home. But seeing his family in the flesh put something different in the air.

His father said nothing, just a civil expression resting on his face. My throat hitched and Evander looked equally as wordless. The hustle and bustle of the market was the only sense of an icebreaker. Unsure if I should extend my hand for a handshake, lean in for a hug as is done back home or most European countries, I inelegantly did both, leaving one hand somewhat extended with the other raised. Only Evander and his father both just looked at me, uncertain at what I was trying to do. To be honest, so was I.

"It's nice to meet you," I said almost expertly in Greek, hoping that that would be enough to save me from my embarrassment as I pulled back to myself.

"It's a pleasure, *Rivka*," he stumbled on my name.

"Rivka," I said once more, politely correcting him, giving me some comfort that neither of us were perfect.

He nodded. "Please accept my apology. I'm Evander's father, Vinicius."

I gave a toothy grin. "Nice to meet you."

This stupid look plastered on my face was so out of character, but this was the most uncomfortable I had been in my entire life—and I killed men for a living. Was this one awkward exchange enough to strip me of my common sense and identity?

As quickly as our words came, they left, leaving us in more silence. Evander's shoulders stiffened as his eyes shifted to anywhere but me. Vinicius calmly gazed at his son, a courteous smile that held riddles on his face. Frankly, this was nothing like how I imagined it turning out. I tried to think of things to talk about, *something*, but my mind hyperfixed on everything that was going wrong, and Evander wasn't helping all that much.

"Did you just arrive in Rome?" Vinicius asked, finally breaking the tension.

"Yes, the ship I was traveling on docked this morning, I made it into the city around midday."

"You made excellent time. Then you must be exhausted and famished," Vinicius said, his deep voice bellowing.

"Yes, I suppose," I replied unsure, even though it felt like my stomach was practically caving in from the hunger I built up from hours of searching. My back was in no better condition, stiff as the wooden planks I'd been sleeping on for months.

He turned to Evander, raising his hand to firmly grip Evander's shoulder again. "Why don't we all go back to our villa, you must join my family for the evening meal," his gray hair reflected against the beaming sun.

"No, I—" Evander interrupted, but stopped there. Whether that was due to the mixed emotions that were written across my face or his father's now noticeably tight grip, I was torn.

His father gave him a hard look. "Let's leave no time to waste."

"I don't want to be a burden," I stated softly. Evander was the reason I came, but this encounter was the last thing that I was expecting. The sense of unwantedness and perturbation wouldn't leave me, making me all the more hesitant.

"Nonsense," Vinicius replied again, his voice a commanding presence.

Almost feeling as if there wasn't much choice in the matter, I gave a simple nod accompanied with the standing smile that hadn't quite left my face, only changed in size, mainly due to the fact of my discomfort. From there, I followed them through the market and towards their home.

—— ✤ ——

The journey back to his villa was an unsettling one, to say the least. His father was polite for a couple of moments, asking about my journey to Rome, but quickly reverted his attention back to Evander, who, on the other hand, hardly said a word to me, let alone even looked in my direction. Whether it was to keep his father's attention from me or his own, I couldn't pin point. Maybe it was both. I just kept internally groaning, thinking that I might have made a mistake in coming here. That being the case, I didn't dare make the first move and direct the conversation towards him.

But that did give me time to take measure of both men. Vinicius's veins were visible below the sleeves of his white linen tunic, resting against his large muscles. His chest was proud and the lines on his face were hard. The juxtaposition between his station, calloused hands, and tan skin was interesting. Being a businessman, having a seat on the Senate, *and* having the look of a common person was a combination of things that were probably not the norm. The only people whom I saw looking like him were the sailors on the boat, the slaves that worked in the fields on the road to Rome, and the soldiers patrolling the streets. There was more to this man than met the eye.

Evander matched his father, in a younger form. He was a soldier, though, so his muscled arms and calloused hands were explicable. His hair had grown since I left him in Jerusalem, the front honey tendrils coming near his eyebrows. They both shared the same green eyes.

It seemed to me that Vinicius was a unique man, even for this time where for many people being physical in one form or another was a natural way of life, that he kept his physique in check. But it put another question into my mind—if he was a man of hard work and strength, what would make him so against his son joining the military? Was his outer appearance a mask for an inwardly soft man, fearful of losing his son to death, or was it something else? Maybe he himself had some sort of past.

I pondered the thought until we arrived at their home. My lower lip dropped, my eyes looking up as we stopped at the base. Their villa was considerably large: cream stones stood as its foundation and walls, with two rock solid posts holding the small awning that covered the steps into the home. It was like nothing I had ever seen before. The destroyed remnants of these homes in Italy gave no indication on just how magnificent these places actually were... or should I say are?

Vinicius led me up the few steps into the entrance as Evander gestured for me to go before him, ignoring the two armed men on the sides. The solid bronze front door was massive, at least twice my size, and showed signs of its strength as Vinicius pushed it forward. Walking inside and entering the small square entrance with two smaller doors acting as a partition into the next room, Evander's father paused, turning towards his son.

"I will bring your mother and sister into the atrium," his father said quickly, giving me a small, tight smile before turning and entering the home. Evander waited until his father left before extending his arm towards the bigger room that lay before us, indicating for me to go in.

We passed the braided doors, two more large men on either side, guarding. It took my eyes a moment to adjust as we passed from the bright sun into the shade, but as they did, they only widened at the size of the room. The four large pillars on the sides held the high ceiling, with a small opening in the center, letting in just enough light. The walls were covered with statues and portrait busts, lampstands placed variously throughout.

29

I momentarily forgot about Evander as I stepped closer towards one of the statues, admiring the intricate detail. A woman with a veil covering her face, her hand pressed against her chest. Giving off a small breath, I couldn't help but relate to her. Having to hide her thoughts, feelings, and dreams that were deep in her heart… always putting duty first.

Evander cleared his throat, pulling me from my thoughts as I turned to face him. "Rivka, please allow me to introduce my mother, Lucrezia, and my sister, Aura."

I gave a soft smile as I looked upon these two women of great beauty who appeared next to Evander. His mother looked quite young to have a son of Evander's age, her auburn hair pulled delicately around her face, enhancing her deep brown eyes. The sister was no different, as she just looked like a younger version of the mother.

"It's a pleasure to meet you," I said, giving a graceful bow.

"Please, my dear, the pleasure is ours," his mother quickly responded, yet a crease formed between her brows.

"Rivka is someone I knew from Jerusalem, mother," Evander jumped in. "I invited her to visit Rome once I knew I was being sent back and she accepted."

His mother nodded as the sister assessed me, eyes moving from my hair down to my toes. No one spoke for a moment, the subtle sound of servants bustling was amplified in the background, making things all the more uncomfortable. We all glanced back and forth, before I finally made it to Evander. His eyes only briefly met mine before he swiftly moved them away.

"Well, Rivka," his mother finally said, clapping her hands together. "I'm sure you must be exhausted from your journey. Why don't I show you to a room where you can get some rest and when you're ready, you may join us for our meal."

"Are you sure? I wouldn't want to impose," I asked sincerely, unconvinced at Vinicius' first answer.

"Not at all," she uttered, gesturing to Aura to lead me on.

Following her daughter's steps towards a small door opening, I added, "Thank you, that'd be lovely."

The doorway hid a decently long hallway, intricate patterned cream tiles ornate the floors. At the end of the hallway lay several sets of wooden doors, designs carved into the dark lumber. Aura led me to the one at the very end, pushing the heavy door aside to reveal a bedroom. Two columns were placed in the center of the room, acting as some form of separator between the two spaces. On the left stood a bed, just big enough to fit two people, standing a few feet off the ground by a wooden bedframe and legs. On the other side stood a small table with what seemed to be a mirror resting on the top. A chair wound in leather was next to it, holding back the grand golden curtains on the wall besides a window opening. Blue mosaic tile decorated the floor and one of the walls, people, animals, and patterns, depicted in golds and creams.

"I'll have a servant bring you a pitcher and basin to freshen up and one of my gowns, if you would like, until we can have yours washed," she said mildly, no hint of admiration or hatred in her tone either way.

I walked into the center of the room as she stayed at the door. "Thank you," I turned back towards her.

She gave a soft nod before closing the door behind her. Making my way to the bed, I sat down, throwing myself on my back and let out a deep sigh, rubbing my cheek.

———— ✢ ————

The servants followed Aura's orders to the letter, giving me everything that I needed to feel more like a human after the long journey on the ship. I couldn't entirely bathe, but I was able to do enough to get the smell of the sea and sweat off me. Aura was close to my size and height, so her dress fit me well, the

31

light blue material resting nicely against my tanned skin. Using one of the combs that was on the small vanity table, I brushed my hair back, unsure if a particular hairstyle would be more proper and just opted for letting its natural form take place, tucking one side behind my ear.

Closing my eyes in a final attempt to muster my courage, I tightened the blue sash across my waist and opened the bedroom door. The light linen found its way in my fingers as I gripped the material between them. With each step I took down the long hallway, I pulled my chin a little higher. No matter what happens, I was here, there was no turning back—not yet anyways.

Having not been given a whole tour of the house, and not wanting to seem nosy, I made my way back on the path I was taken, leading me to the front entrance. My courage waned a little seeing no one was there, but there were still traces of determination. Waiting patiently, it only took a moment for a servant to enter the room, going about their duties. The woman stopped when she saw me, bowing her head low.

"There's no need for that," I commented, without thinking, before continuing. "Have Evander and his family already started their meal?"

"No, my lady," she responded, eyes still downcast, "they were waiting for you."

"Would you be able to show me where they are?"

She said nothing but gave a simple head gesture before she turned and started leading the way. Instead of going through the small door that Aura had led me through, she guided me through the large entrance in the center of the wall. It led into what seemed to be a study, before she took me out another doorway on the other side. My mouth parted as we entered what seemed to be a courtyard, square in shape with no roof. That wasn't the reason I was surprised; I had seen many of these types of homes in Italy in my time. But rather than the stone floors I'd

32

been used to, this large area was designed as a beautiful garden. Flower bushes were decorated into an enchanting design, a fountain directly centerfold with a stone woman pouring water from a basin. Stone benches were placed throughout the design, marble columns surrounding this beauty, hiding the cool hallway in the shade. In truth, the whole area was in shade as the sun was beginning to set, but it was just enough to emphasize the care and preparation that was taken to make this mini oasis.

"Right this way," the servant gestured to an opening underneath the covered hallway, revealing the family as they lay on couches surrounding a table.

"Many thanks," I murmured to the servant as I entered the room. "My apologies, I hope you weren't kept waiting long."

"We just came into the room ourselves," Lucrezia said gracefully, although it looked like that had been there for much longer than that.

I surveyed where to sit, seeing that they left a spot open on the end next to Evander. Tentatively, I made my way over. His lips remained sealed as I lowered myself, his brows rigid as his throat gave the smallest of swallows. Now fully draped, my glance went over the food that was being served, disregarding him as I looked.

"It all looks so… beautifully prepared," I said carefully, my eyes trying not to focus on the small roasted pig in the center of the table.

No one said anything, just politely smiled at one another, before Vinicius raised his glass, signaling that the meal was beginning. Figs, grapes, and various types of nuts were placed alongside the pig. There was also what seemed to be a type of bird, duck possibly. Grabbing one of the stuffed dates, I bit into its sweet and crunchy texture. The combination of nuts balanced the sweetness of the date and drizzled honey. The servants began to serve each of us, pouring a drink into my cup, leaving Aura to be the first to break in the conversation.

"Your hair," she said in awe, her eyes not moving from my tendrils.

I tucked a piece behind my ear, confused at her meaning. "Yes?"

"It's so thick! I think it's the most beautiful hair I've ever seen," she answered, grabbing at her own hair placed in a slightly smaller braid against her shoulder. "I didn't notice it before when it was all hidden, but by the gods!"

"That can't be true," I modestly brushed the comment off, looking down at my plate.

"I must agree with my daughter," Lucrezia interjected. "Most people we seem to see these days are ungraciously losing their hair, men and women alike. Personally, I think it's due to their poor diets, but I am alone in this sentiment it would seem."

Vinicius blew a quiet raspberry, making a comment to himself that only he could hear. I nodded, agreeing with her mentally. Vinicius may think he doesn't agree with her, but the food on his plate showed balance and he didn't seem to be heavy with the wine in his cup either. The same went for Evander and Aura, and all four of them had their own beautiful hair.

"But I will say," Lucrezia added, "I am surprised at just how white and straight your teeth are, especially coming from a place as barren as Jerusalem."

"Jerusalem is anything but barren, mother," Evander chided her as he looked down at his food, making me remember that he actually does have a voice.

"Indeed," Vinicius said grimly.

"Speaking of Jerusalem, how exactly is it that you two *met* there?" his mother asked, eyes surreptitiously peering over her cup, bringing the unanswered question right to the front of dinner.

I glanced over at Evander, curious as to what he'd say, if he would say anything at all.

He cleared his throat, giving a quick glance to me before nonchalantly saying, "On the road, she was in a bit of a situation, and I helped her. We then realized we were heading in the same direction and decided to keep each other company on the way."

"He's being modest," I chimed, my eyes slightly squinted at the under exaggeration. "I was attacked by a lion and he killed it before it had the chance to kill me."

His eyes stayed focused on his food, but they betrayed the emotion he was trying to tuck away.

"A lion?" Aura's eyes went big, mouth open.

Vinicius and Lucrezia shared a look but said nothing.

"A small lion," Evander continued to downplay.

"Did you get hurt? How did you kill it?" Aura questioned, now fully enthralled by her older brother.

Biting the inside of my lip, I wondered what the reason was for his casual display in the matter. Was it about not wanting to worry his parents or something worse, something to do with me. Maybe he really was embarrassed about me, and I had made the wrong choice in coming. My cheeks began to warm in anger, but I took a quiet breath in an attempt to calm myself. There must be more to the story, I couldn't be so naive.

Before Evander or I could respond, Lucrezia jumped in. "I'm glad you're fine now. Let's talk about something not so… harrowing, shall we?" she said with a stiff cheeks.

We all returned to our food.

"I spoke with Pollax in the baths," Vinicius said, putting another bite of food between his teeth before continuing. "It seems he's still angry about my vote against the enforcement of the old law. I told him it would hurt the merchants and common people, but that man is as stubborn as a mule."

"Says it's for your own gain, I suppose?" Lucrezia stated more than asked.

The corner of Vinicius' mouth turned upward in response as he took another bite of his pork.

35

"I thought your father built warships. What would he have to gain from something that supported common people and not soldiers?" I murmured to Evander, unnoticed by his family.

"He does," he answered, the first time speaking to me personally since entering his home, besides his short introduction to his mother. "But while I was gone in Jerusalem, he began to dabble in trade. It seemed to pick up quite well, so now he split his business in half: half warships, half merchant ships."

"This land is going to shambles," Lucrezia groaned, "between the economic crisis and the attack on your vessels..." she rubbed her forehead.

Vinicius took another sip of his drink, giving a pursed analysis. My guess was that he probably didn't want to talk too much about family business at the table with a complete stranger from another land. I could understand.

Evander seemed to pick up on it as well, so he changed the subject, turning it to the famed chariot races. Vinicius and him mostly spoke, with Aura adding comments here and there. In the meantime, I just listened, pretending to ignore what Lucrezia thought were carefully covered stares in my direction. As the dinner progressed, the stress that Evander had in his shoulders seemed to drop slightly, and he even graced me with a few glances. The conversation went long, so long that we completed the meal as the subject was beginning to die away.

A yawn overtook Vinicius and Lucrezia mentioned that there were things she needed to complete in the household before she bid us a well night's rest. I might have believed her, but when Aura said that she wanted to stay and talk with me, Lucrezia gave her a tight pinch on the back of her arm that might have gone undetected if Aura did not let out a yelp. With that, they bid Evander and I a good evening and said they would see us in the morning.

As they made their way down their tiled hallway, Evander and I said nothing for a few moments. The faint trickle from the fountain was the only sound in the night.

That and my racing heartbeat. After how the events of the day had gone, I wasn't going to dare to be the one to speak first.

"Would you like to go and speak in the *peristylum*?" he finally said, motioning to the courtyard.

I gave him a quick glance up and down before I gave an affirming nod. A line appeared between his brows before he called to the servants to bring me something to wrap around my shoulders.

"For the cool air," Evander commented.

It only took what felt like seconds for the slave woman from earlier to appear, bringing me a shawl, and bowing before making her way back into the villa. I wrapped the thin wool around my bare arms, following Evander's lead as he guided us to the courtyard. We stepped into the garden, beginning to walk the elaborate path. Trickling water echoed louder than before into the twilight sky, the lights from the villa giving off a soft glow.

We kept an arm's length distance away, each of us on the ends of either side of the tailored path. The arrangement of the exquisite color palette of the flowers was hardly enough to keep my attention. The orange petals reflecting the torches glow to the violet going hand-in-hand with the speckled sky. Not even the vibrant fuchsia and cherry could captivate my notice as Evander and I walked in silence for a long while. From the corner of my eye, I could just make out him scarcely opening his mouth before closing it, not just once, but several times. My only amazement was that I wasn't visibly doing the exact thing. Potentially giving up, his lips tightened, pulling so firm I thought they may never open again.

I think we were both unsure of what to say, I know that I certainly was. Do we make small talk? Do I point out the elephant in the room and demand an explanation? Do I even speak at all? Small talk seemed to take the win.

"When did you learn Greek?" Evander asked first, hands folded behind his back.

I had already spoken Greek, but not the one he spoke. Never had I attempted it while in Jerusalem and thus explaining why we spoke in the language of my land.

"I knew some," I answered, "but I practiced more on the ship over here. Didn't want to stick out like a sore thumb."

The corner of his lip turned. "An interesting analogy. I guess you did have enough time to master it."

My face remained unchanged, but inside I was relieved he didn't think much of the remark. I thought it would've been one they used here too.

We said nothing for another moment. Slowing, I closed my eyes tightly.

My jaw loosened, a half-formed thought nudging its way out, but Evander's voice hit my ears, beating me to it again. "Rivka," he breathed, "I'm sorry—"

"Don't be sorry," I cut him off. "It was my mistake, Evander," I brushed, trying to salvage what little dignity I had left. "I jumped to conclusions and followed you even after your ship left. I should have taken that as a sign for me not to come. I'm sorry for the intrusion I made in your home and with your family."

"Don't you understand, Rivka? It's not an intrusion, I'm overjoyed that you came."

I stopped walking, partially turning towards him. "Excuse my frankness, but behavior's a language and your actions speak louder than your words. I see that I've put you in a problematic position and—"

"Rivka," he interrupted, stepping closer to me. "I know that my reaction was not what you expected…"

A soft puff of air escaped my lips in disbelief. Expected? Maybe my expectations were a little high, but it was as if I just told him his mother was dying, and I was death to claim her.

"Again, I am sorry. But things are just in a delicate situation with my family, and you were the last person I was expecting to see in Rome. I waited for you at the dock, having the captain of the ship delay our departure because I was almost certain that you would come. And, when you didn't, I had to come to terms with the fact that we…" he paused, "that *I* would never see you again."

His eyes showed sincerity, but he bit his lip as if was holding back. I rubbed my hands on my face, the muscles beneath my cheekbone pulling taut. The sound of leather softly tapping echoed into the night as he took a few steps closer. His hands clasped my palms, carefully drawing them down, leaving me to stare into his own structured features. My hands were like icicles in his warm grip.

I pulled away.

"But how does that explain the past day?" my gaze narrowed. "You would hardly speak to me as we ate, let alone look at me. If I hadn't said anything, or your mother's cues to your family, I doubt we'd even be having this conversation now!"

His face studied my own. Letting out a breath, he took a seat on the nearby stone bench, flowers poking from behind as he looked down at the ground. "I know, I've been acting like an absolute fool. I'm not here to make excuses and I want to be fully honest with you."

Mistrustful, I watched him, unconsciously playing with the hem of my sash. Was he only saying this because we were out of earshot from his family? Maybe I should give him the benefit of the doubt, or at the very least, hear him out.

Making my way to the bench, I slowly sat down, making sure that there was still enough room in between us. "I'd appreciate that. No lies, no beating around the bush."

His brows furrowed, but he seemed to understand my meaning. "As I said before, I wasn't expecting you here in Rome, especially alone. This isn't a very well-kept secret, but here in Rome, Jews are looked at with suspicion and mistrust."

"That sentiment didn't seem to spare your family," I mumbled.

He gave me a look of reproach. Not hard, but one of disagreement. I said nothing, but did mentally admit that they had been kind to me, even under the circumstances.

"To speak plainly," he said in an undertone, "this won't be easy, just your being here. But I'm not a coward to the challenge."

Was that a hidden insult?

"Rivka, you're the same person from our time in Jerusalem and so am I. Again, I'm truly sorry for the way I've been acting, and I want to make it up to you."

I looked down at my lap, the tan shawl slipping from my left shoulder to my elbow. Evander raised his hand, hesitating as it came near my shawl before laying the warm material against my shoulder. He lingered, his fingers delicately brushing against my collarbone.

Saying nothing, I just watched him. His tongue smacked against the roof of his mouth, letting out a sound before he spoke again. "Tomorrow, I have some business with my father, but I will have Aura show you around Rome. And then, once my business is complete, maybe I can take you to a chariot race. There you and I can speak."

I bit my lip. I didn't want to go if this was some sort of pity invitation. But on the other hand, I quite literally left my own world and everything I had ever known to be with him. Don't I owe it to myself to see if there is something actually there, that it wasn't just a high of emotions and all that was going on in Jerusalem?

He seemed to sense my hesitation, because he quickly added, "I *want* to do this with you. Please."

Closing my eyes, I gave a single nod. When I opened them, I found him looking at me, a half smirk on his lips. Rising from the bench, he turned, extending his hand to me.

Pausing as I looked at it, I raised my own hand and placed it in his. Evander's fingers locked around mine and I rose. I tried to pull my hand back, but his grip tightened. My eyes searched his. He looked at me as if there was something about me worth looking at, something deep inside my soul.

Slowly, he began to lean towards me. As I watched him, my eyes moved from his sea green eyes to his lips.

But in an instant, reality and civility took over, the thought pulling his head back.

"Rivka…" he susurrated, his eyes locked on mine—searching, uncertain—shadows of conflict flickering behind them. "I…" The rest snagged in his throat. His mouth tightened, a decision hardening. "I'll have a slave show you to your room."

And in an instant, he was gone, making his way back into the villa.

IV

THE CHARIOT

Streams of light peering in through the cracks of the drapes landed warmly on my face, sweat dripping from it. Taking that as my cue, I stood up from the floor, my muscles sore from the workout I just finished. Using my arm to wipe the sweat away, my lashes batted rapidly, blurred vision focusing on the morning light. Grabbing the pitcher from the table, I poured myself some water, letting the tepid liquid wash down my throat, reviving me. I wiped the rest of my sweat with a cloth that had been left for me and laid down back in my bed, my heartbeat slowly steadying itself.

The clothes that I had worn the night before were laid out by the servant on the settee, its light blue color complementing the wood on the furniture. The smell of bread baking passed through the wooden doors, amplifying my hungry stomach. Giving out a small stretch, I stared up at the ceiling, mind clear. Life had hardly ever gone the way I had expected it to go, a testament which I had made peace with, almost even welcomed. Sure, some things were good and others horrible, but it shaped me into the person I am. Besides, who could ever predict that they would travel through time?

My thoughts trickled again to Evander, our encounters and what to make of them. Maybe my time on the ship, or even while in this century, had made me soft. One of my original goals in not going home was to potentially have an impact on what was to come—to change history. That might possibly be a fool's thought, but so were magical tablets.

I closed my eyes. Never had I ever thought I would have a movie-worthy love; those don't exist in real life, and not for one second did I think that that's what Evander and I have. But what I had thought was so beautiful about it was that I wasn't even looking when I found him. He was noble, determined, and strong. For goodness sake, he was drawn to me, a woman from what he would see as a conquered nation. That took a certain kind of courage in itself, didn't it?

Yet, I could just be drawn to a lost cause. That's what Thana was—a lost cause. A girl of a different nation that I formed a friendship with, thinking I could trust her with anything, but instead was betrayed by her and left to die.

My hand tightened beside me at the thought.

An evil, selfish woman. Bitter over the cards that life had dealt her, even though it was a suitable hand. Too self-absorbed to see what was going on around her and the big picture over what we were trying to accomplish. One of the only benefits I knew about not going back was that her life was spared—one of the few benefits for her, that is. My revenge would know no end.

But soft words came like a gentle breeze over my mind. "Forgive her," it whispered.

Yeshua.

He had spoken these words to me that night on the hill. It was easier said than done.

Pulling me back, the doors burst open, Aura walking in with one of the older slaves following behind her. "Come, come," she clapped, "it's time to awaken. The day is young, and we have many things to do!"

I wasn't unaccustomed to surprise wake up calls, but I was surprised to see Aura awake almost as early as myself. She seemed like the type who would like to lounge about all day in bed, being waited on hand and foot. Maybe I was wrong.

"What are we doing exactly?" I sat up on my elbows, my brown hair pulled on my shoulder.

"Why, spending my fathers earnings, of course! If you are going to stay here in Rome, my dear, then you will need to look the part," she said, unbothered as she pulled the blanket beside me.

"Aura," I started, unsure how to bring up the awkward topic, "I don't really have any money."

"Do not fear, someone has insisted on covering the bill," she walked towards the balcony as the slave pulled back the curtains.

"Who?" I asked in disbelief.

She slyly looked over shoulder at me. "Why, Evander, of course."

Hoping she wouldn't see my soft blush, I stepped down onto the cool tile.

"Before we leave," Aura began as she walked back to my side of my room, the old woman following close behind, "we must have your measurements, so we'll know how much fabric to buy and for your clothes to be made to fit."

Aura pulled me up, lifted my arms, and had the woman take the measurements. Once she had finished, she tsked at the woman who quickly left and returned with a fresh pitcher of water and an empty bowl.

"Make haste and I'll meet you by the entrance when you're finished," Aura directed, walking out of the room, the slave following and closing the door behind her.

I let out a loud sigh and flopped my back onto the bed.

———— ✢ ————

Aura and I were out onto the streets within ten minutes. Expertly, she led the way to the marketplace, specifically in the section where fabrics were sold, a younger servant boy following us behind. Aura said we would need him to carry all of our purchases. We walked with the crowds down the cobblestone street, the rancid aroma of urine occasionally filling my nostrils from the lower class side of the city. But as I said, she was an expert on the path, and we arrived in the marketplace safely and untouched by questionable substances in a matter of minutes.

From what I could tell so far, I liked Evander's sister. Granted, she seemed a little shallow, but innocent, and not too shy to ask any question that was on her mind. She got the ball rolling on problematic questions pretty quickly.

"I heard your country is just a little worm hill," she scrunched her nose, giggling, as we looked at the fabric stands. I made no comment as I saw that she didn't mean it with intended offense, but just basic amusement. She was young, naive, and subject to the opinion of those around her, how could she know any different?

"It is quite small," I smiled in truth.

"I've heard that they all serve one god who's invisible, can you imagine? Is it true? Do you serve him too?"

"Why does that sound so odd to you," I dodged the question.

"Doubtlessly because my family and I serve so many," she answered as if it were obvious. "There's Minerva, the goddess of wisdom, Juno, the protector of women, Neptune, god of the sea, Venus, the goddess of love, Mars, the god of war—he's Evander's favorite—and so many others!"

"I could see how that might be his favorite. That, or his most hated."

"Indeed," she agreed, picking up a pale pallus, draping it against her arm. She admired it in silence before losing interest and dropping it flippantly back to the wooden table.

"But you didn't tell me," she asked again, not forgetting her question, "do *you* serve only one god?"

I paused. The clamoring of the market seemed to go silent in my ears, a bead of sweat slowly trickling down my brow. The thud of my heart was palpable against my chest, the sound carrying up to my ears. Should there be any shame in the truth?

45

"For a long time, I didn't," I said hesitantly, "but recently I've seen His power, both great and small. It was enough for me. Yes, I serve Him."

As the last word left my lips, the sound of the market returned to my ears. I'm not sure what I expected Aura to do, but it certainly wasn't to let out an emphatic giggle.

"That must be so simple! I wish ours was as simple as that," she linked her arm through my elbow and pulled me forward to walk. "It gets so complicated keeping everything straight, when to give offerings, which offering goes to which god, and on and on and on."

I raised my brow. "I guess I hadn't thought of it that way."

"Please, don't tell my parents I ever said such a thing," she turned her deep brown eyes towards me, "my mother will throw me out onto the street if they think I followed the commoner's god."

I didn't even have to reply before her attention turned elsewhere, dragging me down the road. As she shopped, I knew this would probably be one of the few times Aura and I would be alone, so if I wanted answers to any of my questions, she would probably be the best person to ask. Placing my hands behind my back, I laid down the groundwork.

"Do you and your brother get along?"

"Evander and I?" she said aloud, even though she seemed to mostly be thinking to herself. "We don't *not* get along. I'd say we're just not as connected."

"Why is that?" Evander didn't seem like the type of guy to not be close with his family, especially his baby sister, so this news didn't fit my narrative of him.

"My estimation would be that it's because he's been gone for most of my life. First, he went to Germania, then to Jerusalem. Which, by the way, my parents were not very happy when he decided to serve in the army. And when he is home, he's dealing with grief or the family business."

"Grief?" I repeated. "What do you mean by that?"

Before she answered, we stopped at a shop filled with beads, crystals, and jewelry. The silver not covered by the hanging cover glinted in my eyes, making me move to Aura's other side.

"I never thought I'd see Evander with another woman again," Aura commented as she mindlessly looked at the table. I made no outward appearance of notice. Evander and I had talked about the woman he loved when he saved me from Birsha in Machaerus. She had died before they could get married, but I almost forgot about her entirely since he never brought her up again. Almost.

Debating if it was wise to ask any questions about it, I picked up a small bead, pretending to inspect its red color as I circled it in my fingers. If I were to ask anyone about it, it would be Aura; she would be the least suspecting.

"I'm sure he still loves her very much," I noted passively, my eyes fixed on the bead.

"Honestly, I'm not sure," she shrugged, rifling through the other products on the table. "Evander's not one to talk about his feelings. That's probably what makes him such a good military man. He keeps everything inside."

I waited, taking her words in. "I could imagine there's no love to compare to that of one stolen by death."

"I suppose," she put the necklace she was holding down, turning to me. "But what I do know is that—" she stopped, quickly raising her petite hand to her mouth and letting out a small laugh. "Look at me, being a fool and going on and on."

I turned the corners of my lips, although there was no heart behind the smile.

"Come," she said, extending her hand and locking her fingers on my wrist. "There's still many shops I want to show you!"

The hours passed with surprising speed as Aura took me from fabric stand to fabric stand, laying the materials against my skin and commenting on which looked best with my complexion. She pulled blues, olive greens, and whites with ease as she made me her very own Barbie. In my mission I had gone undercover plenty of times, putting on different clothing to match my persona, and that's what this felt like. But having that thought in my head gave me the worst feeling in the pit of my stomach. I didn't want this to be pretend; I wanted it to be my life. Is that all I have been doing up until this point?

Did I trick myself into this world of pretend?

Aura, satisfied with her choices, motioned for the slave to carry our purchases as I followed her to our final destination: the villa.

As the guards threw back the bronze doors, allowing us to enter, a cool breeze escaped from inside the tiled home. I hadn't realized just how warm it was until I felt the crisp villa air. I only had a moment to take it in, when another voice startled me.

"Are you ready, Rivka?" Evander said as he appeared through one of the doorways. He was dressed in leisure wear, a dark blue tunic with a leather belt that held the scabbard of his sword. His sword was in his hands until he placed the weapon into its sheath.

He did look quite handsome.

"Oh, that's right," I mostly said to myself as I smoothed my skirt. "Yes, give me a moment to freshen up," I answered, making my way back to my room as I spoke. Taking only a moment, I returned and found him where I had left him by the door.

Giving a small smile, I followed his hand that he had extended to allow me to exit the villa first. I wrapped the indigo linen shawl that Aura had bought for me loosely around my elbows as I waited for Evander to make his way out of the villa and down the steps, following beside him. Before going down, he offered me his arm. In my mind it felt like I was thinking at a million miles per minute, but it was only seconds before I linked my arm in his, muscles firm in my hold, and we were on our way.

We walked in silence for a few moments. And by silence, I meant the two of us, as Rome was just as loud and as busy as when I had left it with Aura. A pebble found its way into my sandal, but I ignored it. A true way of challenging one's discomfort and I welcomed it. Not only that, but it also brought distraction.

Finally, Evander decided to break the ice. "I thought to maybe ask if you'd want a litter to take you to our destination but, knowing you, I figured you'd probably refuse."

"And why is that?" my brow percolated.

Giving a small laugh, he answered, "Because from what I know of you, you can and want to do things yourself. Besides, I don't think it's something you're used to."

He was right of course. On top of those reasons, I wasn't afraid of exercise. That, and I could keep a better eye as to what was going on around me. Evander seemed to be thinking the same thing.

"Do you always carry a weapon with you, even in leisure wear?" I questioned, already knowing the answer.

He shrugged. "It's a habit, I suppose. The results of being a soldier."

The corner of my lip twitched upward in agreement. I had been doing the same for years and was currently hiding the weapon I had from the boy on my leg underneath my garments.

49

Changing the subject, Evander continued. "How was the voyage?"

It didn't go unnoticed that he hadn't asked me about my trip up until this point, but frankly, I didn't blame him. There were so many different emotions and things to work out, it felt like it had happened so long ago.

"It went by quickly, especially the second half of it," I replied, not really sure what else I could add.

"Oh really?" he turned to me. "For any particular reason?"

"I met a girl on the ship. Sariel. We were in the middle of a long storm when we began speaking. She's the one who helped me with my Greek."

He looked impressed but said nothing else for a while. Weirdly enough, this time it wasn't awkward, but comfortable. The pebble also fell out of my shoe, aided in that feeling.

Within a few moments of the conversation ending, we stood before our destination. I had passed by the Circus Maximus when I first arrived in Rome, though I hadn't known it at the time. Putting a name to the columned building gave me more perspective as to just where exactly I was. We passed through the gated entrances, a mass of people before and behind us. Luckily, Evander knew exactly where he was going, guiding me with ease until we entered the center of the arena. Staring up, I took in the sizable architecture.

"This way," Evander motioned to me, stepping in front as he took the lead.

My eyes focused on Evander's shoulders as I followed him up the steps and to our seats in the stands. The large man next to me paid me no attention as I sat, too interested in figuring his winnings with his friend if his chosen charioteer won. The cold stone was a refreshing contrast to the radiating sun. Having sat down, I could now take in the structure in its full capacity.

The long rectangle shape with the rounded edges of the Circus Maximus reminded me of the tracks for car races. The high seats stacked upon one another like bleachers, the buzz of thousands of conversations rising into the air. Instead of a field of grass in the center of the track, there was marble stacked with a hollow center, water filling it. The golden statues on pillars reflected against the sun, their gods and goddesses intricately designed. I couldn't deny its magnificence.

"The hippodrome of Jerusalem can't even compare to this, hmm," Evander exhaled as he sat down beside me.

"That's for sure," I mumbled, seeing that the advancements of Rome did give him some pride. I would feel the exact same way if I brought him to my world. Just the thought of showing him how a cell phone worked I think would cause him, or anyone from this time, to pass out from fear or shock.

The side of my lip upturned as I remembered seeing the hippodrome of Jericho with Gidon. Evander was right, it was nothing to compare.

"It's fairly full," I observed, watching as the last few spectators found their seats.

"As is the norm," Evander commented, "Not a single citizen of Rome would wish to miss the games. Those who don't make it to the free seats, those who can't afford seats, or once they are already sold out, go along the hill there to get the best view that they can."

Following his finger that pointed past the other side of the stands, I could see shapes of people gathering. My eyes focused on the bronze figure directly in front of us that was partially blocking the view. There were seven dolphins, their snouts high in the air as they were all placed horizontally on a pole of some sort. There was some space in between each, as if for some purpose.

"That's used to count the laps," Evander acknowledged, noticing as I stared at the interesting design. "When a lap is

51

complete, they pull the face of the dolphin down, signaling that it is over to the crowd."

There was something else that was hard to miss—all the people seemed to carry one of four colors on their person: blue, green, red, and white. Clearly, they meant something. Maybe it was their form of an ancient day jersey. I stifled a laugh at the thought of them cheering names unknown to them: Maradona, Ronaldo, Messi, Pele. I didn't keep up with sports, but there were some names that everyone just knew.

Evander took note of my observation. "There are four factions that race, each represented by a color. Blue and green tend to be the favorites."

I learned some things about Ancient Rome from my father, his deep love for the ancient world was an ever-present staple in our home. But unfortunately, I tuned out much of it, only remembering small tidbits here and there. One thing that I did remember was that gladiators and slaves would fight at these sorts of things. Maybe that was only in the Colosseum, but as I noticed on my arrival here, it had yet to be constructed.

"Who is it that races? Freedmen or slaves?" I asked.

"Both. Actually, many a slave have become free because of it. The races can become quite dangerous, but the reward of prestige and wealth is not one to be contended with."

My interest peaked. "Dangerous? Dangerous how?"

"It's not uncommon for the racers or their horses to meet their end doing this. It could be from a hard turn, a bad chariot, a broken wheel, or even a dishonest opponent," Evander pointed to the center. "Many times, the racers get pushed into the wall, crushing them or breaking their riggings."

"Do any ever survive?"

He made a face. "It depends. You see, the racers have the reins of their horses tied to them, usually their waist. If they manage to somehow survive the blow of the fall or evade the broken wood, they only have mere seconds to cut themselves free or be dragged to death by their own team. But even if they manage to get loose, they'll still have to evade any teams from behind trampling them."

"Are the guilty ever sent to compete? That sort of death should deter anyone from crime."

"Not usually," he answered before slowly finishing, "crucifixions are the method of choice."

I paused, debating if my next words were wise. "Then He died a common death?"

A simple question, but one that he wavered before answering. "Crucifixions are a common punishment, but his... It was definitely like nothing I have ever seen before," Evander trailed.

We sat in silence for a moment, thinking back to that day. I hadn't considered what Evander must have been thinking in the days that followed Yeshua's crucifixion. I was so wrapped up in my own emotions, then on retrieving the tablet, to Evander's confession, and then finally hearing that Yeshua was alive. I was caught up in the rollercoaster of emotions myself, how was I to even care about anyone else and their feelings?

"What did you think about it?" he asked me, not turning to face me.

I sighed, debating which way to direct the conversation. "I did hear one of your Roman soldiers say that he was the 'Son of God.'"

That got his attention, his eyebrows scrunched as he turned to look at me. "In all truth?"

Nodding, I watched as he brought his hand to his chin, pondering the seemingly new information that I had just given him. He stayed that way a moment before turning back. "But, Rivka, what did *you* think?"

Swallowing, I couldn't help but note how alike Evander and his sibling were. I already confessed it once today, what's to stop me from doing it again?

"I think your Roman was right."

A slight gloss seemed to cover Evander's vision, his face perplexed. My assumption based on his body language was that he still hadn't fully made up his mind. Either that or that he had made up his mind and was afraid of the answer. Did I dare ask him?

"Does he compare to your Mars?"

As he opened his mouth to answer, two people tried to pass us, their tunics rubbing against our knees as they went to find seating closer towards the center. Being only a momentary distraction, he answered, "I've never seen Mars overcome death."

The band heralded, breaking the conversation. Evander nudged his stubbled chin forward, indicating the entry of a single man in a chariot with an attendant on foot guiding the horses forward. The impressive lineup that followed behind him was also a spectacle. Legionaries, calvary, singers, dancers, priests, and finally the several teams of chariots following one by one, the cheer of the crowd almost overpowering the sound of the trumpets.

"That's the state official who was selected for the games today," Evander yelled over the sound, pointing to the first man. "He decides when the race will begin with a drop of his handkerchief."

The crowd began to stomp their feet against the stone, waving their colored cloths, creating a vibrant display. My bones rattled in my body from the force.

As Evander explained to me what was happening, I observed a man who seemed to take notice of us. He was four rows down, along the aisle, a clay cup in his hand. Watching him from the corner of my eye, I could tell he didn't know I was observing him, and he began to make his way up the steps, his gaze fixed upon us. His tall stature was dressed in a white tunic, an adorned belt was tied against his waist. Defensive, my instincts kicked in and I knew I had to tell Evander.

"That man who's making his way up towards us has been watching you. Do you know him?"

Evander saw him, but before he could answer my question the man was upon us, his hands raised. "Do my eyes deceive me or has that old snake pit finally spit you back to civilization to live a little!"

"Cassius," Evander grinned, clasping his arm as he raised to embrace him.

"You're an old devil, you know this, yes?" Cassius smirked, his clean-shaven face showing his dimples. "You have yet to come to one social engagement since your return from that heathen place and left your old friend to handle all the women of Rome alone."

Evander laughed, patting his back. "You're right, those poor women only left with a scoundrel like you."

Cassius took no offense, the smirk still playing on his lips as he turned his attention to me. "It would seem that the women of Rome will be saddened to hear that they're still stuck with me. Yet, Evander, who is this exotic beauty?"

I gave a polite smile, feeling a little silly and not wanting to embarrass Evander in front of his friend. But his handsome features did not hide his arrogance or his lust.

"Cassius, this is Rivka, she came with me from Jerusalem," he slightly lied. "Rivka, this is Cassius, an old friend. Our fathers have worked together in the Senate for many years."

"Jerusalem?" Cassius interjected. "Tell me then, do you speak Greek?"

"Yes," I replied simply.

"She speaks it quite well, actually," Evander said, as he sat back down beside me. "We'll be working on her Latin in the days to come, as well."

Cassius ran his fingers through his short, brown hair, giving me one more look. "Indeed. Well what better way to immerse yourself in our superior culture than through the feast tonight."

Evander said nothing as I turned to look at him for his answer. Cassius seemed to be doing the same as a quizzical look entertained his brow. "You will be attending the feast tonight, won't you, Evander?"

A tightness creeped into his posture as though the invitation itself made him flinch. I tried to think of the reasons for his hesitance, concluding it must have something to do with me. After all, these past days have been anything but clear. The mixed signals that I was getting were unbelievably confusing, even for a woman of my background.

"You must," Cassius chimed in. "If only to bring your new little friend for us all to," he paused, his eyes looking me up and down, "become better acquainted."

Evander feigned a smile, clearly not to arouse his friends' suspicion on the account of his hesitance. "We'll make a short appearance. Rivka has only just arrived and is exhausted from her journey," Evander said politely, but I noticed the tightness in his voice.

"Indeed," he smiled.

The sound of trumpets thankfully interrupted our conversation, stopping any soon coming tension. Cassius politely excused himself to his seat, assuring us that we would be meeting again soon. When he was out of earshot, I turned to Evander delicately, curious to see what his explanation was, or if he would even give me one.

"I'll be learning Latin, huh?" I began gently.

He gave a soft chuckle, rubbing the back of his neck. "I know, I know. Cassius is a… sensual and lewd man. Before leaving for Germania, I'm sorry to say that I was much like him.

But war and being out in the world changes a person's point of view and responsibilities."

I could see in his eyes that he was being honest, but that still didn't answer my question. "And the feast?"

"A bed of debauchery, vice, and political traps," he said shortly.

"Then why will we be attending? Especially if you disdain it so much?"

"Things in Rome are a lot more complicated than they are in Jerusalem," he said, watching as the chariot racers were taking their positions inside the shortened stall doors. "By going to a feast, you risk saying something that could be used against you, especially me being a Senator's son. By not going, one would be suspected of disaffection to the host and their political ties, usually that of the emperor."

The crowd roared as the trumpets blew once more, the children in the stands rising to their feet giddily. The elected official had dismounted from his chariot while we spoke with Cassius and was now on a platform in the center of the stadium. He slowly raised his hand, the crowd suddenly hushing at the sight. The man lingered, his white handkerchief dangling between his fingers as the delicate wind pushed it to a side. While he waited, a pin could have been heard being dropped, as not even a baby gave out a quiet wail.

In an instant, the cloth fell from the man's hand, erupting a murderous cheer from the crowd. My hands found my ears as the doors to the stall burst open and the charioteers raced out.

V

ROSES

As soon as we returned from the race, Evander wasted no time. While I was still catching my breath and brushing dust from my clothes, he was already listing off customs, names, and rules I was expected to follow. The feast tonight, he said, wasn't just a celebration: it was a test, a stage, and a trap all at once. I was to smile, speak little, and observe everything. Apparently, who I looked at, where I sat, and even what I ate could be interpreted as some kind of message.

Every move mattered.

Evander wasn't drilling this into me for his own gain or to boost his family's standing, I sensed. He was doing it for me. For my protection. Because in a room full of powerful people with sharper smiles than daggers, even the smallest mistake could become dangerous.

Once he was finished, Aura ushered me away to get ready, as she graciously offered me one of her tunics and skill with fashion until my own garments could be completed. Ever since arriving back to their villa, nerves were eating me up inside, except I couldn't fathom why. I was never nervous to speak to new people or be put in difficult situations. My only explanation was that it might be since I am in a new time I may say something that was inexplicable. Either that or the fact that I was meeting more of Evander's friends.

As the sun began to set, my preparations were finally finished. Just in the nick of time, too, because Evander had since sent three servants to check on me, relaying their master's message to finish quickly. Aura placed a pallus, which was much like a shawl, around my shoulders and had the servant take me to the atrium where Evander was waiting restlessly. Entering the ornate room, my eyes locked with him in what seemed to be an agitated state, his arms crossed. But he straightened as soon as I entered, his face changing somehow.

"You look," he faltered as he took in my soft pink toga, the gold trim accenting against my skin. Aura's slave fashioned my hair into a detailed braid, placing gold pins expertly throughout and then later adding minimal makeup to my face. I had to use all I could within me not to think about what possible harmful materials they were using to achieve this look.

"Yes?" I asked, concerned it may be too much.

"Breathtaking," he finally said, his eyes looking across my new attire. It only took him a moment before he cleared his throat. "We best be going if we plan on making an early exit."

He lifted his hand waiting for me to place my own on his before he led me to the litter outside, helping me in. I had seen the people of Rome use these as forms of transportation, but as I entered inside, I noticed there was barely enough room for me let alone the both of us.

"Are you not coming?" I asked, worried.

"I'll be on my horse right beside you," he said, grabbing the reins from a slave. "I didn't think it would be very ladylike for you to ride a stallion beside me and thought you might be more comfortable in a litter."

Forehead scrunched, a frown encapsulated my face. I would have appreciated the extra time with Evander.

Swinging his leg over the brown back covered by the saddle, Evander signaled to the slaves and clicked his tongue, beckoning his steed forward. The top of the litter rose first, my feet following as we began down the streets of Rome. Evander led the way, clearing a small path in the crowds for the men carrying me. Earlier, Evander had mentioned that Cassius lived near the Circus Maximus, but we were not taking the same route we had to get to the races. Instead, he led us down what seemed to be a quieter and more upscale part of the city.

After some time, we finally reached his villa, which seemed to be placed on the outskirts of the city, not particularly near the Circus Maximus, but I paid the minor detail no attention. Stepping down, Evander gave his horse to one of the slaves and helped me out of the litter, guiding me up the abundant steps to the entrance. Soft light escaped from the openings on the side, laughs and conversation resonating outside. Two guards positioned by the door opened it for us, and I followed Evander inside. The entrance alone was magnificent, marble on every wall with torches detailing the beauty of it. It was much grander than Evander's home, but I knew that wasn't from lack of funds on Evander's part. They were much wiser with their money, constantly investing in business opportunities, as Aura had mentioned. Moreover, I noticed a sense of humility in his family, which to me spoke volumes.

A slave girl appeared, bowing before us before motioning us into the next room where the party was being held. We passed through the entrance, following her into the atrium. My eyes widened at the beautiful and creative decorations. All across the ceiling hung roses elegantly, surrounding the room in the sweet essence of their flowery aroma. The occasional petal dropped, making it look like it was straight out of a fairytale. The room was full of people, their conversations now bouncing loudly off the marble walls and pillars. The torches along the room gave it a sense of romance, pairing nicely with the roses. No expense seemed to be spared.

Walking deeper into the room, I felt that I was with some sort of celebrity as I walked beside Evander. The crowd stopped and stared in awe; the women gave him doting looks, but there were other types of looks mixed in with it.

"Why are they staring at you like that?" I whispered to him.

"They're not looking at me," the corner of his lip turned upward, his implication noted.

"Evander, Rivka, you made it!" Cassius exclaimed, walking over to us from across the room, his arms high in the air.

Evander grabbed his hand, embracing him. After, Cassius turned his attention towards me, grabbing my hand and bringing it to his lips. "I'm pleased to see you again, Rivka."

I tilted my head in acknowledgement.

His hand lingered for a moment before letting go and turning to a slave passing by. "Get something to drink for my friends here."

The boy, no older than fifteen, bowed, turning quickly on his heels to oblige his master.

"You finally started expanding your search for slaves, Cassius? Have you finally grown from your rogue ways?" Evander said lightly, chuckling at his remark.

"On the contrary. I've already purchased all the finest slave women in Rome, so the only next viable option was him," he laughed, his olive silk tunic sliding against his tan skin.

Evander laughed, but I could tell it wasn't fully genuine. Odd, I thought to myself. Nevertheless, they continued to briefly touch on the slave trade in Rome while I politely listened until the slave boy returned with our drinks. He lowered his curly head of hair, lifting the platter with three goblets for us to take.

"Thank you," I said quietly to him, reaching first.

He didn't raise his head, but I could see that he was surprised by my thanks. Cassius and Evander didn't notice as they grabbed their own drinks, and Cassius changed the conversation topic. "Come, there are people who have missed you," he said to Evander, gripping his shoulder.

He led us to two men laughing with each other in the corner of the room. Both couldn't be older than thirty, but their balding heads contradicted their youthful skin. The one on the left had a rather large gut, but he seemed content with it as he rested his arms on top of it. The other was tall and thin, practically skin and bones, but had a kind face.

"Rivka, allow me to introduce Quintus," Cassius pointed to the man on the left, "and Gaius," signaling the one on the right.

"A pleasure," I nodded.

"Well, well, well," said Quintus comically to Evander, "you leave for years and come back with a desert flower. Seems your post was not in vain."

Evander laughed, shaking his hand as he introduced me. "This is Rivka, a friend from Jerusalem."

"Enchanted," Gaius smiled,

"Rivka," Evander explained, "Quintus, Gaius, Cassius, and I have been friends since our childhood. Our fathers all serve each other in business in one form or another or in politics, so naturally we all became close."

"I see," I looked towards them, taking stock.

"I hope we didn't interrupt," Evander said.

"Oh, nonsense," Gaius insisted.

"Were you in some form of debate?" I questioned.

"Aren't they always," Cassius muttered, taking a sip from his goblet.

"Come now, Cassius, we know you find our inquiries riveting," Quintus smirked, giving him a hard slap on the back, nearly causing him to spill his drink.

"We were speaking of the Greeks," Gaius answered me, ignoring them.

"The Greeks?" I asked once more.

"Indeed. They have concluded that the land on which we dwell is in fact a sphere."

Giving a small chuckle, I tried to maintain a composed face at what I would consider a primitive question. I kept having to remind myself of the things that have and have not been discovered. In truth, it would be interesting to hear their opinion.

"How is it," Gaius continued, "that two men on different sides of the sphere are on the right side up if they have their feet in opposite directions?"

"The Greeks think they know everything, but it's utterly preposterous that we are all living on a round ball," Quintus fumed, taking a glance over the room. "Wouldn't you agree, Rivka?"

I turned to Quintus, looking into his eyes, thinking quickly of a response. The whites of his eyes were not white at all, but instead yellow, a clear sign of liver damage. My guess would have been the bouts of alcohol that seemed to be flowing at this party, at the very least.

"Well, I'm not a woman who studies such things," I started, trying to get myself out of answering.

"Preposterous. Please, continue,"

"Personally," I hesitated, "I tend to agree with the Greeks. I believe that the evidence that they have given is convincing enough," I stated, hoping they wouldn't ask for specifics. Much to my satisfaction, they didn't, instead Quintus continued on his reasons for doubt. He spewed his speculations for what seemed like an eternity until Gaius leaned close to my ear.

"We tend to argue over such matters," Gaius smiled. "Such as, does a person's flesh decay quicker in the moonlight rather than in the sunlight and what not."

My smile remained, holding the wisdom of the ages deep inside. I watched as they continued their conversation, not noticing that I wasn't an active participant, much to my liking. The two friends were quite interesting characters, mostly due to their odd personalities. Quintus was spoiled, whiney, but up on all the latest gossip. Gaius was much more down to earth, but not far off from Quintus. Their banter back and forth made me curious how they would be able to continue their father's businesses, assuming that that is where their wealth was coming from in the first place. After debating, their topic switched to their ailments.

"My tooth has been bothering me for some time, but I refuse to pay those blasted physicians anything. I'm certain none of them know what they're talking about," Quintus huffed, taking another sip.

"Oh please, Quintus, I know the cure for such a small matter. Cook a black chameleon and you will be just fine. It also works to get rid of mice in the home," Gaius said firmly, his wine sloshing around in his cup.

I had noticed that both Evander and Cassius were only listeners as well, only adding a thought here and there. But the difference between the two was that one continued to steal glances towards me throughout the entire conversation. I pretended as if I didn't notice Cassius, but there was something deep behind his eyes. A hunger of sorts and I was eager to get away from the infatuated man. Evander didn't seem to notice as the topic steered to trade and business, leaving me to continue to play my part.

"Frankly, Evander, between these pirates and the outrageous taxes the government imposes, I don't know how your father is making a living," Cassius chuckled.

"You're not wrong to wonder," Evander joked back, the caution behind his words visible in his eyes.

"At this rate, all our business will be in jeopardy," Quintus huffed. "For having the greatest army in the world, being unable to stop a few bands of rebels is tarnishing our good name."

"Yes, your efforts in the military have become quite strenuous, your labor is thanked," Gaius mocked quietly, taking another sip from his goblet.

Quintus clearly did not approve of the joke, his eyes narrowing on Gaius, before continuing. "I should be more thanked than that old goat Tiberius who just stays hidden away on Capri. If he'd actually do his job and not leave it to the members of the Senate, we might have already resolved this issue."

Evander, not wanting to discuss the subject further, changed the topic, asking what was new since his time gone, as this was his first social engagement since returning.

"Vitus has fashioned himself a musician and has begun to play the flute," Quintus said, in obvious disgust.

Evander sensed my subtle confusion, bending his lips to my ear explaining, "Different than your land, here it's considered degrading to play an instrument or sing."

A shocking fact for any era of time. I was always finding more information that was a surprise to me. Maybe instead of preparing myself for odd facts, I should be alarmed at things that are considered normal. My thoughts were interrupted when a woman bumped into Evander, spilling some of the contents of her drink onto his burgundy toga.

"My apologies, I can be quite clumsy," she said as she dabbed his chest with a small cloth. It only took a moment before she lifted her eyes, catching his own.

"Evander! What on earth are you doing here?" she beamed, grabbing onto his shoulder, pulling him into her.

Evander didn't say anything as he took a hold of her back, tense at the forwardness of her embrace it would seem. It was either that or the fact that she had done it in front of me.

Before addressing her comment, he turned their attention to me. "Rivka, this is Cornelia. Her father, Cornelius Scipio, is in the Senate with mine and he runs the largest slave market in all of Rome."

I gave a polite smile as she just barely took her eyes off him. It gave me a moment to take her in.

Her blonde, loose curls framed her oval face. Her black eyes complimented her dark eyebrows, rosy lips, and pale skin. Her white robe laced with gold almost made her look angelic.

She wasn't heavy, her straight torso and flat chest proving that, but she wasn't slender either. Her figure wasn't fashionable for this time, the countless slender girls around made the fact obvious, but there was still something about her. A certain air or energy that drew you in. It was clear to see that almost every man in the room thought so too.

"Cornelia, this is Rivka."

Her dubious eyes turned to me; intention hidden behind them.

"It is *such* a pleasure to meet you, Rivka," she said sweetly as she gripped my arm, squeezing it before placing both hands around her goblet. My eye caught her gaudy jewelry, a ring on every other finger, each precious stone larger than the one before.

"The pleasure is all mine." She made me uncomfortable.

Cornelia smiled before turning her attention to Evander. "It's been ages since I've seen you, you fiend. It's a wonder the Jews didn't kill you during your time in that wretched land. Your mother told me days ago that you had returned, but seeing as this is the first time I've seen you I thought she must be lying and that you were, in fact, dead."

"No, no, Cornelia, I'm alive and well. I just," he hesitated, "had important matters to handle for my father."

The answer didn't seem to satisfy her, but she pressed it no further. Instead, she turned her attention back to me. "You look just lovely, I must take you for a tour around the room," she purred, grabbing my hands as she pulled me forward. "You don't mind, do you, Evander?"

"Not at all," he gave a small smile, stepping back slightly. Either he didn't see the plea of salvation my eyes gave, or he chose to ignore them. Nevertheless, Cornelia urged me forward, beginning the long process of introducing me to the men in the room. The other women in the room appeared to be watching Cornelia and I, but that didn't seem to bother her.

Instead, she pulled more and more men into conversation. Whether leaving out the women was intentional couldn't be confirmed, but as time passed, it seemed likely.

The men were all captivated by her charming wit and boisterous laugh, divulging in her crude humor and suggestions. Maybe I was the only one who noticed it, in all honesty—the way she held their attention like a lioness prowling into the center of the pride, her presence a silent claim of territory. Still, they all kept both her and I heavy in conversation. I tried to refrain and say as little as possible, which wasn't too hard since Cornelia was doing a fine job of talking for us both. Yet even she had grown tired of the underhanded performance as she finally pulled us away, leading me to the edge of the room near the decorative walls. She grabbed a cup from a servant as he passed with a tray, placing one in my hand as she reached for another.

"*Palmam qui meruit ferat*," she chimed, raising it in the air.

I gave a soft smile, lifting my own into the air, but only watched as she took a hardy gulp down. Giving a sigh of satisfaction, Cornelia turned her attention back to me. "So, tell me, Rivka, how did you cross paths with our long-awaited soldier?"

"He actually saved me from a lion attack in the desert," I responded shortly. Evander had already briefed me as to what was and wasn't appropriate to say while staying here in Rome, especially after our first encounter with Cassius. We both agreed to stick to the truth but leave as few details out as possible.

"Heroic," she laughed. "But that was always *our* Evander, rushing off to be a hero."

I just held my tight smile, scanning the crowd for him, hoping this evening would soon come to a close. That didn't mean I couldn't feel Cornelia's stare burning into my cheek.

Turning back to her, her face changing into a cordial smile. I sensed that she didn't like my short answers, but that didn't matter to me. Still, it didn't seem to intimidate her either, rather giving her some sort of a challenge. She looked across the room as we sat in a moment of silence between us, listening to the laughs of the guests and the clanging of glasses.

"Shall I tell you a secret?" she broke, her gaze never leaving the crowd.

Before I even had a chance to respond, she answered her own question. "Do you know why they hang roses from the ceiling?"

I lifted my brow. "I'm not sure. To make the air smell nice?"

She chuckled, taking another sip from her cup. "Astute, but alas that's not the reason. It's the hosts' reminder to their guests."

"Reminder?" my interest slightly peaked.

"Yes, that whatever happens here, it will stay... confidential. Whether it's due to the influence of wine or if one's odd indulgences reveal themselves, it will all 'remain under the rose.' A sign of secrecy, if you will."

"Interesting." I kept it short; she was alluding to something, looking for a reaction or response out of me. I'm sure she'd make it known soon enough, with the wine loosening her tongue. Or maybe she was just always this brash.

"Indeed," she smirked, placing the cup on a passing tray, grabbing another.

From the corner of my eye, I could tell Evander was looking over at us while two men I hadn't met in his company were visibly in a heated discussion. There seemed to be an uncertain look on his face, eyes scrunched.

"Do tell me, Rivka," Cornelia continued, "Evander seems to be very much smitten with you."

There it was.

After the chariot race, Evander warned me that at this feast there would be a host of prying eyes and gossipers. I didn't argue when he said he would just name me a friend, both for my protection as well as his family business. While the fact still hurt a little, I understood. Besides, of all people, I knew that the less people knew about me, the better.

"We're just friends," I reassured her, forcing my lips back into the courteous smile that had faded.

"You know, after the loss of his first love, Sabina, he vowed to never marry. Raving to those close to him that there would never be another to compare."

She had my attention now. But she didn't need me to say anything for her to continue.

"Oh yes, they were very happy together. She was so beautiful with her light hair and slender figure. Many women were broken-hearted when they heard the news of Evander's vow, knowing that he is a man true to his word."

I bit my tongue.

"But…" she lingered, "I'd say he isn't a god, because low and behold I find him entangled."

"Entangled?"

"Indeed, *dear* Rivka. I've known him for many years. There is nothing that can be hidden from my eyes."

"I don't think—"

"Oh, come now, don't be shy, I see the way you two look at each other," she grinned, tapping my nose. The jealousy was painstakingly obvious, as was the scouting for information, but what was I to say?

"Rivka."

I turned behind me to the sound of Evander calling, grateful for the timely interruption.

"We've had a long day, and I think it's time that we made our way home," he smiled, grabbing my cup and placing it on a table nearby.

"Of course," I replied, pushing back the strands of my dark hair that had made it to the front.

Any hint of Cornelia's jealousy disappeared into thin air, a look of innocence covering her once again, heightening her presence. "Again, my dear, it was indeed a pleasure," she beamed. "This will not be the last time our paths will cross. I'm sure I will be seeing you very soon."

The edge and threat in her voice weren't apparent, but there was something there. Her feigned innocence wasn't enough to fool me.

"Cornelia," I nodded before noticing the blood leaving her rounded fingers as she gripped her goblet, watching as I took Evander's forearm as he led me away.

Evander guided me through the atrium, giving short goodbyes as we made it to the entryway.

"I'll have a servant bring our litter," Evander stated, exiting through the front door as I waited for him. The sound of resounding laughs echoed across the marble halls, the acoustics putting me on the verge of a splitting headache. I placed my forehead against the corner of the cool marble wall, hoping it might help, but it was for naught.

"Leaving so soon?" a voice called from behind.

I turned, slightly startled, only to find Cassius, another drink in hand.

"Yes, I'm not feeling well," I replied, not wanting to put Evander in any difficult situations.

His eyes lingered on me, watching as he took a step forward. "I bet I know what would cure you," he slurred mildly, pressing his free hand on the wall next to my head, cornering me. He clearly wasn't holding his full capacities, which was slightly surprising considering we hadn't been here for all that long. But not for one second did I believe that the look in his eyes was a result of that.

"Cassius," I calmly said, "step aside."

He gave a wily smirk, his intent undeniable. I wasn't worried or panicked over the predicament I found myself in, only

70

annoyed. I didn't want to cause a scene for Evander's sake or do something that might jeopardize his business relationship with this man or his father. But it was plain that I was going to have to do something as he lowered his hand and gripped my waist.

Lifting my hand, I was about to act when out of nowhere Cassius was yanked back, dropping his goblet to the floor.

Evander.

His hand gripped the collar of Cassius' shirt, pulling him towards his face.

"Evander," I placed my hand on his shoulder, trying to stop him from making a decision he might regret, but he just ignored me.

"If you ever come near her again, I promise you, Cassius, friend or not, it will be the last thing you do," his low, firm voice echoed around the small marble room, the torchlight showing Cassius' wide eyes.

He said nothing, only stared back at Evander. It was surprising to see, especially because it wasn't as if Cassius was a weak man. His muscles showed clear dedication to physical discipline, and previous comments about training with gladiators would make him decent at combat, but Evander's commanding presence was enough to make him quiver.

"Do you understand?" Evander asked again, giving him a shake.

Cassius simply nodded, resulting in Evander studying him a moment longer before letting him go, pushing him into the atrium. He turned his head back, giving Evander a hard look before looking me over once more and making his way back into the party.

"Are you alright?" he asked before I had a chance to speak first.

"It seems it's your role in life to pull me out of pernicious situations," I hinted.

"I'm not sure I know what 'pernicious' means, but I think I understand your point," he said, the corner of his mouth turning up. "Shall we?" he motioned towards the door.

He guided me through the door, down the steps, and into the litter that was waiting, helping me climb in. I sighed as he grabbed his horse's reins, and we made our way back to his home. The ride back gave me ample time to think over the night's events: Evander's odd friends, Cassius, Cornelia. One thing that made me wonder was Evander's place in it all. He didn't seem particularly comfortable there, standing out. Now whether that was because I was there or other reasons still remained unclear to me.

I couldn't help but think that his time as a soldier did change his worldview, something that none of those people in that room could ever understand. I still hadn't told him about my past—nor the fact that I was from the future—about my skills, my work, and being an assassin. In a way I feel like that would help us connect on a different level, coming from similar backgrounds, but... I was scared. Scared to change what has already been established and what I would consider to be on shaky ground as it is. The closest he had seen me fight was when I naively tried to free Yeshua from the cross, but I wouldn't even consider that a fight since it was most definitely not my best work: sloppy and based on emotions.

But that nagging feeling stayed with me the entire evening and well into the night. Now back in bed, I stared at the ceiling of my room, the full moon reflecting brightly against the water in the garden.

Ultimately, I would have to make the choice of telling him. But was the gain worth the risk?

VI

SEASHELLS

Morning was a welcome remedy to an evening of restless sleep and night terrors. Over the past few weeks, I had been having this recurring nightmare; randomly it attacked my dreams again and again, with no rhyme or reason. Images from my past, memories that I wanted to forget. Some nights I would wake in a cold sweat, while others I slept as quietly as a baby. I had tried to find a solution to the annoyance, or even a pattern, but was left with nothing.

Pulling my curtains back, the sun hadn't even peaked through yet, meaning the morning meal wouldn't be served, at the very least, for an hour. My first thought to try and get my mind back into some normalcy was to do my morning exercises. But once complete, my heart was still racing, and it wasn't from the training.

Dressing swiftly and freshening up, I pushed my room doors open, the creaking of the hinges sounding through the still hallway. Shutting them behind me, my mind sought the place where I might find true solace: the gardens.

Paying no attention to the servant or two performing their duties, I briskly walked to my destination, relief washing over me as I saw the beautiful vegetation. My pace slowed as I entered its calming space, my mind tranquil as I made my way down its path. Nose tickled with the fragrance of the bright, dew covered flowers, my body sunk to the stone bench in the garden center. Sparrows sang their song, alerting their friends that another day was upon them. My eyelids closed as I embraced the refuge of sweet serenity.

"I didn't expect to find you awake so early," a voice broke my peace.

Listening for a few more seconds to the babbling water, I peeked open one eye. "I could say the same for you. Especially after our late evening."

The corner of Evander's lip turned up, his head bobbing slightly. Smoothing the folds of my olive skirt, I gestured for him to sit beside me. Accepting the invitation, he lowered himself, admiring the garden in the process.

"Truthfully, I haven't had a full night's rest since joining the army," he grimaced, fingers holding onto the edge of the bench.

It wasn't too off to imagine that he would be having night terrors of his own, or better said, PTSD. The horrors of war spared no era of time, each just as gruesome as the last. Only those who had lived through it could really fathom what it was like.

Biting my lower lip, I debated offering some words of understanding, but stopped myself. Any attempt would fall short. We had no shared experience to bridge that gap—at least, not one that I could admit to.

"Why are you up so early?" he asked again.

"Generally, I do like to rise with the sun. But I didn't sleep too well."

He remained silent for a moment. "I hope it wasn't due to Cassius's behavior. While I would like to just blame it on his drink, I'd be lying if I said that it was out of character."

"No, not at all," I answered truthfully. "In fact, thank you for your... chivalrous help."

"Chivalrous?"

"Yes," I nodded. "Valiant. Honorable."

"Ahh, I see," he paused, shifting his position slightly. The tone of the conversation seemed to shift. "Even while that might be his temperament, Cassius is used to women just falling to his will, his features making them swoon."

My dark eyes looked at his flexed jaw.

Was he jealous?

"No, your interruption came perfectly," I reassured him. "I was anything but captivated by him."

Evander relaxed his hold on his jaw, but remained quiet. I pondered if I should explain more, but I couldn't help but give into my own resentful thought. "Your friend, Cornelia, was quite the talker."

He rolled his eyes. "Pay her no mind. I hope she didn't say anything to offend you."

"On the contrary," I said coolly, "she was quite enlightening."

Silence.

"I've known her since we were young. Her father always insisted to my parents that one day our families would unite, but obviously that didn't happen as I was with... with Sabina," he awkwardly finished the sentence.

The name hung stiffly in the air. I wasn't sure if he shared it to clear the tension or to clarify something deeper. Either way, I could feel the green-eyed monster leaving traces in my heart. The longer I stayed in Rome, the more obvious it became that Evander was likely one of the most eligible bachelors around. With his handsome features, kind soul, and familial stature, why wouldn't all the women be finding a way to be with him. In essence, so was I—even if all of my reasons weren't the same.

A knot formed in the center of my chest. "There's no need to explain."

Breathing in deeply, I held the air for a little, trying to steady myself. This was a silly thing to allow myself to be upset over. As I exhaled quietly, I sensed that Evander was thinking the same, honey hair just covering his furrowed brows.

"My lord," a servant interrupted, head bowed to Evander.

"Yes?"

"Your family is waiting for you and the lady Rivka. The morning meal is prepared."

Turning my head to the now rising sun, I couldn't believe how briskly the sun had risen, my conversation with Evander feeling much shorter.

Clearing his throat, Evander rose and extended his hand towards me. Hesitating only a second, I placed my fingers into his calloused hand. With my loose curls falling off my shoulder as I rose, Evander gave a soft smile. A form of apology or will of forgetfulness to our conversation. Giving in, I returned it with a single, low nod and followed him into the dining room.

The table was laid with splendid options for us to choose from. I wasn't usually one for breakfast, but the spread that the servants had prepared for us looked too delicious to pass up; a plethora of fresh delicacies, fruits, and vegetables.

The family had already gathered, waiting only for Evander and me to begin the breaking of their fast. As soon as we entered, the feasting began. Aura began the conversation by asking Evander how the party had gone the night before. He gave minimal details, but I was learning that seemed to be his way with his family. His sister sighed, saying she had wished she had gone with us, but her friends had insisted on visiting the gladiators for their special show in the *ludus* that they held once a month.

"In all honesty, it was quite boring, I don't know why my friends find it so entertaining," she rolled her eyes. "To me it just looks like children playing with sticks since they aren't allowed to use real weapons when women spectators are around."

"Why not?" I asked, finding that note peculiar.

76

"One gladiator killed a senator's wife at one of these matches because he was so bloodthirsty," her eyes widened as she told the story, but it was quickly accompanied with a laugh, "or so the story goes."

"Then?"

"What actually happened was that the senator had promised to speak with the emperor to free that particular gladiator after one of his famous matches but went back on his word. He killed his wife as revenge," Evander clarified.

"Some would almost say that the gladiator's act was justified then," I countered, earning a giddy laugh from Aura. But already bored with the topic, she switched to another.

"Octavia is hosting a party tonight. Rivka, you must come with me," Aura beamed, biting into a fig.

"Another party?" Lucrezia asked.

"Mother," Aura cajoled, "I am young, let me enjoy myself."

Lucrezia said nothing in response, giving Aura the opportunity to talk about what we should wear. I didn't even get a chance to respond before a welcome interruption occurred.

"My lord," a voice called from the entrance of the room. It was one of the slaves. I had seen him during my time here, but mainly near Vinicius. My guess was that he was one of his personal attendees.

"Galen, enter," his master motioned him near him.

The servant bowed before leaning close to Vinicius's ear, whispering the contents of his message. We could all see that it must be bad news, because with each word the attendant spoke Evander's father's face only grew harder and harder. When Galen completed his message, Vinicius waved him off, taking a deep swig of his drink, allowing the liquid to flow until the cup's content was completely gone.

I could see Evander hesitating, but it only took a moment for him to speak what we all wanted to know. "Ill news, father?"

Vinicius' jaw set, his mind visibly filled with a cluster of thoughts, but he granted an answer to his son's question. "The filthy pirates that have been attacking almost any vessel of value on the Mediterranean have managed to take hold of, not one, but two of our ships, along with everything in them."

"Everything, father?" chimed Aura.

"Everything. The cargo, the crew, the infernal rope, all of it!" Vinicius rubbed the bridge of his nose, muttering under his breath.

Like his wife, I pursed my lips, taking account of the situation and everyone's response. Lucrezia was also deeply distressed, knowing the weight on her husband's shoulders, both financially and mentally. Evander, the soldier, was most likely taking in the logistics of the incident, while Aura was only concerned because everyone else was. Still young, it was understandable she would rather get back to speaking about her party. I, on the other hand, was unsure how to feel. It was grave news, indeed, but what could be done about it? In modern day, this would be a quick fix. Nothing that a few helicopters, tracking technology, and weapons couldn't fix. But here in the ancient world? How would we even know where to begin to look?

"Father," Evander called to him, pulling him back into our presence.

Vinicius motioned that he was listening, giving Evander the permission to continue.

"I think it's time that we step in and no longer leave it to others."

His father nodded, hard lines riddled across his forehead. "But what can we do? They're stealing blasted war ships, for Mars sake. What can we do to combat them?"

His words didn't seem to daunt Evander, as a small smirk began to play on his lips, his eyebrow raised. "Come with me to the *tablinum*," Evander said, rising from the table and making his way to the study.

Wasting no time, Vinicius, Lucrezia, and I followed him while Aura called out after us saying she had to buy a new necklace for the party tonight. By the time I entered the room, Evander had already laid out a map on the light wood table, placing weights on each corner. Lucrezia and I lingered near the door while the men dove into their strategies.

"These pirates don't seem to follow any particular order or reason. When we had goods from Egypt, they attacked from the west. When it was Ephesus, the east. Goods from Carthage, they used small boats and attacked from each side," Evander explained, pointing out each location on the map. "Our military vessels are no exception. How they manage to steal an entire vessel, killing the crew, and not being caught by the greatest army in the world is perplexing. No, it's downright ridiculous."

"They are pirates, son," his father reminded him.

"I know that, father. But what's peculiar about it is they must have a drop off location where they sell the goods and ships. I would want to assume it was no Roman occupied city, as they would get caught, but now I'm not so sure."

"Are you saying you want to find their port location?" Vinicius asked, stepping closer to his son.

"It's an idea," he bobbed his head. "Besides, I don't think we gave enough thought to the fact that they may have an informant, whether it's on or off the ships."

"Son, would it not be easier to have them come to you rather than you go to them?"

Evander contemplated the thought for a moment, looking intensely at the map. "It's a strategy, but I don't want to lose the element of surprise."

He thought some more. "We could set a trap for them *in* the sea."

"How?" Vinicius asked.

"By using our merchant ship as bait. It'll be a more tempting snare. We'll send it out, inviting them to rob us, but we'll be waiting with a well-rounded attack."

"That could work," his father pondered, rubbing his chin as he looked intently at the map. "I have some trade going to Egypt set to leave at the end of the week. While the cargo isn't heavy, it's quite precious. Meaning it's probably on the lips of every sailor from here to Crete."

Evander ran his finger along the map, outlining the path of the ship. His finger stopped, finding its mark. "We could wait and ambush them right about here. We're still close enough to Rome, but far away enough from land. There'll be no reinforcements."

"For anyone, that is," Vinicius reminded him.

"I'm not worried about that fact. If we prepare ourselves sufficiently, we just may be able to defeat them. Maybe even bring back a few alive."

"How many men will you need?"

"40 sailors should about do it," Evander calculated.

"So few?" his father asked, his shoulders tensing.

"We must. If they suspect anything is amiss, they won't attack, and this will all be for nothing."

"But why can't you just put soldiers to act as sailors?" I questioned, earning a wide-eyed look from Lucrezia.

Vinicius' mouth was pinched, arms crossed. "I have to agree with Rivka, Evander. Why not disguise them?"

"For one, the soldiers we would have available to us aren't skilled to navigate the sea no matter how short the distance is. If there is even a whiff of oddity, this won't work. These pirates are savages, but that doesn't make them fools. In fact, it's quite the opposite. They've been able to escape us and retribution thus far, haven't they?"

No one seemed fully convinced, but we all kept silent.

"Besides," Evander continued, "those men won't be our only forces. I plan on having two armored military vessels following us from a distance.

"And the emperor, or the Senate, rather, will give you this because…"

"It's a matter of national security, father. Leave the soldiers to me."

Vinicius let out a sigh. "I trust you. Then I will go and make the necessary preparations with the captain. He still may remain the same, yes?"

"I have no objection."

"Then we will speak again once I have finished with him," Vinicius laid a hand on Evander's shoulder, giving it a tight squeeze before exiting the room.

Following her husband, Lucrezia added, "And I will make an offering to the gods for your safety and success."

I listened to their footsteps down the hall until I could no longer hear them. Looking at Evander, I slowly made my way towards him. The lines on his face were pressed hard, deep in thought. Putting my hand next to his, I gave my support. "I'm coming with you."

Evander let out a short laugh, before looking at my face to see just how serious I was. "No, you're not," he taunted, pulling the map from the table and rolling it up in his hands.

My eyes winced; jaw locked. "Why not?"

Evander gave a look, both at my forwardness and demanding tone, resulting in me to soften.

"You mean, besides the fact that you're a woman? It'll be very dangerous, Rivka. You could be killed."

I took a breath, steadying myself. Evander didn't know about me or my past, so I suppose it was out of concern that he didn't want me to come. But I had just as much experience in these matters as him, maybe even more. I knew my knowledge would be useful, and if not my knowledge, my combat skills.

"That's exactly the reason why you need me there," I said collectively. "Without some female presence on a merchant ship, the pirates will grow suspicious. I'll be your safety net."

"Safety net?" he asked, confusion written on his face.

"I'll be there to cover for you," I said quickly.

"Rivka," Evander said, laying the rolled map on the table while spreading his arms against it. "I don't think you realize just how few women are on ships unless it's a passenger ship."

"I know that, but aren't there women on merchant ships? I was when on my way to Rome."

"Sometimes, I suppose—"

"And wouldn't seeing a woman make them believe that they have a better chance at conquering the ship? Believing we are all the weaker and more defenseless?"

Watching him, Evander slumped on a leather chair, rubbing his face. Softening, I crouched down in front of him, pulling his hands down with my own. My eyes finding his, I spoke quietly, "It'll be alright and be your best chance at capturing these… villains. Besides, if there's a way I can help, I want to do that for you."

His eyes searched mine as his lips pressed into a hard line. We sat in silence as he pondered the option before finally conceding, "Alright, you can come. But, Rivka, you have to promise to listen to whatever I tell you. This isn't a regular situation—this is war."

I nodded, knowing that once he saw my capabilities he would relent in the circumstances.

———— ✤ ————

Preparations filled the next few days, everyone having some role to play. Evander was busy securing the military forces we may need, Vinicius setting up everything with his captain, Lucrezia preparing Evander's belongings, and Aura, well, just being Aura. I filled my days with learning all I could about Rome, pirates, and political tensions going on. Some I received

82

from Evander, but much was from the servants. They had warmed up to me. Mostly because I was an outsider myself, I thought.

During this time, I had also managed to run into Sariel when shopping with Aura. Our conversation wasn't long, but she reminded me that I was in her prayers and hoped that all was well with me. I didn't get a chance to speak of anything in depth before Aura pulled me away.

Now back at the villa, only a day before our journey was to take place, I found myself a little idle. I had just finished speaking with Evander as he told me the plan for the pirates capture and our role to play. Mine was to stay on deck until the pirates came and then to take cover underneath. I nodded along with his strategy knowing that I wouldn't take heed. On that day, I would see wherever the need for me was. In war and espionage, something unexpected always comes up; you can't plan for everything. He'll be glad someone's there to help quietly keep things in place.

Since our garden encounter, there was a gentleness to the way he spoke to me, a quiet attentiveness I hadn't noticed before, even in these types of conversations. Our exchanges flowed more easily, touched with the kind of familiarity that forms not from grand declarations, but from shared mornings, passing smiles, and the comfort of silence that didn't need filling. Whatever was unfolding wasn't rushed. It moved gently, like sunlight creeping across a floor. I wasn't sure what it meant yet, but I found myself looking forward to the next moment we'd share, however small it might be.

In search of a little quiet before dinner, I found myself making my way once again towards the garden. The gentle patter of the water always seemed to give me peace. Entering, the flowers that were in bloom gave a magnificent scent, their vivid array of colors placed as if they were a mosaic unto itself. I took one full breath of air, taking in its fresh sweetness, until I saw that I wasn't alone.

"My apologies, Lucrezia," I bowed my head. "I didn't mean to disturb you."

"No disruption caused," she tilted her head to one side.

Unsure of what to do next since my plan of isolation failed, I began to make my way back into the villa until I heard her call after me.

"Please, sit with me," she motioned to the free space on the bench.

Somewhat reluctantly, I obliged her. Evander's mother and I had exchanged few words during my time here, and anytime we had, there was always someone else present. She seemed like a force to be reckoned with, making me a little uneasy.

"Have you been enjoying your time in Rome?"

"Yes," I responded politely.

"Especially with my son," she stated, more than asked.

Her forwardness caught me off guard, making me a little lost on how to answer. Instead, I just held my tongue, giving a small smile. That seemed to be enough to allow her to start what she truly had on her mind. Clicking her tongue, she began, "You're not the first woman in Evander's life. Did you know this?"

So that was her angle. "Yes, I know."

My response seemed to have taken her aback. "You do?"

"Evander told me."

She leaned back, straightening her shoulders. "Then let me tell you what I'm sure he hasn't. You see," Lucrezia began, "Evander was very much in love with Sabina. They had grown together as children, her parents being close friends of the family."

Looking down, I clasped my hands on my lap as she continued her story.

"She had always loved him, but was a quiet, patient girl. When Evander went to Germania, she went down to the temple of Mars to pray for his victories and his safety every single day, lest she miss a day, and he should perish. Upon his arrival home, he realized that they were meant to be together too," her mouth twitched.

"I'm sure her death was very difficult for him to bear," I said softly.

"Oh, indeed. Her gentleness soothed his temper, her smile brightened his gaze, and her tenderness touched his heart. Their love reminded me of Vinicius and I."

I slowly looked back up at her, her brown curls softly blowing in the breeze.

"And now, here you are, the complete opposite of her…" she trailed. "I can't help but wonder if what attracted him to you is out of purity or if for the sole reason that you do *not* remind him of her."

I swallowed, the new dark thought beginning to plague my own mind. "What makes you think he is attracted to me? In truth, I would have thought quite the opposite since coming here."

"Rivka," she placed her hand on top of my own, "a mother knows. It's not just in how he looks at you, but rather in how he does not look at you. He doesn't want to disappoint us, marrying someone we might disapprove of. But I still know. He can't hide anything from me."

I looked at her, not sure if I should take what she said as an insult. Then I caught on to the tail end of her sentence. "Marry?"

Lucrezia nodded, pulling her hand back into her lap. "When Sabina became gravely ill, Evander was not here. He had business to attend to and by the time he returned she had passed into the next world and had already been burned on the pyre. Once his official time of mourning was complete, he made a vow to his father and I," she gazed off into the garden, tears filling the rim of her eyes.

Holding my breath, I waited for her to continue, bracing myself for Cornelia's warning.

"He swore that he would never look at another woman, unless he intended on marrying her. The truth of it is that he did believe that meant he would never look at another woman, for none compared to his Sabina. And yet, here you are."

I bit my lip. Cornelia had said that Evander vowed he would never marry, period. My instincts were to believe his mother over that girl, but still, something wasn't adding up.

"That's interesting," I sat straighter. "Because at the banquet I was informed that his vow was to never marry at all."

Lucrezia gave a small laugh. "Did Evander tell you that?"

I hesitated. "No."

"Then don't believe it. What he said to us is the truth. The only reason he *might* have even said such a thing is because many women were shamelessly glad at Sabina's death, meaning that my son was back for the taking," she clenched her jaw. "It was likely just to have the lions pull back their claws."

Lucrezia's love for her son was as plain to see as the blue sky. Could I fault her for doing and planning things for her son in the way she thought best? Her candor should be something to admire. Even in her frankness, she still did something that few women might do.

"I don't know much about you, Rivka," she turned to me, her eyebrows scrunched. "I don't know your past, your family, your thoughts and feelings. The only thing I know is that you're a Jewess, much to our dislike."

Pursing my lips, I turned my attention back to my clasped hands, waiting for the rest of her blow. I knew there was prejudice in Rome, but nevertheless, it was still difficult to face.

"That, and..." she continued, "that you've made my son very happy. The only source of happiness that he has been able to find since her death all those years ago."

My heart softened, her words like embers warming my soul. My lips parted as my mind searched for words to say, but nothing came.

"For his sake alone, I will welcome you into our family should he decide to spend the rest of his life with you."

It wasn't exactly the blessing one would hope for, but I could see that Lucrezia was doing her best to extend an olive branch. Having lost my own mother so long ago, this was the closest thing I would have to replace her absence. Her love and kindness were there, even if she was having difficulty accepting me. But the love she bore her son overcame even that hesitancy.

She pulled me into her embrace, her warm skin caressing my own as the smell of lavender graced my nose. Even in this unlikely exchange, I felt... secure. I basked in Lucrezia's motherly tendency, for one moment imagining she was my mother.

"Please," she whispered into my neck, "take care of my son."

"I will," I responded, the words leaving my mouth before I had time to fully register.

She held on a little longer, giving one final squeeze before pulling back and letting out a sigh. Wiping her tears with her thumb, she continued. "There's much to be done before your journey. Best not have idle hands," she rose, walking back into the villa without looking back.

———— ✦ ————

Our last moments in Rome before boarding the ship were a whirlwind. Having to leave at dawn, I said my goodbyes to Evander's family the night before. Lucrezia was polite, Vinicius stoic, and Aura slightly bothered. She said that it would be boring until we returned, so to make haste so we could tell her all about our adventure.

This wasn't a final goodbye, so Evander didn't treat it as such, just a business trip. I took with me the few things I brought with me to Rome. From the knife, to the hair tie and belt I kept hidden, to one of the simpler outfits that Aura had made for me.

Wearing another simple, linen material that I had chosen while we were out, I made my way up the gangplank following Evander. The thick leather belt that I had purchased sat snuggly against my waist. Little to Evander's knowledge, I chose this outfit with great purpose. Should trouble arise, the tunics that the women wore here would give me little movement. This way, I could pull my dress from the back and tuck it into the front of my belt, making myself a makeshift jumper. I had also purchased a new pair of leather sandals that I tested for their flexibility. It felt good to feel like I was doing my duty once again, my military instincts on the cusp of being used.

The ship was similar to the one I had boarded on my way to Rome. A flat wooden deck with the mast in the middle, a slightly elevated back for the ships steering, quarters down below as well as a galley for the sailors to row the ship. The goods that Evander's father had were securely fastened below deck, hidden in one of the compartments while decoys were wrapped on the top, just daring for pirates to come and take them.

Waving to his family at the dock, we watched as they got smaller and smaller, our ship pushing out to sea. Once they were no longer visible, Evander had us settle into the task at hand.

Our Captain, Adad, was an interesting man, an Assyrian with a thick, long black beard. He had shells tied into it, with his equally thick head of hair tied back in braids. He was small in stature, but his muscles showed he had the life of a sailor. He had some oddities, but was always willing to impart wisdom, even to a woman. I took advantage of that, asking and learning all I could. A few days into the voyage he even explained why he wore the shells. I had assumed it was for decorative purposes, but he quickly corrected me.

"It's for the wind," he taught, "keeps the eyesight clear and hair out of the way should a quarrel arise."

Made sense, like a weight.

As the days on the ship passed, Evander and I had been able to do some learning of our own. While he was still busy reminding the sailors of the plan and keeping guard on the sea, we did manage to have a few conversations together. I had noticed that being away from Rome welcomed back the Evander that I knew, the one from Jerusalem. He wasn't exactly carefree, as in every situation I found him in he had a mission of some sorts, but he was more... free to be himself.

This separation was good for him—good for us. Never had I craved attention, until I tasted his. It was like we were back in the gardens of Machaerus, untethered. But every so often, I caught myself. Was this right?

Now a week into the voyage, I was about to find out.

The wind blew wildly against our faces, the smell of the salty sea filling our nostrils. The dark blue water contrasted beautifully with the ship's wood and white sails. It was like something out of a dream, birds still flying high above us. Evander and I sat against the deck in silence, taking in the natural beauty. I could hear him taking a deep breath, but I assumed it was to just embrace the fresh air. Only the breath turned into words.

"Rivka, I've been a bit of a fool."

His frankness caught me unexpectedly. Did he mean right now or when we were in Rome? Because if he did mean back in Rome, I was the one who felt like the fool.

"What do you mean?" I asked for clarity.

"With my parents, my lifestyle, my home," he shook his head as his eyes searched over the water.

Then the most uncontrolled sound came from my mouth. My lips pursed as I shut my eyes. I had just snorted from my laughter. But, within seconds, my own benign laugh was accompanied by Evander's as well.

"I know, I know," he repeated, turning to face me.

"It wasn't exactly subtle," I chortled.

He smiled. "For that, I am sorry. And I want to be honest with you, the good and the bad."

Bracing myself, unsure of what he was going to say, I gave my response, "I'd like that very much. Lay your cards on the table."

He looked at me quizzically for a moment before continuing with what was on his mind. "Rivka, you know about my past. How I went into the army, about Sabina, now about my family and their business, the people in my circle, and how I react in situations. You saw firsthand that I haven't handled things well since you've arrived. I'm not trying to shift the blame or make excuses for why, I know that it was wrong, and I hope that you can forgive me. It's just… my life in Rome, my experiences, they've shaped me. But it's not who I am."

My brows crinkled together, not being entirely sure as to what he was trying to say. Evander noticed, because he tried to explain it better.

"War changes you. Experiences change you. People change you. The lifestyle you saw, the people you saw—my family included—are part of the old Evander. My post in Judea, meeting you, Yeshua… they've readjusted my priorities and my goals. When I returned to Rome, I forgot that and didn't know how to balance the two. But now I know and I'm never going to let that disorientation happen again. Who I am is the man that you knew in Machaerus and Jerusalem, the man that asked you to come with him to Rome."

His hand brushed against my face, pulling my hair tenderly behind my ear. I could feel my heart begin to race as he lingered, his rough hands against my own soft skin.

"Rivka," he began, his throat catching slightly.

I knew what he wanted to say. At least, I think I knew. But was it something I'm ready for? I cared for him too, but was this right? Maybe this was all a mistake. Our days in Rome had only left me more confused rather than giving me clarity I have longed for, hoped for.

He pulled his hand from my face, resting it near mine on the wooden edge of the ship. "I know we haven't known each other for a very long time, yet it feels like I've known you for a lifetime," he paused, taking a moment to look at the crashing waves.

I bit the inside of my cheeks, the anticipation only growing. This was where the conversation was going to end, I shouldn't let it go any further. He hadn't said much yet, but I knew it was only a matter of time. Only, when I went to open my mouth, no words came out. He must have not sensed what was going on, because he continued, his sea-green eyes finding my own.

"Rivka, you're fierce the way a wildfire is—unapologetic, unstoppable. Your determination... it's not loud or dramatic, but it's there, deep in your bones. And yet, for all that strength, you feel with every inch of your heart. I've seen it—in the way you love, in the way you protect what matters to you..."

A flush crept up my neck, painting my face.

"And, Rivka, you're... you're beautiful. The kind that lingers in your mind long after you've left the room. Your dark hair like brown silk, the way your eyes spark when you're passionate about something... You're not just beautiful. You're rare."

A warmth took root in my heart, slow and radiant, starting in my chest and spilling outward until even my fingertips felt alive.

"You coming back shows me that you care for me as well. You must; otherwise, what would be the point of coming? Either way, you know that I have feelings for you. After our time in Jerusalem, our experience together, how could I not. You deserve to know that I have grown to care for you. Deeply," he hesitated.

My own brain flooded with a thousand things to say to him—especially after a beautiful confession like that.

Stop, we should just be friends.

I care for you too.

We shouldn't be having this conversation.

I'm from another time.

I love you.

But the words just wouldn't come out. They caught somewhere in my throat, tangled up in fear, hope, and everything in between.

It didn't matter, it seemed the silence gave him the courage he needed. Because he didn't retreat. He didn't hesitate. Instead, he continued, as if the quiet between us wasn't emptiness, but an invitation. He placed his hand on top of my own, grasping it slightly, giving me no room for escape.

"Rivka… I'm falling in love with you."

Rarely did a moment like this happen, one where I didn't have any words to say. Or rather, I didn't have any words that would come out of my mouth. I stared at him; his dark, dirty blonde hair moving with the wind. He didn't look away, and that steadiness undid me more than the words had. Truly, I tried to get the words out. My mouth was open, my brain was sending the signals, but they just weren't working together. It seemed like an eternity before he finally spoke again.

"Please, say something. I've lived in your silence for so long, so long that I don't know how much longer I can stand in this deafening stillness."

His eyes searched mine, but still no words came.

He shook his head. "You don't have to tell me that you love me. I know that it may not be as much as that. But, please, Rivka, just tell me something."

My own voice croaked against my throat. Finally, the words were coming. It's now or never.

"Evander, I—"

VII

PIRATES

My words were cut short with the sound of an ominous shriek coming from the water. Evander and I both spun toward the sound, but before we could make sense of it, a brutal force slammed into the side of the boat, throwing us off balance and sending us crashing to the deck. Lifting ourselves up with our forearms, Evander's eyes widened.

"Pirates!" Evander shouted, giving me a quick look before turning to his crew. "To arms! To arms!"

We were still a few days sail from the most likely place of attack that we had configured. This was still close to port. They dared to attack this near?

The few soldiers we had on board grabbed their weapons, throwing extras to the crew of the ship. I hadn't felt comfortable having so few skilled fighting men on this ship, but Evander was right. If the pirates had even a hint that we were filled with soldiers they wouldn't attack and then our plan would be for naught. I just prayed that the battleships that were supposed to be trailing us would come help before there was too much damage, or worse. Better yet, that our secret weapon would work.

Looking to the back of the ship, I locked eyes with him—the ace up our sleeve. Marcus was an archer who had been under Evander's command while in Germania. He was gravely injured while in active duty, losing one of his legs, and was sent back to his family in Rome. But that injury didn't make him lose his skills; he was still one of the best archers Evander said that he had ever known. That and he was fitted with a wooden leg. Once

THE ABYSS BETWEEN

our men spilled some oil onto the pirates ship, Marcus would
shoot a fiery arrow into it, bringing it up in flames.

I pulled myself up, eyes locked on the incoming pirates
that were beginning to board.

"Rivka, get behind me and go below deck, now!"
Evander commanded, gripping his sword in one hand and knife
in the other.

Knowing that it would just waste time to explain, my
eyes scanned the deck, making sure everyone was in position.

"*Now!*" he yelled again, giving me a firm shove towards
the direction of the stairs. I gave him a quick look and began
making my way there. Proceeding down the steps, I checked
behind to see if my stash was still there. I had left a sword and
simple knife tucked away in case the need should arise. Well,
arise it did and my weapons thankfully were. The leather
wrapped handles felt good in my hands, giving me a decent grip.
Lastly, I flipped the hem of my tunic into my belt, ensuring that
it was secured.

Not wasting a second, I ran back up the stairs to join
Evander and his comrades. The pirates had already boarded the
ship, the hand-to-hand combat spreading among the men like a
disease. Some more of the pirates were still swinging in on the
right of the ship. Flipping the knife in my hand, I threw it,
landing square in the chest of a boarding pirate. Grunting, he fell
off his rope and into the sea.

I ran into the fray, iron smacking against iron as the
fighting commenced. Between blows, I could see that Evander
wasn't far from me. He was battling against what seemed to be
the largest pirate on deck, each giving hard blows to the other,
but Evander held his ground.

A sword came swinging, which I barely dodged. The
man kept swinging at me, forcing me back as the sword was just
inches from me. Just managing, I brought my sword up to block
his swing, leaving him open. Snatching the opportunity, I

95

jammed my elbow into his face, sending him down as he held his bloodied nose. Spitting to the side, I turned to find my next opponent, adrenaline rushing through my body.

I didn't get two feet away when a veiny arm slipped its way around my neck, putting me in a headlock, while the other hand pressed against my head holding it secure. His arm pushed against my vocal chords, making it impossible for my lungs to receive air. Forcefully, I raised my own arm and dug my elbow hard into his stomach, earning some release to the pressure around my neck. Using the momentum, I locked my fingers behind his sweaty neck, gripping his hair, and hurled him over my shoulder, his back making a loud "thud" as it hit the ground. He lay unconscious or dead.

Picking up my sword from the ground, I looked to see if Marcus had set fire to the ship, only to see it still intact. My eyes scanned for him on the upper deck, finding a harrowing image.

Two pirates were attacking him, cornering him against the railing. He was already at a disadvantage, but having two men to fight instead of one made the odds of his survival even slimmer. One of the pirate brutes landed another blow to Marcus, knocking him on his back. Marcus managed to swing his good leg behind the pirate, bringing him down, but the advantage was momentary. Within seconds, the pirate got on his knees and tried to bring his knife down on Marcus. Marcus resisted for a little, but pushing up was more difficult than the force going down and within seconds the pirate's blade landed in his heart.

With everyone else occupied in their own fight, I seemed to be the only one who saw, meaning it was my job to take his place. Stabbing the pirate in front of me, I tried to run to that side of the ship. Another pirate came from my right, trying to land his sword on my side, but I rolled out of the way, sliding my sword against his calves. He screamed in pain as he fell to the floor.

Getting up, I continued through the chaos, trying my best to take out any pirates I could on the way.

In the meantime, one of the sailors seemed to have taken notice that Marcus was dead and grabbed the bow and arrow, trying to find the flint and iron pyrites to light the tip to send it over to our enemy's ship. But speed was not on his side as I saw the disaster unfold. The pirate that had killed Marcus appeared behind him, sliced the back of his legs, sending him on his back as the bow went flying through the air next to the ship's steering. The arrow went in the other direction, landing near the mast. I didn't wait to see the raider land his final move.

I was halfway across the ship along the side, just parallel to the arrow. The only thing in my way was a dozen men fighting. I didn't even have a second to think of the best way to get over to the mast when another pirate thought he'd try his luck with me. Giving a forceful grunt, I used all my might and pushed my opponent back, flipping his sword through his hand and just barely managing to knock him over the side and into the waves below. The taste of sweat found its way onto my lips, salty and warm. Wiping my mouth, I turned around.

"Rivka!" I heard my name called through the commotion. I squinted as I tried to find the source.

"*Rivka!*" it rang again, my eyes finally landing on Evander on the other side of the ship. He cut down the man he was fighting and began to make his way over to me.

"Get below!"

Disregarding his command, I called back to him as I pointed to the mast, "The arrow!"

He found sight of it, its tip lodged in the base. Having the clearer path, he made his way towards it as I tried my best to meet him there. Within a couple of minutes I had arrived just as he dislodged it.

"Marcus is dead!" I yelled over the noise. Evander instantly looked up at the deck and saw his fallen comrade. He looked back at me and knew what had to be done, but didn't want to accept it.

"Where are the soldiers?" I asked. The military reinforcement ships that Evander had gotten for us hadn't come to our aid. In fact, I hadn't even seen them once since we began our journey. My assumption was that they were following behind at a distance.

"They were going to meet us closer to the rendezvous point!"

Reality hit—they weren't coming.

"Look out!" he screamed, pushing my head down with one arm and swinging his blade into the pirate behind me. The enemy defeated, Evander looked back at me.

"Cover me!" I yelled again and waited only a second for a single nod from him before I ran towards the bow. I almost reached the stairs when my sandals began to slip on the water that had found itself onto the deck.

Or maybe it was blood.

I had just gotten my balance when two men fighting smacked their backs into me, sending me to the floor, my sword sliding before me. Grabbing it, I tried to get up, but between the rocking of the ship, the slippery floor, and the fighting men, I couldn't get a grip. I had to do the next best thing.

Crawling, I just made it to the base of the stairs, trying to pull myself up as the boat shook again from the pressure of the pirate's ship and the waves. Somehow, I managed to grab the railing and hoist myself up the stairs. There were two separate fights going on up here, but I reached the bow without them realizing I was there.

The flint and iron pyrites were still on the ground. Picking them up, I swung the bow over my shoulder and placed the arrow in between my legs while I tried to light the material wrapped tip. One, two, three times I striked it, but to no avail.

Finally, the material lit. Wasting no time, I swung the bow off, nocked the arrow, and looked down the shaft. Taking a deep breath, my eyes locked on the floor of the pirate ship. One of the oil filled barrels was cracked next to the mast, a perfect target. Steadying my hand, I released the bowstring from my fingers, the arrow leaving towards its mark. It took only seconds for the arrow to land flawlessly, instantly lighting the oil. I watched as the fire rapidly spread up the mast and onto the sails, sending what few pirates remained on the ship into a panic. They didn't even have time to grab anything to quench the fire before the other oil barrels that were thrown were lit as well, bringing the whole ship into flames.

My smug grin was knocked off my face almost instantly when I felt something jamming into the back of my head, knocking me to the ground. My eyes shifted out of focus, but out of instinct, I rapidly rolled to the right. As I did, an axe was brought down where I had been, splintering the wood. Still dazed, I tried to get up but was knocked down as the pirate ship was slammed into ours again by the waves. By this point, the pirate had dislodged his axe and was already raising it again to bring my life to an end. I turned my head and saw my sword was just out of arm's reach from where I had left it to pick up the flint and iron pyrites.

As the axe started its downward swing, a sudden flash of light exploded before my eyes, momentarily blinding me. Metal hitting metal, I saw the outline of a sword stopping the axe from coming down. Captain Adad let out a low growl as he pushed the pirate back.

"Get out of here!" he yelled at me, stopping swings from the man twice his size. Semi-obeying, I tried to get up, but struggled as they fought over me.

The pirate towered over Captain Adad, a brute force of muscle and fury. Within a snap, the fight turned savage. Steel clashed, and then the axe came down—merciless, precise. A cry tore from the Captain's throat as the head struck true, and with agonizing slowness, he sank to his knees, the light fading from his eyes.

Taking the opportunity, I managed to grab my sword. Now full of rage, I sprang to my feet, taking revenge for the loss of the Captain. The anger mixed with adrenaline gave me a boost of momentary strength, making me able to knock the handle of the pirate's axe from his hands, its head still lodged in Captain Adad. Using the advantage, I swung at the raider. He was quicker than his size gave him credit for. Swing after swing he evaded.

A harsh screech fractured the air, sending a jolt down my spine. Instinctively, I turned my head just for a second and the pirate capitalized on it. He swung his legs behind my own, sending me up. Landing on my back, all the air was knocked out of my lungs. I tried to get up, but he put one foot on my sword and the other on my chest, pressing down hard. Trying to use my free hand to push his foot off of me, he took it as a challenge to press down even harder.

A cheer erupted around the ship, but I could hardly focus as I was just trying to hold on to dear life. Without warning, another foot came on top of my sword hand, a hand releasing my fingers from its grip. I tried to hold on, but I wasn't strong enough, and the leather handle was ripped away.

Sword now removed, the pirate released his foot from my chest, making me instantly gasp for breath. I didn't even have a chance to fully regain my capacities before he grabbed a fistful of my hair and held my arms behind my back, dragging me down the stairs. I breathed through clenched teeth, trying to think as quickly as I could as to how I was going to get out of this, but my knees hit the ground before anything came to mind. My hands rested at my side, palms on the wooden floor. Fingers twitching, my brain scanned for any ideas, any solutions, to get myself out of this.

I now realized that the piercing sound from earlier was a horn, a horn that seemed to signal our defeat. All of our surviving men were lined up alongside me, pirates behind them

100

with their hands on their swords. Panicked, I looked down the line for Evander, not seeing him. When my eyes finally found him at the far end, a knot twisted in my chest. I didn't know whether to feel relief or worry. At least we had both survived the attack—thus far.

I went back to trying to find a way of escape, but it only took a matter of seconds before I was interrupted by a proclamation.

"*Gentlemen*, I cannot thank you enough for your ship and supplies. It seems that we were in great need since a group of ruffians decided to burn down ours. I know how badly you wanted to share it with us."

That voice.

It sounded frighteningly familiar, making my entire body freeze. Slowly, I looked up to find the owner of the belligerent sound. My eyes found the source and in that moment, it was as if my entire life force was knocked out of me. Worse than when the pirate took me down. My mouth was like sandpaper, my heart was racing while my eyes wouldn't leave their point of interest.

Its owner walked in front of the men all the way on my left, looking down at them with a sneer.

"I'll give you that you've done the most damage to my men and ships then any before you, so give yourselves a pat on the back. But unfortunately, long-term, that doesn't mean good news for you."

Before me was the person I was least expecting.

My best friend.

My greatest enemy.

Thana.

She reached for her sword, the silver metal reflecting against the hard sun. I hardly recognized her, but I suppose she was always good at that. Her dark hair was pulled back in braids and around her eyes there seemed to be charcoal smeared. Her belt around her tunic held a variety of weapons, but something was hidden on her back underneath, slightly bulging out, almost undetectable. She passed the crew of our ship one-by-one, slowly tracing the short, curved blade gently across their necks, only drawing some blood occasionally.

She couldn't know I was here.

She'd likely execute me on the spot.

I tried to surreptitiously look around for something to cover or hide myself with, but there was nothing! She was only five people away from me now and I knew if I was going to do something, I'd have to do it fast.

I bowed my head low, but just enough for her to drag her blade against my throat, lest she get suspicious. I kept my eyes downcast. Maybe my Roman clothes and adornments would be enough to keep me hidden. Her leather shoes tapped against the wooden floor, until they finally came before me. Her blade grazed my smooth neck. I didn't flinch, knowing it could grab her attention. Her blade left my throat and she moved onto the next person. I wouldn't dare give a sigh of relief, but the knots in my stomach loosened.

But my joy was premature.

The brown leather stopped, slowly turning, toes landing towards me.

Step.

Step.

Step.

She stood in front of me, unmoving. An eternity seemed to pass by, millions of thoughts running wildly. Then the cool steel rested under my chin, lingering only a moment before it pressured me to raise my head.

"Rivka."

VIII

SILVER CLAWS

Thana's eyes gave the imitation of control, but I knew her. Deep down she was surprised, panicked even. I said nothing, biting my tongue and slightly pursing my lips. She stared only a moment more before an eerie sound escaped her lips.

A laugh.

A few of her crew began to join her, but whether they knew why they were laughing was a mystery to me.

She moved her blade, slightly tilting her head as she stared at me. My eyes were stones, determined not to give her the reaction she so obviously wanted. She crouched down in front of me, not breaking eye contact before she whispered, "I knew you were down here."

A smug smirk dancing on the corners of her mouth. My stoic expression stayed. Her stare lingered on me before she finally rose and walked towards her men.

"Kill the crew, just keep enough alive to help our slaves man this ship."

I dared not react.

"What about her?" her man said just loud enough for me to hear, gesturing towards me.

She hesitated only a moment before replying. "Chain her to one of the posts in a room which can be locked. I'll deal with her later."

He nodded and began shouting orders to their men. Our own men's eyes widened with fear as the evil pirates obeyed their leader's orders. Screams and whimpers came from those of the unlucky, begging echoing.

I finally risked a glance at Evander, wondering which fate would be his. A pirate grabbed him, pulling him from his knees and pushing him towards the steps that led below the deck. He was safe—for now, at least.

From behind, a pair of burly hands grabbed my shoulders, lifting me from the ground. He tied my hands and pushed me forward. I already gave up on the hope to fight him. I could take on two, maybe three men, but I was unevenly matched. The others would kill me before I would even make it to the edge of the ship. Even if I managed to escape, what about Evander?

Possibly being brash, the thought of confronting her here and now crossed my mind. Could it hurt our situation? Maybe. But could it also help our situation? Again, maybe. Nonetheless, the more I thought about it, the greater the itch became.

"Thana!" I yelled over the sound of pleadings, but she didn't hear me—or chose to ignore me—as she made her way to the other side of the ship. "Thana!" I screamed again, louder and more determined than before.

She paused, her back still towards me as her men leaned down to her ear, whispering something. Thana shook her head before slowly turning around, her sword pointed towards the ground as if it were a cane. I said nothing at first as we stared at each other, curious if she would make the first move, but that was uncharacteristic of her. Through all our missions together, she would always push me to be the instigator, the spokesperson, the enforcer, while she just quietly stood back and watched. At first, I thought it to be her timidity, her lack of leadership skills, that made her that way. But as time passed, I realized it was her cunningness, making sure she always had a scapegoat, and I was the lucky sucker. Well now she didn't have me to hide behind, she'd have to come and face me herself.

"In the flesh," she took a mocking bow, rising and making her way towards me.

Studying her, I waited for her to speak again, having already practically begged her back. I wouldn't demean myself lower and give away my vantage point too.

"Speaking of flesh," she continued, "here you are. Between the two of us, you are the one who's supposed to be dead. But here I find you—*alive*."

"Miss me?" I lifted my chin, mockingly.

She scoffed, not taking her eyes off me. "Endlessly."

"Well this was no warm welcome. Already you're trying to get rid of me and we haven't even had time to catch up."

"My deepest apologies."

"You made it through alright? No cuts or bruises?" I asked through a face of feigned concern, trying my best to both stall for time and find out as much information as possible.

"Me? What do you take me for? Not a scratch, I'm a survivor," she raised her sword, earning a cheer from her men, feet stomping against the wooden planks.

"That's the thing about survivors," I interrupted, earning silence from the crowd. "You never trust one… not until you understand what they were willing to do to survive."

A tight smile spread across her face, eyes shrewd and unwavering. "You know, I've done quite well for myself here," her white teeth glistened, using her sword to point at all of her men, one large, scarred brute in particular. "Atticus here served as a gladiator down in Ephesus. He escaped by killing his trainer during practice, feeding his bones to the dogs."

She moved to another with golden hair and just as many muscles. "Baldilo is from the mountains of Germania. He was captured fighting the Roman army, but he never made it back to Rome before killing all eight of his armed guards and escaping to Gaul and finding me." Thana pointed to the man next to him, his tan complexion offering himself as a force to be reckoned with. "Demetrius is a Greek who was a slave to one of Rome's prominent officials. He worked in the fields until he killed his master to come and join my crew," she paused. "Need I go on?"

I stared at her, chin level as I gave a small smile. "If your men are so good, then why don't we place a little wager?"

She paused, lifting an eyebrow as her men offered up a chuckle, most likely entertained by the thought of a bet.

"What kind of wager?" she asked.

"Me against one of your best men," I smiled as the thought must have amused her crew as their chuckles grew to a roar of laughter. Only Thana wasn't laughing. Instead, her cold eyes stared into mine; she knew my capabilities and that the fight would practically be evenly matched. What I lacked in size and strength, I well made up for in strategy and experience.

Still, she seemed to entertain the thought. "To what end?"

I licked my lips. "Our freedom. If I win, me and anyone else that I came here with go free. If your side wins, then we'll do whatever you want, no questions asked, no problems made."

Her men snickered, softly insisting that she take the deal. Her gaze never left me as she considered my proposal. In truth, we both knew that taking it would weaken Thana, a thought that I'm sure she wasn't too thrilled about. But the pressure from her crew seemed to be working in my favor, each eager to see my, what they believed, easy death.

"Enough," she held up a hand to her crew, silencing them. "Rivka, my men are the best in the world, each a heartless killer in their own right. I feel that it is only a waste to have your body so quickly tossed overboard as fish food."

"Scared, Thana?"

Her men went silent as her jaw set. Her brow raised as she scrunched her face, contemplating her next move, the wheels turning inside her mind. "Alright, Rivka, I'm intrigued. I'll take you on your deal, with one minor adjustment."

"Which is?"

"I would feel just awful taking advantage of you, a small young woman, against my giant attack dogs. Why don't we even the odds a little bit. One of my men against one of the ones we spared downstairs," she grinned as she spun her deceit.

Her crew seemed confused at her proposition, but I knew.

Before I had time to protest, she cut me off. "Take it or leave it. But rest assured, this is the only chance of freedom you'll have."

I clenched my jaw. She was right. Anything I tried after the fact would either end in failure or I wouldn't be able to save everyone. Besides, we could try this and if we failed, we could still try to escape another way. The only problem was, how great would our chances be? From what I could tell, most of the men they spared weren't fighters. There was Evander, but could I risk putting his life on the line? On the other hand, he is a soldier and could probably hold his own. Again, assuming they even chose him.

"Fine, we have a deal. But you let the men volunteer; you don't choose, they do," I demanded, thinking at least this way Evander might offer himself. A cruel thought, but a practical one. He was our best chance of getting out of here.

She hesitated as her men gave soft murmurs. "We have a deal."

A cheer went up as I kept my eyes on her. She motioned to her men to go and grab a fighter and told others to pull me to the side of the ship. As her men went down, others began clearing the area for the fight. I stared at them all, curious who would be their warrior, all looking up to the challenge. After some time, the creaking of the stairs echoed against the sky. I tried to look past the three men blocking my vision to see who had been chosen, but they were too large. It wasn't until they were all up that I could see who was picked.

"Evander," I muttered, his head held high as they undid his chains and directed him towards me. We made eye contact, and he pressed his lips.

"You filthy dogs, who is ready for a fight," Baldilo roared, causing the men to join him.

"In the true tradition of a pirate fight, let's keep things interesting, shall we?" Thana chimed in. "Atticus will be our champion!"

The men roared, banging against the wood of the ship causing all the things around to shake.

Evander, now shoulder to shoulder with me, stayed silent as one of the men tossed him some cloth. It seemed odd, but Evander gripped it tightly in his hand.

"I'm sorry I got you into this," I mumbled, "but I figured you would be our best chance of survival."

"Don't be, you did the right thing—"

"Bring out the weapons!" Thana yelled, lifting her sword into the sky.

My eyes widened slightly, but I shouldn't have been surprised. Thana always did have some kind of trick up her sleeve.

Baldilo brought a small wooden case, bending on his knees before Thana and lifting the box to her. Thana opened it, staring at the mysterious contents as a smile percolated her lips. Grabbing it, she lifted the weapons into the air earning a cheer from her men. I flinched as the silver reflected against the sun before I realized what they were. The metal was fashioned into two claws, four points with a handle on the side. I glanced at Evander, but he seemed unphased. I sighed, knowing I had to trust in his confidence.

"Atticus," Thana shouted, "come claim your weapon."

"Are you sure about this?" I questioned, looking the savage over as he grabbed the silver weapon into his hands. His black beard was the only hair he had, which seemed to hide some of the many scars that encompassed his face. He smirked at me before hocking the saliva from the back of his throat and onto the wood planks. I turned away in disgust.

"I'm a soldier, remember?" Evander reassured me. "I've fought hundreds of men just like this one. It's just another regular day for me." He wrapped the cloth around his knuckles before placing the claws Baldilo brought him in between his fingers.

"Really? You fought every day, regular soldiers with steel knives between each of your fingers?" I asked sarcastically.

He gave a soft chuckle. I couldn't help but wonder if he was as good as he said he was. After all, the only instance I had ever seen him fight was when Thana first boarded our ship, and even then, I didn't see much since I was busy with my own opponents. He seemed fine, but this man was clearly a skilled fighter, the marks on his chest showing just how many times he had escaped death. His history as a gladiator only enhanced the fact.

"I'll get us free," he said, gripping his weapon tightly in his fingers. He gave me one final affirming nod before walking towards the inside of the man-made ring as one of Thana's henchmen pulled me to the side, the coarse rope cutting into my wrists.

"Are you ready," asked one of her men standing between the two fighters. Evander gave a small nod as Atticus let out a hoot, met with a responding sound from the pirates.

He raised a small cloth into the air, pulling it down as he yelled, "Begin!"

They took their stances, each shifting their weight on their feet, hands protecting their face. All of Thana's thugs were practically foaming at the mouth as they cheered their comrade, throwing out slurs at Evander. I watched Thana's arrogant lip curl, an obvious tell that showed she thought she had already won. Clenching my teeth, I turned my attention back to Evander, sending a silent prayer that he would make it out alive.

Atticus took the first swing, quick and skilled, but just slow enough for Evander to duck, circling around him. He wiped his nose with his thumb as he studied his competitor. Once again, the brute attacked first, and once again, he missed Evander.

Not wasting the opportunity, Evander lunged, blade inches away from Atticus's chin as he stepped back. Atticus swiped his claws in the air, giving a battle curling yell, but Evander managed to block him and push him back with his body weight as he slammed his side into the man's chest.

The crowd booed as a small trickle of hope began to seep into my thoughts. Evander grabbed the momentum, lunging forward again, but a hushed gasp escaped his lips as the man's claws came in contact with his side. Again, the crowd cheered their ally, leaving me to worry as I watched Evander assess the damage. He winced as he placed his fingers on the bloody cuts.

Seeing that he gave enough reprieve to his opponent, Atticus circled him once again. This time coming on the offensive, he charged at the hunched Evander, claw hand high, as he let out another battle cry.

My heart sank: was Evander doomed?

But Evander turned just in the nick of time, swiping Atticus's side. As he gave out a yelp, Evander jumped at the chance without delay to sink his claws into the man's shoulder. Glory was short-lived as the opponent turned around, landing another set of cuts into Evander's chest, pushing him through the crowd and into the side of the ship. He tried to attack one more time, but Evander managed to block that hand. Unfortunately, that left his side exposed as Atticus countered with a hard punch to the face. Again, he tried to stab him, but Evander held both of his arms back, as they slowly inched closer and closer to his face.

The sun showed the sweat dripping down from both of their faces, a small amount of blood pooling at their feet. I hardly felt the rope chafing my wrist as I watched over the sound of the crowd calling for Evander's death. He had to do something quick, otherwise he would be getting just that.

Suddenly, Atticus was with his back on the ground and Evander jumped on top, landing blows to his face with his unarmed hand. I hadn't even seen him swipe his leg under the man. Louder yells filled my ears as the pirates pushed closer and closer into them, almost obstructing my view. But Atticus's bloody and dazed face was visible between their legs, enough to know that Evander had won. A sigh left my lips, knowing that he had just bought our freedom.

That feeling was temporary.

The angry pirates pulled Evander off the man, ripping the claws from his grasp, and began to beat him, punching and kicking as if he were some wild animal.

Horrified, I yelled, "Thana! Stop this! We had a deal! We had a deal!"

Our eyes met, but hers were cold and lifeless. She stared at me as the men continued to attack him. I knew if they continued any longer, he would die. She knew it too and seemed to enjoy the pain it brought me.

"Thana!" I screamed again, making my fury known.

She cocked her eyebrow before holding up her hand. "Enough."

Immediately on her command, her men stopped, not one landing another blow to him.

"We had a deal. He would have won had your fiends not interfered. You know that's the truth!" I challenged.

"Do I?" She asked smugly, earning her a small laugh from her men. "He never did finish the fight, so I suppose that we will never truly know."

"Thana! We had a deal!"

111

She didn't say another word, instead she just motioned to her men next to me, who grabbed me and began pushing me towards the steps that led to the belly of the ship.

"Thana!" I screamed, "We had a deal! We had a deal, Thana!"

My screams rang out in repetition as they took me deeper and deeper. I had no idea what waited ahead—only fear, and the terrifying uncertainty of what would become of me... or Evander.

IX

ESCAPE

Thana's thugs took me below the deck, pushing me into the room that held the grain and spices for the voyage. The post in the center of the room seemed to be where they intended on putting me, as the chains were already clasped around it. Pulling my tied hands, they secured me to the post and gagged me. I choked on the dirty contents, not wanting to totally figure out what was actually on the cloth for fear I would vomit all over the creaky floor. Based on their current reputation, these men would have left me to live in any mess that I would make.

Once they were positive that I was secure, they left me alone, closing the door behind them, leaving me in almost complete darkness. After a few moments, my eyes adjusted and saw the little light that peeked through from underneath the door. Stiffening, I tried to look around the room and see what was there, but it was to no avail. My hands threaded through the shackles, the short, rusted link that held my cusped wrists pulled through a hook in the middle of the post. Finally giving up, I slumped against the post, confused at the situation all together.

Time dragged on in that room, the hours blurring as I sat bound. I tried to think of how we could escape, but no matter what I came up with, it wasn't enough. Even the hairpin I had holding my hair that could be used to pick my lock was unreachable. At one point, I gave my mind a reprieve, leaning my head against the post, the waves crashing against the boats' sides as the light from under the door was beginning to fade. I sighed, finally letting my mind wander to where I did not want it to—Thana.

They beckoned; question after question, each one met with suffocating silence. What was she doing here? How did she come? Did the tablet bring her here? Did she find it because she went back to rescue me? Or worse, kill me? What did she plan on doing with us? Did she actually know I time traveled? Does she have the tablet here?

I softly tapped my head now against the pole that held me. Closing my eyes, I tried to picture the old days, the days when we were a team. Maybe there were some signs that I had missed, or there was something that could help me now. But my thoughts just seemed to drag, nothing particularly helpful coming to mind. Instead, it just brought up the feelings of betrayal once more.

I thought that I had let it go—my decision to stay in this time was proof of that—but now… seeing her, I wasn't so sure. I wanted to believe Yeshua and the words He spoke to me on that night which seemed so long ago. He told me that she was led by her feelings of hatred, that she was blinded from the truth, to forgive her. But as I looked into her cold eyes, I could only feel the anger boil in me once more and a sense of sadness.

I dwelt on these feelings for some time, just trying to make sense of it all, until I could feel an interruption coming. I straightened as heavy footsteps reverberated as they walked down the hall towards me. They stopped at my door, struggling to open it, a soft light seeping in from underneath. Once it finally gave way, a gruff man who I hadn't seen yet in Thana's crew walked in, scars all along his face and bald head. He gave a toothy, devious smile – toothy in the sense that he revealed his few rotten teeth. His eyes suggested the rest.

"Don't even think about it," I muffled through the gag.

It didn't deter him, his hearty laugh a telling sign. But instead of continuing towards me, he stopped at the barrel across from me that held a simple, flat, clay lamp. He shook the small object, not turning to face me. "You're lucky. Someone recently

114

filled this. Had it not been filled, I wouldn't have bothered," he huffed.

My body tensed as I watched him lean his own candle to the cord hanging from the lamp. It only took a couple seconds for it to catch, bringing some more light in the room. The man turned to me and looked me up and down a few times before giving into another of his screechy laughs as he turned to leave the room. He didn't say another word as he closed the door hard behind him, his cackle ringing as he made his way up the stairs.

Coming into my own surroundings, I realized that the lamp not only offered illumination, but little warmth as well. The sea night air was proving to becoming colder by the hour. I suppose I was considered blessed since I was being held away from the sea's winds, but its coolness did not spare those of us who were tucked below. The lamp was still a ways away, but every little bit helped. The smell of mixed spices tickled my nose as I tried to find a more comfortable way to stand in this hull.

No, I had to get out of here.

Once I was out of these chains—who knows how—I'd free Evander from wherever they were keeping him, assuming that he was still alive.

I pushed the thought away.

Grinding my teeth, I tried to think of what the best way would be to approach this situation. I knew I had to leave sooner rather than later. The longer I waited, the better the chance that Thana would interrogate me or, at the very worst, get rid of me. And if not me, she would most definitely harm Evander, if she hadn't already done so.

If I executed this plan during the night, I would have a greater success as most of the crew would be sleeping, leaving only a few out for the night's watch. Evander and I could easily take down any guards that may catch us and we could get to the rowboat that was attached to the back of the ship. I knew that it would come in handy and was grateful that they listened to me to install it in the first place. As for Thana, I would have to leave anything that would be done to her for another time. I'd probably never get the opportunity to escape again, let alone execute my revenge on her *and* flee with my life. I would just have to find her again.

Staring into the lit clay jar, I tried to concentrate on releasing myself from these iron cuffs. When they removed the rope to chain me, I did receive a break from the coarse chafing against my wrists, but now I had a different problem at hand—no pun intended. How could I get out of metal?

A figurative lightbulb appeared in my mind.

The light.

My heart began to race at the hope that this might actually work. I would use the oil from the jar as a lubricant for my hands, sliding them out from my chains. They weren't locked so tight around my smaller wrists that with a little help I just might be able to wiggle free.

But with that idea came another problem. How was I to get the jar with my hands behind my back? The barrel was parallel to my side, but I was incapacitated.

Clenching my tongue, I concentrated on finding the easiest path to make my plan work. Using my feet would prove dangerous, for fear that it might knock the lamp over, along with the barrel. But as I looked around, I saw that there were few other options at my disposal. That was going to be a risk that I had to take.

My brows knit together as I took a deep breath, preparing myself. I gripped the chains behind me, knowing that I'd have to put my full weight on it in order for it to work. Giving one final quick breath, I put my weight on the chains as I lifted my legs, each one grabbing onto the sides of the barrel. The exercises I had done over the years, especially for my core, now aided me in my mission. As I hung horizontally, I knew that this would be the most difficult part. Slowly, I began to rock the barrel back and forth, pulling it towards me. My wrists burned from my body weight, but I ignored it.

Against all odds, it actually worked. After a couple minutes, the barrel was leaning against the post. I sent out silent praise, having half of the plan complete.

Now, for the grand finale.

I blew out the light from the jar and I turned my body so that my back was against the barrel, the chains rustling with the turn. Not moving for a moment, I listened to see if anyone had heard anything or was coming. Convinced I was in the clear, I continued, feeling for the jar. I used the faint heat of the cooling oil as a guide. Feeling the clay against my fingertips, I let out a soft sigh at its surprisingly icy surface. Trying to grip my hands, the final phase was about to be complete. Ensuring I had a strong hold, I began to pour out the contents against my wrists and hands. I sucked air in from its still warm liquid hidden inside, but I pressed on, continuing until I could pour every last drop. Finished, I dropped the jar and began trying to wiggle my hands free. It took a little time, but as I folded my hands into themselves, they were ultimately able to give way, freeing me from my chains. After rubbing my wrists, I ripped the gag from my mouth and used it to wipe the oil from my hands. I spit to the side of me, happy to be rid of it and its nasty contents.

My eyes had already adjusted to the darkness and I was orientated with the room. From what I could tell prior to blowing out the lights, there were no weapons here, no knives, swords, not even a fork. No matter, I'd get by without them.

Placing my hand against the rope door handle, I tested the door gently, making sure there was nothing hindering my path. To my relief, it was looser than when the pirate opened it, and it swung outward with ease, moonlight spilling down the stairs. Contrary to what Thana thought, there weren't any rooms that locked on the ship, but I thought for sure that they'd at least put something to brace the door. The pirate must have just been lazy.

I scanned the area, making sure the coast was clear before making my way down the hallway. Snores babbled from closed doors along the hallway, proving my plan already to be accurate.

My first destination was the deck; it had been the last place I had seen Evander and thus made it a good place to start. Tiptoeing up the stairs, my eyes just nearly leveled the floor as I surreptitiously looked about. Overall, the deck was flat and there wasn't much hidden to the eye. There were a couple crew members manning the ship, but other than that there was no sign of Evander anywhere.

My next guess was below. If they weren't holding him on the deck, then they probably put him to work underneath it with the rowers. I sent out silent thanks for Evander having shown me where some of the things were on the ship beforehand.

Once again, I tiptoed down the stairs, making my way to the other end of the hall where there was a ladder that led underneath. Taking a quick look for Thana and her men, I proceeded down the ladder to the back of the room. My eyes adjusted to the torches attached to the wall, revealing over thirty men leaned over their oars with their overseer knocked out in the corner. It took me a moment to scan the area for Evander, but when my eyes finally landed on him, I couldn't help but let out a small gasp.

There he was in the front bench, seat closest to the aisle. It wasn't the harsh conditions down here that disturbed me; half-starved men chained to their seats, sitting in their own filth with that very malodorous aroma filling the air. It was Evander's shredded back, dried blood sticking to it as almost black bruises covered the rest of the exposed areas. Little sways evident, I knew that he had to use all his strength to sit upright. I had seen worse done to men, but it was never a man that I cared for.

Scanning to see that the guard was still asleep in the corner, I took silent steps towards Evander. The gaunt men didn't seem to notice me, each looking down at their oars. I didn't recognize most of them, figuring that they must be slaves of Thana's, but I did know a few: our chef, the first mate, and two others. They watched me as I walked down the center aisle to Evander, hope filling their eyes. I would try to save them if I could, but my first and main priority was Evander. Finally reaching him, my hand gently grazed his shoulder. He didn't make a sound as he lifted his head, barely catching a glimpse at me.

"Rivka," he breathed before wincing at what I was positive was unimaginable pain.

"Hey," I whispered, trying not to let my face reveal my true thoughts. "Don't worry, I'm going to get you out of here."

Evander's lip was cut, along with other cuts along his face, his right eye already swelling and turning purple— the evidence showing that even after the fight and his beating, they forced him to work.

It hurt me to see him like this, especially knowing that I was the cause. I attempted to give him a reassuring smile, but it turned out more somber than what I would have hoped for. Brushing my mouth gently over his bare shoulder I moved the oar from his lap and I got on my knees, trying to work the lock on his feet with my hairpin. Curiously, this lock wasn't much easier to pick than one from my own time, but I just scarcely managed to pry it open, the shackles slipping down from his ankles as they released. A couple of the other chained men noticed me or felt the weight of the chains shift at their feet, but they were either loyal or too weak to bring any attention to us.

Pressing my finger to my lips, signaling Evander to be silent, I unclasped the chains and placed them onto the foul floor.

119

The easy part was over—now comes escape.

Before I could get up to help Evander, something oddly familiar pressed up against my back. The cool steel was felt through my tunic, the circular shape an ode of death. My fear and suspicion were right.

"Going somewhere?" Thana asked from behind me.

I closed my eyes, outmatched. Slowly rising, I turned to face her as she lowered the barrel of the gun into my stomach.

What could I possibly say?

"I know their restraints are primitive at best, but I'm still curious as to how you got out of your manacles," she said, locking her jaw.

"What's with him," I nodded towards Evander, ignoring her question. "You promised that we'd be free if he won the fight. Not only did he win, but you all cheated and beat him near to death for it?"

"Oh, you think I just *gave* those to him? He earned those when he continued to fight my men after they brought him down here so he could look for you. I thought his fiery spirit should be put to better use."

He got those because of me?

My gaze narrowed. "Liar. I saw you mercilessly beat him."

Thana dismissed me completely.

I swallowed. "What do you plan to do with us?"

"I could just kill you, now couldn't I," her head tilted, reminding me that she held the power as she pushed the barrel deeper still. "But after such a long history, that might be in bad taste. I could just kill your friend, though."

My face stayed expressionless, even though my mind was doing the exact opposite. We were at a standstill, with Thana having the upper hand.

I had to change that and fast, but the only way was a gamble. Still, I had to try.

"Please, you need me," I rolled my eyes.

"*I* need *you*?" she chuckled. "Why would I need you?"

"Isn't it obvious?" I said smoothly, trying not to overplay my hand. "You came here by accident, and you want to get back, your problem is that you don't know how. That's why."

She studied me, not saying anything as the only sound was shallow breathing. She might just be on the verge of calling my bluff and as more time went the more likely it seemed. Our life was in her hands. The torch from her henchman who was mere feet away illuminated the side of her face, a red spot sparsely visible.

"You know how to get back?"

Checkmate.

"Yes. And if you kill me now, you'll be stuck here."

"I don't need to kill you. But what would I need your friend for? He's not worth anything," she challenged, shifting the gun slightly to rest on my hip and point at Evander.

"He's insurance," I said quickly, "that I help you."

I knew that I had just confirmed that he could be used as leverage against me, but better that than him being dead. I could have tried to take the gun away from her, but even if I managed it and killed her, there was no way that I could get rid of her entire crew while taking Evander with me, even with a gun. The risk was too great and Evander's life wasn't something I was willing to bet on.

Thana's jaw set as she decided if it was worth it and if she should trust me, but what other option did she have? She apparently thought the same, because she simply responded, "Go back to your room."

"I'll go, but you have to give him proper medical treatment," I said firmly.

"Why would I do that? I can make you go and not do anything for him," she clipped, turning the gun back into my stomach.

"You're right. The difference is that I wouldn't be giving you any trouble. I'd be going willingly."

She hesitated, but I could see in her eyes that she knew I was right. Not only that, deep down she knew I was a woman of my word. Still, she said nothing.

"Please," I whispered to her. "You know that if his wounds aren't cleaned, he'll die from infection. All I ask is that he is properly cared for. And by care, I mean by *our* standards."

She looked at Evander, studying him for a moment before turning her attention back to me. "Fine, you have a deal. I'll let you clean him up and then both of you will be locked up."

She motioned to her henchmen to grab Evander as she spun me around, pressing the gun into my back and pushing me forward. The sound of Evander's feet dragging and struggled breathing flowed through the air as we climbed up the ladder and walked down the narrow, wooden hallway. It didn't take long to reach Thana's desired room before she stopped us and opened one of the small doors. She motioned for me to enter, pushing Evander in behind me. It was a sort of mini storage room, three barrels along the wall, rope and unfamiliar items hooked on to the remaining two. Together, Evander and I could barely fit. It would be a challenge to bandage him.

"Someone will be back with the supplies," she said aggressively before slamming the door closed. I could hear a pair of heavy feet positioning themselves against it, knowing that there was no way out of this predicament.

"Rivka," Evander mumbled, being the first to break the silence. "You shouldn't... have done... that."

I hushed him, helping him onto one of the barrels, his teeth clenched and brows furrowed. "Trust me, this is best. I need you strong if we have any hope of getting out of here."

My heart broke as I gazed upon his broken body. The damage was considerable. And the truth of the matter was that even if I properly cleaned him, infection could have already set

122

in. It had been hours since the fight and his condition in the galley were abominable. His swollen eye wouldn't meet my own, instead they focused on the floor. I softened, carefully raising my hand to rest against his cheek. He winced at first before resting into it.

"Hey," I murmured, "thank you for what you did for me."

His eyes still wouldn't meet my own and my only conclusion was from shame about his broken appearance or for not being able to get us out of here.

Gently, I raised his chin, compelling him to look at me. "I'm sorry for what they did to you. If it weren't for me…" I trailed.

"It's not being beaten… that bothers me. Even though I obviously didn't enjoy that," he winced, his eyes moving in and out of focus. "It's that…" he hesitated. "It's that I couldn't protect you."

"Evander—"

The wooden door pushed open, interrupting us and just barely hitting me from behind before one of Thana's men gave me a basket with supplies, an empty bowl, and a pitcher of what seemed to be boiled water. Gruffly pushing it into my hands, he let out a snort before shutting the door behind him.

Now having the supplies, I wasted no time. The back of my hand found his forehead, which burned up with fever; a common sign of infection. My other hand on his shoulder felt his cold sweat. There wasn't much I could do, but I would have to try my best. I laid the basket and other supplies neatly on the remaining two barrels. In the basket were some clean cloths, a bar of goat's milk soap, a cup, a small bottle with some form of liquid, a salve, and a small knife— which was surprising. Pulling off the small cork, I held the bottle to my nose, inspecting the contents.

Alcohol.

For a day and age without antibiotics and general hygiene, this would all have to do. I looked over at Evander as he leaned his head sideways on the wall, his side facing me. Quickly washing my hands in the basin with the hot water and soap and using the knife to cut the cloth into strips, I knew that this next part wouldn't be pleasant for him.

"Evander," I said, trying to grab his focus as his eyes struggled. "What's going to happen now is going to hurt, but I'm going to be as gentle as I can. Alright?"

He said nothing, but just gave a simple nod.

Placing the small bottle against his lips, I uttered, "For the pain." He took a long sip before giving his head a tiny shake. That was my cue. Taking a deep breath, I washed one of the cloths in the hot water and braced myself before taking to his back.

"Here I go," I murmured, trying to give him a heads up. I tenderly placed the cloth on his back, earning a small jolt from Evander, no sound escaped his lips. At first, I tested the waters, so to speak, on his comfort and pain before I fully immersed myself into the cleaning. I tried my best to remove all the dry blood as delicately as I could, but in some spots, there was just no helping it. Evander weathered it quietly, though the tightness in his expression betrayed how much it hurt. But I knew the worst was still to come. Placing the cloth aside, I picked up the small bottle.

"You're going to have to prepare yourself. This might feel just as bad as when you got the wounds."

Evander didn't say anything for a moment, but I could see him swallow. He gave a deep breath before finally whispering, "I'm ready."

Biting my lip and gripping the small bottle, I slowly began to pour the liquid down his back. He gave a sudden jerk, but I knew I had to do this, if not there would be no saving him. I tried to finish as quickly as I could before I grabbed the salve, carefully applying it, and wrapping the wounds on his back with a dry cloth. I repeated it all again for his hands, chest, and face. But by the time we neared the end, I could see that he couldn't go on for much longer. His face was drawn, his unswollen eye hardly open. Washing the cup, I filled it with some of the boiled water, beckoning him to drink as much and as slowly as he could. It was a challenge at first, but he managed to finish the entire thing.

Wiping the sweat from his face and rinsing it with the last of the water, I tried to see how he was mentally.

"Can you tell me your name?"

He didn't have to open his eyes to show that he was confused by the question. "What are you... talking... about. Don't you know... my name?" he winced.

"Humor me."

"Evander."

"Do you know where you are?"

"On a ship. Taken hostage."

"Do you know where we were supposed to be going?"

"Egypt."

"And do you know who I am?"

"Rivka."

I nodded, thankful for the fact that he didn't show signs of head trauma. I'd still have to keep an eye on him, in case it was delayed or if something worse were to happen.

Giving him a look of reassurance, I turned and began putting the supplies back into the basket. We seemed to finish right on their schedule because just then the door swung open, only this time Thana was on the receiving end. "Finished?"

There wasn't much I could do in this situation except tell the truth. I'd have to find some other way out of here, although the chances began looking slimmer and slimmer. Giving a nod, she grabbed my arm, pulling me out as her men grabbed Evander.

"Grab the knife," she said to one of them, taking no chance, and pushed me forward.

We walked down the hallway, barely fitting, before she led us to the stairs leading up to the deck. Nerves started coursing through me as the possibilities rushed across my mind. She couldn't be throwing us overboard; she wouldn't have wasted the supplies on Evander. Not only that, but I was also too valuable.

As we reached the top of the stairs, my eyes slowly adjusted to the darkness, small traces of moonlight shining through the cloudy sky. I looked all across the deck but saw no indication of where she was leading us, just two of her men standing in front of the mast, working with their backs towards us. Then I finally put the pieces together, the men moving to reveal my already formulated idea. There were chains linked at eye level. She was going to chain us to the mast, on full display constantly.

Our chance of escape was now next to none.

Pushing us down, they rested our backs against the mast, lifting both of our hands above our heads before they clasped the heavy, cold metal against our wrists. I could hear Evander wince. I was anguished that I couldn't do anything to help and upset that I pulled us into this situation. But I hadn't really, had I.

It was all Thana.

My blood bubbling, the thought began to dawn on me. Some would say that I should be grateful that she had kept me alive, allowing me to give care to Evander, but they wouldn't understand. She was keeping me alive for a purpose, a purpose that she had yet to reveal. One that was more than just trying to get home.

She stared at me as they secured our locks, almost no life reflecting behind her eyes. As they finished, she walked toward Evander, offering a small kick to his thigh as she let out a snicker. "Some champion," she scoffed.

126

Her men joined her with a laugh as she made her way over to me. She crouched down, placing her lips against my ear. "Just try something, I dare you, *Zionist devil*. It'll give me an excuse to kill you now."

Fighting the urge to spit in her face, I had to physically bite my tongue to hold myself back. I knew what Thana was doing by locking us up here. What's worse is that Thana knew it too. Letting my emotions get the better of me would do nothing but get us into trouble. I had been doing a decent job until now and wasn't going to let Thana get to me. I had to be strong. The taste of iron slowly filling my mouth the harder I bit as I reasoned with myself.

But temptation grew too great. I turned to the side, spitting the crimson liquid next to her, my eyebrows pressed in fury. "You want a battle, Thana? I'll give you a *war*."

Thana looked me in the eyes, studying me, before giving me a final smirk as she rose, motioning some of her men to follow her.

"Sleep tight, Rivka," she called behind her before disappearing down the stairs.

I let out a sigh as I pressed my head back against the mast.

This couldn't be defeat.

X

THE CHOICE

Thana now out of sight, I dared to look around. There was only one lantern near the stairway that provided a dim light, a small help against the cloudy night sky. Only a few of her men were left on the deck, none that she had previously named. They glanced at us, faces full of contempt and controlled rage. Their gazes were mainly pointed towards Evander, probably because of him beating their man. But whether Evander could tell was doubtful, his brainpower more focused on his wounds, I assumed. Even with that pain, it didn't take long before he began his questioning.

"What were you thinking, Rivka?" he whispered, not diminishing the sternness from his voice.

Silence hung heavy as I stayed frozen, my blood pounding like a war drum beneath my skin—still raging from Thana. What were we going to do now? How could we possibly get out of this? I might have had a chance if Evander wasn't injured, or if I was alone, but now...

"Rivka," he rasped, pulling me out of my thoughts.

"I was thinking they were going to kill us and that we had to do something!" I snapped, pointing my anger against the wrong person. I closed my eyes. "I'm sorry, I just... I was just trying to save us."

"It's alright," he softly comforted me.

I scoffed. Here he was, beaten, battered, and bruised and he was comforting *me*.

"What happened to you after they separated us?" I asked timidly. Obviously, I got the gist, his broken body being a statement piece, but maybe Thana said or did something else.

128

Maybe she slipped and gave some hint as to what is going on, what she's doing here, what she wants.

"Not much that you can't already tell. They dragged me down... to work with the other men after the fight... although they continued their violent pleasure," he grunted painfully. "The whip and I do not get along."

"Did the woman say anything to you? Or did you hear her say anything to her men?" I pressed, hoping that there would even be a sliver of information.

"No, just that she was going to use you," he panted. "She didn't say how."

Use me? I suppose that made sense, considering she found me. But then comes the question of was her finding me accidental or something she had carefully planned out once she figured out she was back in time? That would alter our circumstances drastically. Was there something bigger going on that included Mossad and Kidon? Did Thana already know somewhat about time travel? Some of it must have been by chance, if her response to my bluff was any indication.

We gently swayed with the ship, trying to make sense of this puzzle, my mind filled with all one-thousand pieces.

"Do you have... any idea what's going on?"

"No," I whispered, technically being truthful.

Speculation? Sure.

Facts? None.

The questions in my mind kept coming and coming with no sign of it ending anytime soon. We sat in silence for what seemed like hours, but it was probably only moments before Evander pulled me back, the voices in my head finally dimming down.

I could hear his teeth grind before he spoke again. "I just can't believe that the reserve... ships didn't come. We would have destroyed these pirates once and for all."

Pondering the thought, I myself couldn't figure out why they hadn't come. Evander had talked over the plan extensively to me and it seemed like he did everything perfectly.

"Do you know what might have hindered them?" I asked, curious as to his answer.

"My only suspicion… is that either I was lied to or that this pirate gang is… bigger than we first suspected. That they fought them on a different front."

Nodding at the observation, I bit the bottom of my lip, sinking back into my thoughts of what had happened and what might still be coming. Evander honored the silence for a little, using it to muster his strength before he spoke again.

"Rivka," he breathed, "there's something you're not telling me."

"What do you mean?"

"I saw you out there. I've hardly ever seen my own men… fight the way that you did. Where did you learn to do that?"

"Oh, that?" I said softly, trying to gauge how much he knew and wanted to know.

"Yes, that," he winced, taking deep breaths. "To add on, you… seemed pretty distressed by that piece of metal that woman had. Like you knew something nobody else did."

I said nothing, waiting to see if he'd say more. He didn't, only sat there, his strained breathing just barely covering the sound of the calm waves. The ship rocked back and forth, the single lantern at the edge of the deck swaying with it. The few men that Thana left on duty were nowhere near us, each towards the rim of the boat, keeping their eyes peeled on the sea.

My thoughts rocked just as easily as the ship. If I told him the truth, would he even believe me? I'm an assassin and this is my best friend who betrayed me. Oh, and by the way, I'm from the future, two-thousand years from now to be precise. I mean, if someone were to tell me the exact same thing, I would think that their heads weren't screwed on properly. On top of that, that would be with our modern-day advancements. There had been plenty of books, films, and other creative works that had some form of time travel in them. My world had been desensitized to that fact. But this world? These people? Evander?

Being able to handle pressure was something that was needed in order to do the job I have at Kidon. But pressure builds up.

No, I wouldn't crack. We were trained not to crack. If we crack, we die, our nation dies, and life as we know it could cease to exist. But that didn't mean the pressure wasn't there.

"Everything is so messed up," I pursed my lips, knocking my head against the wooden post. My right pinky finger was already beginning to go numb from its raised position.

I could feel Evander scooching up behind me, his shoulders becoming higher than my own. He must think I'm pathetic in all of this. That thought ran laps through my mind, over and over and over again.

His body shifted, his side coming near to my own, but not enough for us to see one another. His fingers grazed over mine, slowly and tenderly grasping them as if to calm me.

"Rivka," he finally said through labored breaths, "you can tell me. Every flower has its thorns."

It was as if my heart instantly slowed, the world stopping, and there lay only Evander and I. No pirate crew, no Thana, no chains; only us, side to side, hand in hand. Biting my tongue, I couldn't help but feel my heart begin to open, the floodgates of truth wanting to be released.

"Evander, I…" I started, trying to pick and choose the right words. "Thana, their leader, and I have known each other for quite some time. We actually grew up together."

He didn't say anything. Whether that was because he was giving me time to explain or he physically couldn't, I wasn't sure, but I continued, "When we grew older, we actually joined our nation's military force, as secret operatives… spies… and assassins. We were best friends. We were on a mission together, when she betrayed me, stealing the information I had to give to our enemies and then left me in the bottom of a pit to die."

Now for the tricky part. "I managed to escape from there and then made my way to the nearest city. I went to Jerusalem, stayed for a little then left, and after you found me in the desert."

The taste of salt was faint in my mouth, but I rubbed my cheek against my shoulder, making sure it wasn't coming from my eyes. No, it was the spray from the sea.

Evander's calloused hands squeezed my own.

He waited a moment before speaking again. "You're an assassin for your land? Working for Herod?"

Technically, I suppose that would be correct. "Yes."

"Herod has secret assassins… that he withheld from the Roman authorities?"

My face scrunched. The Romans and Herod did seem to work hand-in-hand. I opened my mouth to speak, but he luckily cut me off.

"That's no surprise, every leader usually has their own secrets," he grunted softly.

Another pause came.

"When I found you on the road… And in the palace… Were you going to kill someone?" Evander hesitated. "To kill me?"

"No!" I blurted. "No, when you found me, I was done with all that. I wasn't working for anyone anymore. I was leaving to get away from it all."

Truth? Lie? Both?

I tried to come up with the right words to say, but they were all falling short. I could feel the tenseness in Evander's body, working through everything I just said. Maybe leaving him to work it out for himself would be best. After all, I could barely make sense of it and I had more facts.

"A soldier, an assassin," he finally said, slowly but surely. "We're all just following orders from our commanders. We're not all that different... except that we were working for the opposite sides."

My pulse quickened. Needing to reassure him, I continued, "I left that life behind when I met you. I came to Rome to find you because I knew there we would find a fresh start, together. Evander... I gave it up for you."

The lantern knocked against the wood, the waves splashed against the boat, the men patrolled the edges, all while I waited to see where Evander stood.

Would this change things?

He took a staggering breath. "I believe you."

I let go of my tongue, not realizing I had been biting it until now as the metallic taste teemed my mouth.

"I'm not sure fully why, but I do."

I nodded, even though he couldn't see me, feeling the weight that I had been carrying on my shoulders from this secret slightly alleviating.

"What do you think we should do with... this Thana girl? If you worked with her, what do you think her next move is?"

Truth was, I had no idea.

Uttering the words aloud would only make my thoughts into a reality.

"Whatever it is," I finally said, "it can't be good."

The moon peeked through the clouded sky, showing that we only had a few more hours until sunlight. Our chances for sleep dwindled as I was sure it wouldn't be long before Thana was back here and turning our lives into a living hell.

"You should get some rest. She'll be back soon," I said to Evander, knowing that his weakened state needed it most. Whether he wanted to protest or not didn't matter as his body couldn't physically do it. Instead, I could feel him slowly slump as much as his raised, chained hands would let him.

Swallowing, I lay my head against the post looking towards the sky.

———————✣———————

Sharp pain shot through my thigh. My eyes scrunched, not wanting to break my dreamless sleep, it being the only escape from the real world. Again, the pain came, shooting down my leg. There was something familiar about it. I half-peeked one eye open, landing on the recognizable footwear. I squinted at Thana, astonished that she would be so brazen to wear her military grade issued boots in this time, but she was clearly taking more and bigger risks than I ever did, having hidden my own in a covered hole outside of Jerusalem.

"What's with the boots?" I mumbled, being the first to speak. The sun hadn't even fully come out yet, its luminous colors just barely lurking over the subtle waves of the water.

"Wake up," she commanded, accompanying it with another hard kick.

"I'm up," I groaned, pulling myself into a more upright position. "What do you want?"

"We've got work to do."

"What work?" I yawned, pretending to show a lack of interest.

"You're gonna tell me everything you know since coming here. Actually, even before that."

"Tell you what?" I questioned, the charade continuing.

She snorted, looking over to Evander before delivering another quick, hard kick. Only this time, she found my stomach instead of my leg. As I gasped for air, Thana crouched down, pulling my hair to make me look her in the eye. She tilted her head at me, my chin high, jaw set. She lingered for a moment, savoring the power she held over me, before finally rising and making her way to Evander.

"You want to play this way, huh?" she asked, her shadow looming over me as she stood in front of Evander. I couldn't see her, but her kick to his side and his stifled grunt were enough.

I locked my jaw, doing all that I could to show no emotion. I let her get the better of me last night and I wasn't going to let that happen again. I glanced at the two men that were posted near the stairway, close enough to see everything but hear nothing.

"Let's try that again, shall we?" she susurrated, the sound of the chain unlocking clicking into the air. Mightily, she yanked Evander in front of me, then shoved him to his knees. Grabbing a fistful of his hair, she tilted his head back, exposing the vulnerable curve of his neck.

His teeth were grinding as she pulled a knife from her waist.

"How'd you get here, Rivka?" she asked.

"What are you talking about?" I fired back, now genuinely confused. Had we not come the same way?

"Wrong answer." Her blade tightened against his neck, blood slowly beginning to travel down his throat.

My eyes widened. "Thana, I'm serious. Did we not come the same way?"

"And how exactly did you come?"

I could see she wasn't playing around. One more wrong move and she would kill Evander. I'd seen her do it a hundred times with our assignments. She was good, she knew how to draw out information and it didn't matter who she killed through the process. She could get anyone to talk.

And I had helped her.

Only, the situation with Evander was different. He wasn't just another target. He was someone I couldn't bear to see broken or exposed. The thought of her tearing into him made my chest tighten.

135

"Easy, Thana," I said cautiously. "I used the tablet, same as you."

Her eyes peered at me, showing no emotion or thought. There wasn't another way to come through, so why was she so curious as to how I made it? Did she think I was dead? After turning it over in my mind, the only explanation I could find was that she had come back for me in the cave. Whether it was to save me or to make sure I was truly gone didn't seem to matter. When she didn't find me, she must have discovered the golden tablet and been transported here. Didn't she?

"What tablet?" she asked carefully.

I bit my tongue, realizing my mistake. I looked down at Evander, stuck in her grasp. His jaw was locked, eyes not leaving my own as I could see him breathing steadily. He wasn't afraid for himself, but I knew he was concerned about me. I knew the thought of leaving me alone with her was too much, and I knew this because it would be the same for myself if it was the other way around.

"Don't be afraid, Rivka," he said calmly, his eyes holding mine with quiet reassurance. "You don't have… to tell her anything."

Thana ignored him at first, before a small smirk percolated the corner of her mouth. Her eyes looked down at Evander. "How about you and I make a little deal?"

I remained emotionless, knowing even a twitch would give Thana an idea, an inkling over what I truly felt and I couldn't do that. Doing that would put Evander's life at risk.

"Not interested?" she asked, feigning concern over her contempt.

"For what?"

Her smirk lingered. "Help me, and I won't kill your little boyfriend here."

"Help you how?"

136

She tsked. "It's a take it or leave it deal. All you need to know is that if you help me, your boyfriend here gets off scot-free."

I hesitated.

Thana's eyes narrowed. "In this instance, my word is as good as the Bedouins."

My lips pursed; my lack of options clear. I glanced once more at Evander, already knowing what he would think. The moment he mouthed "don't," I knew I was right. But Evander's life was more important. *He* was more important than anything else.

"Alright," I began slowly, "you have a deal."

"Very good," her lips curved. She wore a smile like a loaded gun. It didn't help that she had one of those too.

"But one wrong move, one hint at betrayal and…" she glanced down at Evander, releasing his hair and wasting no time delivering a swift and hard kick to the back, knocking him down on his hands, gasping for air.

I winced, looking at him before turning to her blackened eyes. "What do you want?"

———— ✦ ————

Thana had motioned for her thugs to take me down to the captain's chambers, having others chain Evander back up to the mast. Thana did nothing to change the small room, as Baldilo forced me onto the small stool, keeping my hands tied with the rugged rope and linking it to the leg of the table. He stayed beside me until Thana returned, who then sent him out to give us time alone to talk.

Closing the door behind him, she turned to me, victory clear in her demeanor. She tossed the brown leather bag that she was carrying from her shoulder and pulled a stool for herself directly in front of me. We both said nothing for a moment, each seeing who was bold enough to break the silence. We'd played strategies like this for hours while training, each trying to break the other. The longest we had ever gone was a little over a week, and even that was only due to the fact that Rav Aluf gave us a new mission. But this wasn't like old times. There wasn't time to waste, Evander's life hung in the balance. Even with the care that I had given him, I knew it wouldn't hold for too long. He needed rest and attention, and I would do anything in my power to give it to him.

"Where do you want to begin, Thana?"

She tilted her head, the same smile that she had when she held Evander was still playing on her lips. She raised her eyebrows to go along with it. "At the beginning. Tell me everything you know. What happened after I last saw you?"

The floor creaked as I studied her. I knew I had to tell her the truth, she was a smart girl, and she knew me well. The next best thing I could do was to try and keep as much information to myself as I could. "After you threw me in the pit, I found this tablet. When I touched it and read the inscription, it knocked me unconscious, and I was transported here. I thought it was a dream at first, but as we can both see it's some type of reality."

Thana reached for the bag, quickly finding her desired item—a Lotar Combat knife, black steel and hilt.

"How about you?"

She didn't look at me, toying with her knife instead.

I sighed. "Thana, this isn't going to work if I don't have all the facts. If *we* don't have all the facts."

She stayed quiet.

"Thana!" I said harshly.

"I don't know," she barked, huffing, her smiley demeanor finally over. "Okay? I don't know how I got here. All I know is when I went back to the cave, into the pit, my feet hardly touched the ground before I was suddenly in the middle of a desert. I didn't see the tablet, didn't read any incantations, none of that."

Holding my breath, I dared to ask my next question. "How long after you ditched me did you go back?"

Again, she remained quiet.

"Thana, how long?"

"Maybe an hour, half an hour, I'm not sure," she shook her head, leaning forward in the chair.

Nodding, I confirmed my original theory. Either she was making sure I was dead or checking to see if I was alive. While the answer for that was crucial to how the rest of this would play out, I didn't dream of asking it. Whatever her reason was, it didn't change the fact over how she had treated me since arriving.

Probably sensing my internal debate, she brought the conversation back into her power and asked a question. "Do you think this tablet can take us back?"

"Truthfully, I'm not sure."

"Alright, do you know where this tablet is?"

I remained emotionless, but again, she knew me.

"Let me just remind you that you're doing this to save your little *habibi's* life. So let me ask again, do you know where the tablet is?"

Looking over to the empty table, I licked my lips. "I don't know exactly where it is, but I know where I last saw it not too long ago."

"And how would you know that? How did you see it?"

I closed my eyes. "Because I was stealing it trying to get myself back."

She studied me. "And did you fail? Is that why you don't have it? Or did it not work?"

"I didn't try it."

"Then why don't you have it?"

Striking a chord, my tone roughened. "It doesn't matter. Do you want my help to get the tablet or not? I'm clearly your best shot. Without me, you won't even know where to start."

She didn't say anything, and I closed my eyes again, already regretting my harsh words, knowing that it would only bring me farther away from my goal.

"Look," I began, more nicely this time, "if we do this, then you're going to have to trust me."

She continued to play with her knife, the boat's creaks surrounding us with each sway.

"Where'd you last see it?"

"In Jerusalem," I responded more cooperatively, "with Birsha, the son of Herod."

"Herod? Is that a ruler?"

"Yes."

"That means it was in one of his palaces, huh? Where else would a royal family stay?"

I nodded.

"How'd you get in?"

"I'll show and tell you, Thana, but first untie me," I said, raising my hands for her to cut.

She looked at me, eyebrow raised, and tense lipped.

"Come on. You know I'm not stupid enough to try and escape. Even if I got out of this room, how would I beat your men while toting Evander?"

"I don't know, you were pretty tough in Serbia for the Abdullah mission," she smirked.

I looked back, giving a small laugh while I saw the Thana I knew coming out. But as quickly as it came it disappeared, replaced with a face of a life bitterly lived.

"I promise, it's in both of our best interests if I cooperate," I reassured her, raising my hands one more time.

Her grip tightened around the knife, eyes locked on mine, searching for a lie. Then, almost reluctantly, she brought the blade forward and severed the rope. As she pulled away, her hair moved off her neck, exposing her jaw with a small glint of redness and sores that I vaguely saw the night before. Before I could get a good view of it, she pulled back, quickly adjusting herself so it was no longer visible.

Rubbing my wrists, I continued. "Do you have a map?"

"Always," she said, turning to grab her bag that was laid across the bed, pulling out a handmade map. Spreading it across the table, I looked at it. There were two shades of black ink, one more faded than the other. The faded one seemed to be the original coordinates while the darker seemed to be things that Thana added. Luckily, it was all correct, just more defined lines of land edges and so forth.

Smoothing the page, I knew that there was something more important that we had to do first before getting into the palace. "Before we get into the palace, we need to get into the city. The Golden Gate is the easiest way," I said, pointing it out with my finger.

Oddly enough, I could sense some reservations from her as she held her comments to herself. Not uncharacteristic, but indeed for this circumstance. I tried to think what could possibly be bothering her, until the lightbulb finally turned on.

"Have you been to Jerusalem? Since the tablet, I mean," I asked, looking up from the map. Her eyes wouldn't meet mine, making it clear that she hadn't and that I had the advantage.

"It can't be all that different from our own time, can it?" She stated defensively.

I let the silence linger, knowing that I could, if needed, play things against her.

"It's not," I fibbed. Sure, the basic landmarks were the same, but there were so many corners and secrets hidden in this city. I didn't even know them all, but at least I was one step ahead.

Trying to gain the advantage again, Thana added, "It makes sense that The Golden Gate would be open for use, since it isn't for years that the Muslims will close it up, stopping your rumored Messiah."

I grimaced at the small word.

Your.

Interesting how such a small word, almost insignificant, was salt in my wound, making it once again plain that she had turned her back not only on me, but her people as well. It wasn't even about Yeshua being the Messiah or not. She had given up on even waiting for one, believing in one. Had she ever truly believed? I had to brush it aside. Or better yet, use it as my motivation.

"You'll need clothes to blend in: head coverings, tunics, leather shoes."

"I'll get my men on it," she commented.

"We'll need other supplies on top of that. You know, the usual: knives, rope, something to pick the locks, some medical equipment, and anything else you brought with you," I slid, hoping that she might mention any extra tools she had. An extra gun or bullets, some ether, parachute, literally anything that could help us or be used against me. Unfortunately, she didn't take the bait. Getting any information out of her would take a lot more work than just a well-placed comment.

Thana leaned up from her post. "We should be docking within the hour. The moment we do, we'll make our journey onward."

I nodded to her as she turned, opening the cabin door and shutting it tight behind her. This mission promised to be nothing short of interesting… and almost certainly uncomfortable.

XI

TUNNELS

The route from the port of Jaffa was smoother than I'd expected. Thana's men had bought us supplies, upon her orders, including proper walking shoes for her. She did put up a bit of a fight, but slowly relented as I explained how while, strategically, her military boots would have been more comfortable and durable, she would draw unwanted attention. Thana laced the straps of her sandals with that same steely focus she wore like armor, then moved ahead without a word.

It took us a little over two days, but we made good time. There was even a family that let us hitch a ride in their cart for some of it, giving our legs some rest. She left her men with instructions to watch over the ship, also issuing other orders she kept to herself—but I was certain one of them was to make sure Evander didn't escape. Throughout the two days, Thana and I barely went over our plan for once we reached Jerusalem. It was a little odd. We would always analyze our missions, setting our target, course of action, and leaving nothing to chance. That is before she betrayed me. Now she was an entirely different person. Wasn't she?

As we neared Jerusalem's walls, now back on foot, I could hear her breath hitch. Whether it was the nerves of the mission or the sight of seeing our great city in its ancient form, I wasn't sure. We trudged along behind a slew of travelers up the rough road and pulled our veils further across our face as we neared the gate.

"Here we go," Thana murmured.

Scanning the area, I could see that something was not right. Both of the heavy doors under the double archway gates

143

were closed. There were over a dozen Romans guarding it, each seemingly dealing with the other travelers ahead of us. All but one. He began to approach us, a silver helmet covering half his face, giving the indication that he was their commander.

"The gates are closed," he said roughly, not giving us a chance to speak.

"Why?" I asked, my voice cutting through the murmurs as a crowd began to swell around me, faces turning curious.

"Governor Pilate's orders: no one gets into the city."

"I don't understand," Thana interjected. "We're here to see our sick mother. They think she'll be dead by days end."

"That's not my problem. Be on your way."

"Kind sir," I mused, "do you know when the gates will reopen?"

"It'll be at least a few more days," he bellowed, his voice booming over the crowd, tinged with irritation at our relentless questions. His glare was sharp, cutting through the murmurs like a blade. "Now, move along."

We didn't get a chance to say another word before he was gone, pushing some other travelers from their destination. As quickly as people were being turned away, new travelers kept on coming.

"All the other gates are closed as well," a couple stammered as they walked past us.

Thana heard them too as we shared a look at their bleak news.

"What now, genius?" she folded her arms.

Giving a sigh, I grabbed her elbow, pulling her away from the earshot of the Romans and the other travelers. I had to come up with something quick. Evander's life hung in the balance. I watched the passersby, hoping one would just come up to me and reveal some big plan or march us straight through the gates. That didn't happen, but something almost as good did. My eyes connected with a little girl as she drank from her father's canteen, water dribbling down her chin.

"I've got it," I mumbled, earning a quizzical look from Thana as she pulled her elbow from my grasp. "We could go through the tunnel."

Thana rubbed her arm, eyes sharp and guarded as suspicion flickered across her face. Her brow drew together in a tight scowl, lips curling slightly. "What tunnel?"

"Hezekiah's Tunnel," I said, the idea slowly expanding in my mind.

"You don't think there will be something blocking it off? I'm sure it's no tourist destination anymore."

She was right. Hezekiah's Tunnel was built centuries ago as a form of defense from Israel's attackers. The King didn't want their enemies to cut off the city's water source, so he had his men construct an underground passageway that brought the water from the Gihon Spring outside of the wall into the city. In our time, it is still standing and is a popular tourist destination. I hadn't even seen the tunnel in this era, but at this point, what other option did we have?

"We've both been through, so we know the basic structure. Any other obstacles along the way we'll both just have to handle it together."

Thana's expression turned unreadable, but something in the stillness of her gaze—too focused, too quiet—hinted she was far from convinced.

"Besides," I continued, "it'll take us into the Old City, which is probably where I'm most familiar. It's our best chance."

She exhaled sharply, her patience clearly thinning. "Fine," she said, voice low but commanding. "But don't forget who's giving the orders." She turned, feet striking the ground in steady rhythm as she marched ahead—leaving no room for argument, and no glance over her shoulder.

Rolling my eyes, I muttered a "Yes, ma'am," before catching up behind her.

We moved quietly along the outer walls of Jerusalem, hugging the stone as the sun cast a narrow shadow just wide enough to conceal us. The heat clung to our backs, keeping low, eyes forward.

Up ahead, our target came into view, impossible to miss. The wall, which had run in a straight line for most of the approach, widened and curved outward into an inverted "U." It was a subtle break in the fortifications, but a noticeable one. From where we crouched, we could make out a couple of guard helmets glinting at the top edge, heads shifting lazily as they scanned the horizon. We stayed low, blending with the scattered rocks and debris that littered the base. The terrain here worked in our favor, giving us just enough uneven cover to inch forward undetected. Every few paces, we paused—watching the wall, watching the guards—until we reached the curve's corner, cloaked in deeper shade.

The stone here was smoother than expected, worn down by time and heat. There were few natural holds to grip, making the climb ahead anything but easy. The wall loomed above us, at least forty feet high—daunting, silent, and still.

What was an advantage, though, was the fact that there were no guards on the lower portion. This corner was also blessed with some shade, making them cool to the touch. Our only difficulties would be once we got to the top.

Having been training partners for years, we had been put in similar situations before, so we naturally went into our instinct mode. I pulled two freshly sharpened knives Thana's men had given me from my bag, dropping them onto the ground. After securing my bag on my back, I pulled the lower parts of my tunic into my belt. I tightened my leather sandals and picked up a handful of dust from the ground, rubbing it into my hands. Thana did the same, making sure not a single trace of sweat remained.

She nodded to me as I bent down, retrieving the knives and gripping them in my hands. Thana knelt against the wall, folding her hands, waiting. Taking a deep breath, I cleared my mind and mentally prepared. It was all about speed. If I had enough speed, it would all be over in seconds.

Taking a final breath, I sprang into action. As my foot connected with Thanas' hand, she used all her force to hoist me higher into the sky. Using the momentum, I stabbed my knives into the hardened mortar, securing my weight against the wall. Wasting no time, my arms carried me higher and higher, the muscles in my back beginning to burn. I tried to focus on my breathing, rather than the Judean heat, and what my next course of action was.

Just making it to the top, I hung from my knives, trying to listen to where the guards were. Based on the footsteps, I gathered that there were only two there. Letting go of the knife in my right hand, I gripped the wall's edge, using it and my other knife to pull me up. Peeking over, my calculations proved to be true: there were two guards to my right, leaning against the wall engaged in conversation. They were either green soldiers, careless, or some unfortunate mix of the two. Their smooth faces confirmed the former.

Biting my lip, I pulled myself over the wall and managed to tackle one of the guards in the process. Before the other guard realized what was going on and could alert others for help, my knife found his leg and my fist found his jaw, knocking him out of consciousness. I looked around to see if they had anything up here to tie them up with and found some of their own thin, three-stranded rope lying in a corner. Quickly gagging and tying them up, my thoughts couldn't help but drift to killing them. It seemed like a lifetime ago that I would have gotten rid of anyone who was in my way, but now… now things are different. It felt wrong to kill them just for my own convenience.

147

I pushed the thought back and undid the bag from my back, pulling out our own rope. I tied it securely around my waist before throwing it over the edge for Thana. For how small she was, her weight still made the rope tighten around me as I braced my legs against the wall for aide. Finally pulling herself up, she wiped the perspiration from her brow with her veil, nodding towards the two soldiers. I knew what she was asking. Rather than dignifying her with a response, I just commented, "We'd better get going."

Sighting no other soldiers, we walked across the flat surface of the wall roof, trying to figure out exactly where we were. Rather than there being a small cafe with a ticket stand near stairs of aluminum taking us down to the cave, we just found a small hole in the roof. Peeking through, we spotted a set of stone stairs, but they led only to another stretch of wall, carrying us forward in a straight line with a large, gaping hole yawning to our right.. Only it wasn't just a gaping hole. Instead, it was *the* gaping hole we were looking for: the entrance of the Gihon Spring. Eager to escape both the treacherous sun and any suspicious eyes that may come about, we hurried down.

To our fortune, the passage remained deserted. No soldiers, no civilians, just silence and stone. Flickering torchlight lit the narrow, uneven path ahead, casting long shadows that danced across the jagged walls as we descended deeper into the cavern. Thana and I had walked this tunnel before, more than once, but without its recent reinforcements, it felt completely unfamiliar. Raw. Treacherous. Each step demanded caution; one slip could send us spiraling down to our deaths.

We moved forward cautiously, every step measured and deliberate, until the unmistakable roar of rushing water confirmed what we'd hoped. At the end of the narrow, straight path, a worn set of stairs clung precariously to the wall, twisting down: the dark mouth of the tunnel. We exchanged a brief, hopeful glance, a silent acknowledgment that this might actually work, before we got to work.

Carefully, we tightened our tunics higher around our thighs, determined to keep every inch dry and avoid any trace of moisture that might betray our passage once we emerged. I leaned forward and peered into the black void ahead, straining my eyes for any flicker of light, but the cavern remained an impenetrable shadow, utterly void of illumination.

I glanced back at the torch wedged somehow in the stone wall. I grasped it and tugged, but there was no moving it.

Darkness was our only companion now.

Preparing myself, I turned back to the abyss, ready to disappear into the black.

Pushing that somewhat vexing thought behind me, I unstrapped my sandals, securing them in my hand, before I dipped my toes into the water. The biting chill slammed into my skin like a blast of frozen wind, accompanied by the faint drip-drip of water echoing around me. My muscles tensed instinctively, and a sharp gasp caught in my throat as a wave of cold seeped into my bones, but my body eventually adjusted. Thana must have thought the same as a soft "yelp" escaped her as she joined me.

Mustering my courage, I descended into the entrance that took me deeper into its mysterious mouth. Once I was fully in, the water came only to my calves, thankfully, proving that we were indeed the summer months. During the winter, the waters can reach the top of the tunnel, which would have submerged me as I was only a couple of inches shorter than the top.

Thana splashed in behind me, the small waves dashing against my knees.

"A flashlight would come in handy right about now," I muttered to myself, plunging myself deeper into the unlit cave, the last torch disappearing behind us leaving us in utter and complete darkness.

At least, it was that way for a moment, before something all too familiar and something that I missed appeared before me—an LED blue light.

"Where'd you get that?" I asked, turning around as I shielded my eyes with my hand. Instead of responding, Thana moved around me and took the lead, now illuminating the way. I pursed my lips. If she was hiding something as small as a flashlight from me, what else could she be hiding?

"You didn't happen to bring deodorant, did you?" I teased.

Ignored again, we continued on, my hands guiding me as they rested on the sides of the tunnel. Our feet slid against the slippery rocks, constantly trying to avoid the random holes that would appear, pulling us deeper into the water.

We walked in silence for a few minutes, the only sound trickling water. But several questions had been nagging in my mind ever since I realized that Thana came to the past. Truth be told, those doubts had lingered even before, but the moment I saw her, they sharpened into something urgent, impossible to ignore. The real problem wasn't what to ask, but whether I even dared. Would she turn hostile? Would she refuse to answer? Could I accidentally expose something about myself, something that would put me in danger? Yet, the more I wrestled with those fears, the less I cared. I needed answers. No matter the cost.

"You know, I don't get it."

"What?" she grumbled, not taking her focus off the path ahead.

"You working with Hassan."

She scoffed but said nothing.

"Truly, I don't understand," I continued, determined to get my answers. "It baffles me to think that you would betray your own people like that."

"They're not my people," she said through clenched teeth.

"Thana, just repeating it over and over again doesn't make it true. Your mother was a Jew. She was born in Jerusalem, for goodness sake. I don't see why you have such an issue when your father clearly didn't."

"Enough."

I paused. Maybe I was pressing her too hard.

No, I wasn't pressing her hard enough.

She clearly had some twisted thoughts on the matter, and I wanted to know why. "Why would you join an organization that was responsible for the murder of your parents?"

She scoffed, trudging through the water. "Murder?"

"Yes, what else would it be?"

She stopped. I had struck a nerve as she slowly turned around, her fists clenched.

"They deserved their deaths."

I stared at her, silent. Never did I imagine this side of her.

She continued, "My father turned his back on us, my true people, the day he met my mother. The day he converted. We are well to be rid of them."

She turned back around, pressing on through the water. Swallowing, I followed behind realizing just how deep in she was. I couldn't back out now that I had opened this can of worms.

"Is that why you joined the Islamic Movement? Joined Hamas? To get back at your father?"

I could hear her low, rasping chuckle; a soft echo rang through the tunnel.

"You don't get it, do you? There's a much bigger picture at play. It's not just about my father, my mother, me, or even you! This is about history and the one that is to be made."

"Attacking the innocent is the history you want to be remembered? The one you want to be a part of?"

"No, it's the liberation of my people. The freedom for my country. It's something I'm willing to die for—to be a *shahid.*"

"Oh, believe me, I understand," I quipped. "We were doing the exact thing. Doing it together, in fact, just for the other side. Except we don't indoctrinate children, target and murder civilians, we—"

"Enough, Rivka!" she turned, water splashing against us. "You don't have to agree with my reasons, or even know them, for that matter. It's my business. You shouldn't be focused on my ties with Hamas, or any other movement. You should just be happy I didn't kill you that day in the cave and focus on keeping your man alive."

We stared at each other for a moment before she continued forward.

"You've changed, Thana," I whispered.

"No, I didn't change," she said lowly. "You just never knew me."

She turned partially, eyes hooded in shadows. "And besides," she said, her voice like a blade, "are you really going to stand there and pretend the horrors we committed were any better?"

I blinked.

Thana didn't wait for a response. Just turned and trudged forward, her legs splashing through.

She was right. The thought had haunted me before—late at night, after missions that left the air thick with ash and blood. I'd lie awake, staring at the ceiling, wondering how far gone we really were. Wondering if we were any different from the monsters we fought.

Were the Kidon or Mossad any better than Hamas?

Before God and man, I didn't have an answer.

Only a sick weight in my chest that told me we were

never as righteous as we claimed to be. War had a price. And it was always the innocent who paid.

We walked the rest of the way in silence, moving forward until a soft light appeared ahead, one that didn't come from Thana's flashlight, signaling we were finally nearing the end. An iron gate blocking our exit confirmed it.

"Unlock it," Thana said, peering through the bars at the steps of the pool of Siloam.

Looking at it, I simply gave it a small push as the gate swung open, hinges squeaking. Thana rolled her eyes as she pushed past me, walking towards the steps. At least this part was familiar: the shallow pool glimmering quietly on our right, the worn stone stairs winding upward to our left.

Signaling her to follow me, I walked cautiously up the stone stairs, still not coming in contact with anyone. But we knew they were there; we could hear the soft hum of conversation which only grew louder and louder as we trekked up the stairs. Conversations layered over one another, laughter mixing with sharp commands, the clink of armor beneath casual chatter.

By the time we reached the top, the full picture unfolded.

Below us lay a large, square pool of water, its surface rippling gently beneath the open air. Steps framed each side, leading down into it, and the space around it buzzed with life. Roman soldiers stood guard, unmoving and watchful. Jewish civilians clustered in small groups, their voices rising and falling in conversation. The entire area pulsed with a strange rhythm, like a public square—no, a meeting hall, suspended between sacred ritual and military order.

It felt like we'd stepped into another world entirely.

We nodded to each other and went to the separate sides of the pool. I sat on the steps, wading my feet in the water while she walked around. Listening around at the pool for any information that could link to Birsha, his father, or their treasures, Thana and I stayed as long as we could without drawing suspicion to ourselves, the better part of an hour. Not only that, no one there seemed to have anything that could be useful. Pushing our way out, my next best guess to where we could find this information was the marketplace. In fact, we probably should have even started there first since all sorts of people go there, including staff from the palace.

We trudged uphill towards the market, finally arriving. I could sense Thana's awe as she looked around, taking in the ancient city. She physically stopped as we passed by The Temple Mount, watching the people coming to and fro. If she truly had converted, I'm sure that this wasn't a pleasant sight, since the Dome of the Rock had yet to take its place. I decided to leave it alone and instead let the market be the first place we talked. The hubbub was just as I remembered it, loud hagglers, different spices filling the air.

Turning to Thana, I whispered, "We have a better chance of getting the information we need if we split up."

She didn't say a word, but the way her eyes never left me said enough. She wasn't going to let me out of her sight. Or maybe it wasn't just about trust. Maybe she was nervous, nervous about being stranded in an ancient world without the safety net of her time. No maps. No phones. No GPS. No familiar signs to guide her if things went wrong.

Still, Thana understood what I did: if we split up, our prospects of success would only grow. And that was the gamble we both had to take.

"Alright. We'll meet by the Temple in one hour," she said, adjusting her veil on her head.

Nodding, we went in different directions, her north and I south. My muted tunic did well to blend me in as I pushed my way through the crowded streets, not making eye contact with any of the vendors as I kept my gaze on their products and my ear figuratively to the ground.

I didn't just enjoy the distance—I needed it, the relief of finally being away from everyone settling into my shoulders. The market buzzed around me, but I was alone: free to move, free to choose, free from anyone's control. And I savored it. But it was short lived as someone in the crowd bumped into me, knocking me back slightly.

"Excuse me," I responded without looking up, but a hand gripped my arm, pushing me back.

"Hey, let go of me!" I said, turning to the towering, hooded figure. It ignored me as it pulled me around the corner of the wall, into a small hidden opening. Before I had time to protest and push away, he lowered the cloth that covered his mouth.

"Gidon," I breathed in disbelief.

But there he was; short dark curls framing his tan face. We both didn't say anything for a second as we took each other in, memories I didn't realize I had flooding back.

"Gidon," I repeated breathlessly, trying to find the right words to say.

Instead, he cut me off. "I'll waste no time: why are you here?"

"Gidon, I…" my words drifted off, people bartering in the market being the only sound between us.

"Is that all you can say? '*Gidon*?'" he snapped brashly, his hand still gripped on my arm.

He had every right to be upset. We hadn't left on the best of terms. I thought about him on my journey to Rome, thinking about how I broke his heart, but I was certain that he would mend. Maybe even find some nice girl who would make it as if I never even existed.

"I'm here looking for something," I finally said.

He studied me for a moment, brown eyes winced.

My face softened. "It's good to see you, Gidon."

The comment got him slightly off guard, face showing that he was weighing his next words. Finally, he spoke. "Do you know what risk I'm taking for even speaking with you?"

My brows furrowed. "Risk? Why? Has something changed?"

"I've joined an Order. If you're here, I'm sure your little Roman is not far behind."

"An Order?"

"Yes, for the Zealot Cause."

"How is that any different than what you were doing before?"

"Before I was acting alone, some friends and I. But now... now we are trained. We are a political group. Now, we are discipled. We are *Sicarii*."

"Getting more radical, I see," I trailed.

His face hardened, insulted by my remark.

He withdrew his arm. "Trying to free your country from tyranny is anything but radical. I'm a patriot for God and His people."

"I didn't mean to offend you. I'm sorry," I said with sincerity. "But I don't understand. Why would it matter if they saw you speaking with me? I'm still a Jewess, after all."

"But you're friends with Romans," he reiterated, showing that that alone was enough to jeopardize him and his position. "We have not only gotten rid of Romans, but of their Jewish sympathizers as well."

"I suppose I am, but how would they even know that?" I raised an eyebrow. "Did you tell them?"

He hesitated slightly, peeking over me to scan the area. "No, but it wouldn't take them long to find out who you are. They know everything about every person who sets foot in this city. It's a matter of safety."

"Alright, fine. But couldn't they just think that I was an old friend from another town? That much is true, isn't it?"

Gidon's eyes met my own from under his hood, before he looked away, rubbing his hand against the nape of his neck. Another pause of silence came, only this one was more awkward than the first.

I opened my mouth, but he broke it first. "You didn't really answer my question. Why are you here? What are you looking for?"

Did I owe him an explanation? Probably. Maybe if I explained what was going on he might help me. Then again, why would he even want to after how I left things. I would just be making things worse for him, getting him entwined with pirates. Or worse, Gidon might want revenge for my rejection. Maybe his hatred ran so deep that he would do anything to get back at me, including letting the pirates finish the job with Evander. I couldn't help but think about him, all battered and bruised. I had to get him out of there and I knew I needed to use all the resources in my power. I couldn't do this alone… If that meant taking a risk with Gidon, then so be it.

"I'm here for a golden tablet."

"A golden tablet?"

"Yes," I affirmed, looking around for any signs of Thana. "One that I saw in the palace the day we broke in."

"And you are doing that alone?"

I bit my tongue in hesitation. Do I tell him about Thana? Or was that his way of asking if Evander was here with me?

Before I could respond, he cut in again, "I saw you here with a woman."

I crossed my arms, upset both at the fact that he didn't approach me sooner and that I hadn't noticed him in the first place. "How long have you been watching me?"

"I saw you both at the Pools of Siloam. I've just been waiting for the right moment to catch you alone. So tell me… why are you looking for it? What's in it for you?"

Going back and forth, I weighed my options.

"You deserve complete honesty," I took a deep breath. "I'm being blackmailed by pirates. They're holding Evander hostage until I retrieve this golden tablet. Their leader is here with me in the market to make sure that I get it. Once I find it, I'll exchange it for his life."

He stayed quiet, eyes fixed on me—not with shock, but with caution. "Pirates?"

I let out a breath. "Yes, raiders, marauders. It's a long and complicated story."

"Well, I can't say I'm not pleased with his situation, but I am sorry that you're caught in the middle. I'd never want any harm to come to you."

To my surprise, I could see that he meant it.

"Thank you."

"So the leader is the *woman* who was with you before?"

I nodded. I didn't want to get into the nitty-gritty details of our complex past and thankfully he didn't press it.

"I know this is a lot to ask," I hesitated, looking up into his dark eyes as the wind moved his hood gently. "But do you think you could help me?"

He shifted his weight on his legs, looking out again towards the marketplace. "Rivka…if I could, I would, but it's not just me anymore. If I help you, I put the entire Order at risk. As I said before, I shouldn't even be speaking to you."

I couldn't blame him. If I was in his situation, I probably would have done the same thing.

"But I can tell you this. The guards patrolling has increased in the past few weeks," Gidon paused. "How did you even get into the city? How long have you been here?"

"I arrived just this morning."

"Through the gates?" he tested, clearly trying to judge my honesty.

"They've all been closed, as I'm sure you already know. And no, no Romans let me in. I snuck in."

He didn't push for the details of how and I cut in before he could. "But my question is why? Have there been revolts?"

"Not necessarily. It was more at the pressure of the Pharisees."

"Pharisees? At the gate they said it was Pilate."

"At the behest of the Pharisees."

"That doesn't make any sense," I pondered. "I thought Pilate was done with the Pharisees, or at the very least, annoyed with them."

"My guess is he's desperate to keep the simmering tension from boiling over into chaos. Locking down the city is his way to maintain control—shutting gates, doubling patrols, and shutting out anyone who might stir the unrest further. It's a heavy-handed move, suffocating the daily life of every citizen under the weight of suspicion and fear. But in his eyes, if that's what it takes to hold the fragile peace together, then so be it. The Pharisees are scared of these 'new believers.' Besides, Pilate returned to Caesarea soon after the execution."

Believers? "Believers of what?"

"Your Yeshua. The Pharisees have been keeping a tight rule over any mention of Yeshua, but that doesn't stop the people from spreading the stories."

"What stories? I haven't heard anything."

He squinted, looking if there was truth in my words. "They say he has risen from the dead—that since then, he has appeared to his followers and hundreds more. But as quickly as he comes, he disappears, as if he was never there."

I pressed my hand to my chest. Could it be true? I believed Yeshua to be alive, but to actually see Him…

"In any case," Gidon continued, scanning the area, "you will have a difficult time finding what you're looking for.

Nodding, I processed the information he had given me. But there was a question that had been gnawing in my mind since realizing it was him. I knew I had to ask, or I would never forgive myself.

"How's Tamara?" I finally said, the guilt of my question settled over me like a dark shadow. I had abandoned her and there was no beating around that bush.

Gidon seemed to be thinking as much, letting out a short breath. "She's fine. My mother and Safta have been taking care of her and she is getting along well with my brothers and sisters."

I pursed my lips, giving a small nod.

"Rivka," he said in lowly hushed tones, making me hold my breath. "Is the tablet the only reason you're here?"

Taken aback by his question, my heart began to race. I thought I was, but now that I was actually back, I felt… conflicted. Or maybe it was just selfishness, feeling the heavy weight of this burden that I had been carrying for so long. Not just this dilemma with the pirates and Thana, but being away from my own time and from everything I had ever known. I hadn't slept in days, my mind slowly chipping away. I had been trained exactly for these types of situations, having complete control no matter the lack of food, water, sleep, or energy, but that didn't mean the burden was any easier to carry. My patience was thin and as was my control.

"I'm so sorry, Gidon," I finally caved, rubbing my face.

Even with every nerve in me stretched taut, his hesitation was obvious. His hand moved deliberately, pulling mine down with a gentle but steady grip. The unexpectedness of the gesture caught me off guard, as did the calm look in his eyes. It made me pause despite everything happening around us.

"Gidon, I'm so sorry for everything I've put you all through. For everything that I did to Tamara, to Safta. Abandoning you all."

I was alluding to more than he could ever know, but how could I ever explain? How could I ever put it into words?

"Rivka," he broke firmly, pulling back and gripping my shoulders solidly. "You need to pull yourself together. Self-pity doesn't become you."

I stiffened, eyes widened at his toughness. Pulling my shoulders away, I leaned deeper into the stone corner behind me. "What if it's coupled with sincerity? What then?"

He clenched his jaw as he watched me regain my composure.

"Forgive me, Rivka."

I scoffed silently, barely able to believe his words. "Please," I said, shaking my head, "you have nothing to apologize for."

"I do, I—" his deep voice caught, but he didn't continue his sentence. "Had you never come, Tamara would be walking around with only one arm, assuming she would still be alive," he said instead.

I gave a small smirk. "That is true."

Gidon pursed his lips and then opened his mouth to say something, only I interjected before he could. "I'm sure she will be looking for me," I mumbled, peeking around the stone corner.

"The pirate leader?"

"Yes, she…" I sighed, committing to the whole truth. "She was my best friend who betrayed me, and now is the leader of the crew."

He simply gave a nod. We both didn't say anything for another moment, my heart beating fast against my chest, curious as to what this all meant. Or if it even meant anything at all.

"I have to go before someone recognizes me," he said, pulling the cloth back over his mouth. "I can't help you, Rivka, but I'll leave you with this. Your best chance of finding that tablet is in the palace. The prince may have moved its location, but it's a good place to start."

He paused, his gaze locking onto mine, as if searching for something deeper. After a moment, he finally spoke, his voice low but steady. "If you ever feel like you have nowhere else to turn, go to my mother's and I'll get word. I'll do whatever I can." Another flicker of hesitation crossed his face—an unspoken struggle—before he reached out gently, his hand finding mine in a warm, reassuring squeeze. Without another word, he slipped from the shadowed corner, melting into the street like a wisp of smoke carried off by the wind.

I leaned my head back against the stone, eyes slipping shut, one hand pressed to my stomach as I tried to shake the sensation that my wide leather belt was cinching tighter with every breath. After a long, steady inhale, I pushed off the wall and stepped back into the road.

All this time, throughout all the travels I had been on these past months, waves of homesickness would come over me. The conveniences of the modern world and all that it encompasses. But now after seeing Gidon, a new realization came over me and I knew—you could become homesick for people too.

XII

THE UNEXPECTED

Returning to the Temple steps, I wrung my hands together. Blending in with the women in the crowd, I tried to be inconspicuous, watching for Thana and thinking about what we were getting ourselves into. The last time I had made it into the palace was by being stuffed into a bag of grain. While that option provided stealth, it lacked speed, and time wasn't something that we had much of. Moreover, I wasn't even sure if there was anything that was going to be taken into the palace.

Catching a glimpse of Thana's veil, I met her on the other side of the steps. We didn't speak, only moved to a more secure location where we could discuss more openly. Finding some stairs, we climbed until we reached the roof of what appeared to be an unoccupied home. Dust lay undisturbed beneath our feet as we stepped under a tattered, sun-worn awning, hidden from the street. Deep orange and red hues spread across the neighboring mud thatched roofs, evening coming upon us.

"So," Thana asked, after we both secured the spot, "what did you find?"

"Not more than what I already knew," I answered honestly. "You?"

She frowned. "About the same."

"The only reasonable place to assume it's at is the last place that I left it—the palace," I sighed.

"Do you know how to get it?"

I told her how I made it in last time and why it wouldn't work this time.

"We'll keep that as a backup plan," she instructed.

I thought for a moment. "Why don't we just do what we did in Baghdad?"

We'd had several successful missions there and were lucky to have used the same technique each time for getting to our targets.

"It could work," she started slowly. "The worst they'll do is turn us away."

"Or imprison us, or execute us," I finished.

Thana laughed to herself.

Caught off guard by her unexpected humanness, I looked at her.

She didn't catch my look, but did elaborate. "Maybe this time don't fall into an abandoned fox hole filled with scorpions."

An impulsive snort came out. "If you didn't rush me in securing the perimeter, that wouldn't have happened. And besides, I was so quick in jumping out of there that they didn't even know I was inside."

"I'm sure they realized once half their nest was gone," Thana laughed. Shaking her head, she paused, coming back to the task at hand. Bending down, she began to draw a gameplan in the dirt.

Pity blindsided me, creeping up into my thoughts. I'd known since her betrayal that she wasn't the person she used to be. That whatever remained of her former self was buried so deep, it might never surface again. And yet... *buried* was the word that lingered. Because buried isn't gone. Maybe, just maybe, some part of her true self was still in there, waiting.

The nostalgia of our friendship and the facts of what happened overwhelmed me. Past her rough edges were deep scars. From what, I wasn't entirely sure. But they must be there, her life as evidence of it. Watching her as she drew the plan in the dirt, I opened my mouth. "I hope you heal from the things you don't talk about."

And for a moment, I saw it.

There, deep behind the curtain over her eyes, was *her*. They ever so slightly glossed, making me think that maybe I had broken through to her. She closed her eyes. But as soon as Thana opened them, anger rushed in, eclipsing whatever part of herself had been there before.

"Don't pretend like you know me," she spat, holding her gaze a moment longer before turning her attention back to the dirt.

Literally biting my tongue, I forced myself to stay calm through her tough act. I pushed past it—not because I wasn't irritated, but because I could see the insecurity behind her bravado. We didn't have the luxury of getting tangled in attitudes, not with what was coming. So I steered us back to the plan. It didn't take long before we pieced together a solid strategy.

Like it or not, we worked well together. It wasn't just the years of partnership. It was our minds, working towards a common goal, thinking the same way. Our life experiences, most of them being shared. I always had her back, and I thought she would always have mine.

———— ✤ ————

My shoulders pressed against the cool stone wall as I pulled the black material over my nose. Thana, standing beside me, did the same, locking her dark eyes with my own. Closest to the edge, I peeked around the corner of the building, the torches from the palace exterior providing little light in the inky night. Two soldiers stood guard at the vast wooden doors, their swords reflecting against the glow of the flame. Besides them, there was hardly anyone else out on the street.

All was quiet.

Seeing the opportunity, I gave the signal into the road.

Yells echoed. The soldier's attention was brought to the two beggars on the palace steps, their conversation escalating with each phrase said. The dialogue was hardly understandable, just a few words such as "mine" and "leave" made sense. But none of that mattered when they started laying hands on each other, their shoves and punches making quite a spectacle. One of the two guards at the door rushed to break up the fight, with little success.

Seizing the chance, Thana and I slipped along the wall, our footsteps barely whispering against the dusty ground. As we neared the corner by the steps the beggars amplified their scuffle, keeping the soldier occupied.

Reaching the top of the steps, Thana and I got into position in the darkened arch. The remaining guard wasn't too hard to fool, either. Fortunately for us, he was also positioned perfectly on the left side of the door, away from the door latch and handle. Expertly, Thana hurled the hand-sized rock beyond the guard's line of sight. The sharp crack of stone striking stone echoed off the walls, snapping his attention to the right. He shifted, just slightly, to investigate. It was all we needed. We slipped through the opening unnoticed, vanishing into the shadows before he drifted back to his post, none the wiser.

With the hulking door quietly shut behind us, we pulled ourselves against the wall, anticipating more guards stationed along the halls.

Sharing a look, Thana and I could almost hardly believe our eyes. Down the massive columned hallways, there didn't seem to be a guard in sight. It wasn't just guards we weren't seeing, but no servants or people of any kind. The few lit lamps and torches gave the hall an eerie presence.

"This can't be good," I said more to myself than to Thana.

Giving a small stretch of her neck, she raised her eyebrow.

"Better get moving," I whispered, feeling as if I'd wake an unknown beast.

Thana cautiously nodded, confirming the plan was still in motion. With a quick point down the hallway, she signaled she'd take that route, then motioned for me to head the opposite way. I responded with a subtle gesture of agreement, and without a word, we split off. Thana seemed to be heading towards the throne room, although I wasn't entirely sure. That left me going the other way, where I'd hope to find the kitchen. Once I found it, I would know how to find Birsha's room, the most likely location for the tablet.

The previous time I had managed to sneak into the palace, I came inside through a completely different direction. That being my starting point then, I wasn't sure where anything was without it.

Not letting my guard down, I kept my eye on my perimeter. From what I could tell, it seemed like there was no one of political importance here, thus explaining the lack of attendants. Still, wouldn't the house be kept in running order even if Herod wasn't here? The lack of security in this palace was suspicious.

Leaving no stone unturned, I methodically searched each room I passed, scanning every shadow and crevice. Within minutes of splitting up, faint murmurs reached my ears—low voices drifting through the halls. As I rounded corners, finally the occasional servant would appear, their footsteps light, their conversations quiet. I slipped into alcoves and behind doorways, narrowly avoiding detection. The further I went, the fewer people I encountered—just a handful stationed in corners, scattered and sparse, like ghosts clinging to the edges of silence.

One thing I had managed to get right: I finally found the entrance to the kitchen. A soft, golden glow from the stove spilled into the hallway, accompanied by the muffled clatter of cookware and the low murmur of voices—likely the chef and a few attendants, judging by the rhythm of their back-and-forth. Listening for a moment to see if any of what they were saying might be useful, I shook my head as I realized it was just basic talk of how to properly store certain foods. Waiting for my chance to cross, I bit my lip. In perfect timing, one of the servants dropped a clay pot in the corner of the room. The chef yelled at her as I used it to my advantage. Passing by them unnoticed, I crept down the hall.

My fingers traced against the smooth stone. His quarters were coming close. The only major obstacle left would be the great hall. Reaching the last column before the opening, I rested my shoulders on its coolness. Peeking past it, I surveyed the room.

Squinting, I noticed another person hiding behind a column across the room when they stuck their head out for a skim.

Thana.

There must be a way that the palace loops around, connecting it in various ways. That or she didn't trust me, chose to follow me, and I just didn't detect it. I chose to believe the former, not wanting to hurt my ego.

"Rivka?" a voice quietly called out behind me. Spinning around, my eyes landed on the last person I would expect to see here.

"Sariel?" I whispered, looking at her in a new cream tunic with a wheat-colored sash.

She opened her mouth to respond, but before she could, I raised my hand and tightened it around her arm, looking around to make sure that there wasn't anyone else there, or at least who noticed us.

"What are you doing here?" I asked once I was sure, pulling her behind the large column. "Last I saw you, you were in Rome."

"I was, but my father's business unexpectedly brought me back here."

"As a servant to the king or a lady in his household?"

"Not exactly… but my father does have ties in this city with certain people here and he sent me to aid them," she answered softly, tucking the wisps of brown hair that escaped back underneath her veil. "But I could ask the same thing about you. What are you doing here?"

Pursing my lips, I had to think of something quick. "I'm here on business too. Only this isn't for my father…"

"Is it with that woman you're with?"

My face stiffened. She saw us; meaning who knew who else might have. "Yes, she's… a friend."

"I take it that this is something that is to be meant to be kept quiet," she tilted her head sideways.

"Yes," I gave a polite, but tight, smile. "I would be indebted to you."

She nodded kindly. "I'm sure you're here for a good reason," she said almost easily.

I held my smile. "Yes, a delicate matter."

"Of course," she responded. "What's her name?"

"Her name?"

"Yes, your friend."

Looking at her, I tried to look as deep into her soul as I could with obvious hindrances. There wouldn't be any harm in telling her Thana's name, I thought to myself. She might have already heard me call her and this may be some form of test. Better to play it safe than sorry.

"Her name is Thana," I susurrated, glancing around, half-expecting her to appear at the sound of it.

"Thana," she rolled the name on her tongue, her eyes winced. "Is this your friend who betrayed you?"

I gave a single nod, trying to remember if I had mentioned it when we traveled. I know I told her a little about my life, the basics. It wasn't what one would consider a lot, but it was for me.

169

"Never mind that," I abruptly said. "You won't tell anyone I was here, yes?"

"I would never betray your trust like that," she responded, gently gripping my arm, sincerity clear on her face. "But…" she trailed.

"But what?"

She paused before raising her gaze to meet mine. "How was it for you the first time you saw her?"

A sudden, almost inexplicable sense of security washed over me—warm, grounding, and unmistakably familiar. It was the same feeling I'd experienced back on the ship the first time I met her, like a silent signal that I could finally let my guard down, even if only for a moment. There was no trace of calculation in her eyes, no hidden agenda woven into her words or gestures. I didn't believe that she was manipulating me, trying to pull some emotional string or extract classified information. No, there was something sincere in her presence, something uncommon. She seemed to care. Not out of obligation or curiosity, but out of genuine, unforced empathy. And that struck me as strange.

In my own time, trust was a currency too expensive to spend freely. Yet here, in this strange era I'd found myself in, people like her kept showing up—people who were open, earnest, and kind in ways I wasn't used to.

Yohanan. Evander. Gidon.

Yeshua.

It was disorienting. Comforting, yes, but also deeply unsettling. I couldn't help but wonder what it said about me, or about the world I'd left behind, that such kindness felt like a foreign language.

Closing my eyes, I gave a small shake. "I want to let it go. I thought I *had* let it go." The feelings bubbled up again inside me, my mind the boiling cauldron that was spilling over, making the fire underneath it only to grow more and more.

"What do you feel?" Sariel asked as if she was reading my mind. I tried to steady my thoughts, put the lid on the cauldron and just walk away from it. But if I tried to cap it and push it away into a corner with the fire of emotions still there, there was only one thing that would happen—I'd boil over and explode.

"Anger. Confusion. Rage…Hatred," I answered slowly, gripping a handful of my scarf tighter and tighter with each confession.

She nodded, not saying anything for a moment. "I don't blame you. You can hate her."

My eyes widened at her answer, those being the last words I would ever hear from a sweet girl such as her. "I can?"

"Yes, you can hate her."

My heart sank at the unexpected answer, showing me that if she thought that then all hope truly was lost.

"But," she paused, "this hate that you have, how does it feel?"

I swallowed, closing my eyes. "Not very good."

Sariel nodded. "Hate is a hungry beast that will devour you, leaving no room left for love. God understands this and takes the burden off of our shoulders if we want."

"How?" I asked, exasperated. "I thought I gave it to Him, only to find myself back in the same place where I started, if not worse since seeing her after what she did to me."

"Rivka, every person will stand before Him for their actions. Why burden yourself with something that will just consume your life?"

I pondered her thoughts, my current situation completely leaving my mind.

Sariel rested her hand on my shoulder. "You may feel this way again, but there's something you're going to do when hate begins to sink its teeth into your heart."

"What's that?"

171

"Choose to forgive again. And again. And again, if necessary. Until it's finally gone and given to The Lord."

"And if I can't?"

She paused for a moment, her eyes softening as she looked at me. "Just be careful to not let sin *against* you produce sin *in* you."

I opened my mouth to speak when a clanging sound interrupted me, reminding me where I was. Leaning in closer to the post, I pulled Sariel beside me and risked a quick glance around it. Two servants were kneeling on the floor, quietly gathering a tray's worth of spilled fruit. A clumsy lot, I thought to myself. Past them, I could see that Thana was hiding herself behind a pillar as well, scoping the scene, exactly like me.

"Is that her?" Sariel asked, her head suddenly next to mine as she looked past me and straight at Thana.

Eyes wide, I yanked her back, silently praying Thana, or anyone, hadn't seen her. "Yes," I said through clenched teeth, furious at the stupid mistake.

"She's beautiful," Sariel murmured, looking at me with a sweetness that briefly softened my frustration. My thoughts flickered to the red mark on Thana's neck before I forced them away.

"Sariel," I said firmly, "you won't tell anyone I'm here, right?" I needed her to understand completely.

"On pain of death," she pulled my hand into her own, gripping it and giving a squeeze. "You'll be in my prayers, Rivka, that you may find the peace of everlasting forgiveness and that this will not be the last we see of each other."

She hesitated a moment, something else on her mind. "Can I help you and Thana with what you have to do?"

Clenching my teeth, I knew that even as a newcomer, she might have information I could use. But could I trust her with it? Mentioning theft from a monarch might turn her against me. Still, if she did betray me, I'd likely be gone with the tablet by then. Maybe I didn't need to tell her everything; just start small and see where the thread would lead.

Her round eyes looked back at me, waiting patiently.

It couldn't hurt to try. "I'm looking for Herod's son, Birsha. Do you know where he is?"

I knew where his room was, but if he was in there that'd probably make things a little more complicated.

"I do," she nodded, "but you won't find him here. Him or anyone else in his family, for that matter."

"What do you mean?" I asked, perplexed.

"They've all left. Herod Antipas went back to his main palace with most of his household."

"And Birsha with him?"

"No, not him."

Some hope? "Is he still in the city?"

"He left for Alexandria yesterday. His father had some royal matters for him to look into."

My heart sank. Gone. Just like that.

Sariel's lips parted, but then closed again, retrieving whatever it was that she was going to originally say. "I must go, Rivka, but I pray blessings upon you."

I opened my mouth to respond, but another noise came echoing through the halls, pulling my attention away. When I glanced back—just a second later—Sariel was gone, without a trace.

Birsha's room wasn't far.

This was it. My last hope. A final, flickering flame in a storm I could no longer control.

I caught Thana's eye and gave her a quick gesture to wait before slipping off, each movement sharp with urgency.

Like many of the rest of the halls, there were no guards near his room. I slid through the door, breath held, heart hammering. The room greeted me in eerie stillness—untouched,

173

undisturbed. Exactly how I had left it. That should have comforted me. It didn't.

I moved fast. Methodical at first. Then frantic. Gilded drawer handles clinked under my grip as I tore them open one by one, the wood groaning in protest. I shoved aside embroidered linens dyed in royal purples and rich indigos, their silken folds catching on rings and carvings of gold and silver that adorned the furniture like jewelry. Torchlight glinted off inlaid bronze trim and filigree, flickering across shadowed corners as I searched every hidden space, every crevice veiled behind opulence. I willed it to be there. Willed the tablet to reveal itself.

But it didn't.

And as I stood in the wreckage, chest heaving, panic creeping in like poison, the truth settled over me like a cold, heavy shroud.

The tablet was gone.

And with it, my only way of saving Evander.

Closing my eyes I leaned my forehead against the wall, dreading what would come next. I would have to tell Thana. There was no predicting how she'd respond, only the sinking certainty that it wouldn't end well.

I had to get it together. Gidon said it, and he was right.

Rolling my shoulders, I secured myself and covertly made my way to her, escaping the indolent servants around the corner still cleaning their mess. Making it without much strain, I tapped her shoulder. She turned to look at me, confusion on her face.

"It's not here," I susurrated.

"What do you mean it's not here?"

"It's not here. The royal family must have taken it."

Anger filled her eyes, her lips becoming a thin, white line. "Are you trying to trick me?

I couldn't believe her. "What are you talking about? Are you blind? Everyone is gone! Most of the royal family left to a different palace, others elsewhere. They took everything with them."

Thana looked around the column, ensuring that we hadn't been spotted. She grabbed a piece of her hair, playing with it between her fingers.

"Look, we can stay and search all you want, but you can't find something that's not here!" I bellowed harshly.

"How do you know it's not here?" she asked, obscurely losing some confidence.

I raised my eyebrow. "Would you leave your gold behind?"

Her eyes locked with mine—the decision was hers.

XIII

ZEALOT

Escaping the palace, we found our way to an inn in the lower part of the city. The only inn in the lower part, actually. It smelled of stale drink and manure, but it looked like a place where we could lay low. All of this was supposed to be a "get in, get out" operation. But now, with everything unexpected thrown at us, we needed time that we didn't have to figure out our next move.

The proprietor, upon seeing us, gave us a hard time at first. But his attitude changed when Thana threw a heavy pouch on his wooden table, a few silver coins spilling from inside. My eyes almost widened as much as the unsavory man. Being a pirate notably had some monetary benefits. It didn't take him long to lead us to our room, saying it was the best in Jerusalem. Door creaking open, the unchanged straw from the bed in the corner and sorry excuse for a table and stool in the center made me wonder what the other rooms must then look like.

Exhausted, Thana closed the door to the room while I undid my cloak, placing it on the stool and slumped on the straw. Thana rubbed her temples as she sat down beside me. Neither one of us spoke for a while, drained, and frankly, just not wanting to speak to one another. Nevertheless, the obvious had to be brought up and discussed.

"What do you want to do now?" I said, breaking the ice.

She continued to rub her temples, making me almost believe that she hadn't heard me the first time.

"Thana."

"What?" she responded sharply.

"What's the next step?"

Grunting, she turned towards me. "There's only one step—get the tablet. How doesn't matter, only when. And 'when' is now."

"Okay," I trailed, thinking of a plan. Herod and Birsha leaving made things much more difficult. Them both going to different places was already a challenge in itself. What if Herod took the tablet with him? Should Thana and I divide and conquer? It was a gamble picking who would have the tablet. On one hand, in every instance that I had encountered it, it was always with Birsha, meaning it was his. On the other hand, it was solid gold, valuable, meaning he might have sent it with his father for protection or his father took it from him, wanted or not. But there was one thing that was clear.

"If you ever want to get back, this will be our last chance," I said to her.

Again, she didn't respond.

I gave a huff. "It's a miracle that I found it the first time, let alone this second time. We will not get this chance again."

"How do we even know who has it?" she finally said, dropping her hands on her lap and looking at me. I hadn't noticed before, but now it caught me off guard. She looked so...old. The bags under her eyes were dark, darker than I'd ever seen them. Wrinkles formed against her forehead, her eyebrows in a tense pose. Thana had been beautiful—was beautiful. Was the stress wearing her down?

Or a better question, was it the stress of this era or our own time?

"We know where they are, right?" I pointed out, tucking the thought in a deeper part of my mind.

"Yes."

"Then, let's use that to our advantage."

Thana took a breath. She knew even a small advantage was better than none. "What are you thinking?"

"There are only two options of where it can be. That being the case, we're going to have to take a little bit of a gamble, but our best bet is Birsha. Anytime I've ever seen the tablet was with him."

"He's the son of a public official, Rivka," she rolled her eyes.

"And? That's stopped you before?"

"He'll have guards and, not only that, he's sailing out of Caesarea."

"And that matters because?"

Her brows furrowed, eyes growing big. "You're not the only one who's learned a thing or two since being here. Caesarea is the Romans of Judea's headquarters. All of their government officials are there, probably including Pontius Pilate. Jerusalem is just a vacation spot for them. On top of those guards, I'm sure Birsha will have his own royal guards surrounding him. That means that security will be top notch. And then, of course, the cherry on top is that he's on a ship."

"Your men can attack the ship at port, while I go and search for the tablet, that way it's semi-secluded."

She scoffed. "You think I'm going to let you go and look for the tablet yourself? Not on your life."

I pressed my lips together. "Fine, we can go together. My point is, while they're fighting, we're looking."

Thana began rubbing her temples, thinking it over. "Let's pretend that's a foolproof plan; I don't know if I have enough men to defy an entire port, even with the promise of gold and riches."

She wasn't wrong. Between the Romans and Herod's guard, we'd be finished.

"We'll iron out the details of how we get on the ship without their notice later. First, I think I have an idea of where I can get more men," I said. "I'm not sure yet, so don't count on it, but it's a start."

She shook her head. "No, Rivka, you know how this works. Even if we had enough men, we'd start a revolt. This isn't something worth starting one over. They cause chaos and uncontrollable chaos means an infinitely small chance of finding the tablet. Getting to Birsha, no problem. Finding something that's probably not on his person, crazy small chance."

I thought for a moment. "Then we need to get him isolated. That's the only way."

"How would we do that?" she asked semi-sarcastically. "Do you want us to follow him to Alexandria, or stop and attack his highly trained guards on open waters?"

Lightbulb.

"Yes, exactly!" I stood, forming the plan in my mind.

She stared up at me in disbelief. "You're joking..."

"I'm being serious. We get him on the ship. It's isolated, no extra help from anyone around."

Thana didn't look convinced,

I scoffed, putting a hand on my hip. "Aren't you a pirate? Isn't this literally in your job description?"

She paused for a moment, before shaking her head. "The military surrounding Birsha, the men on the ship, will signal for help the second they see us coming on the horizon. There's bound to be a ship around that will come to help and that's assuming we're far away enough from land."

"Then how did you manage to capture us?" I asked, irritated. "We had two battleships trailing us and you still managed to conquer our ship."

"Not to divulge too much, but let's just say we had a work around and connections from the start. I wouldn't have that here, thus meaning the same tactic wouldn't work."

Thana had a point. I said nothing for a minute, trying to think of what would work, putting a pin in that piece of information for later. The wheels in my brain began to turn as I thought of our missions from the past. Caesarea being the location of our headquarters, we'd left out of there through various ways: helicopters, cars, small planes, boats. Anything by air we never used for stealth, only speed. Even if we had that option, it wouldn't work to use them in this situation. Cars were sometimes good for stealth. Again, not an option.

An idea mumbled out of my mouth.

"What'd you say?"

"Row boats," I spoke louder, the details forming.

"What about them?" Thana asked, not getting the picture.

"We use them. Just like that mission we had in Crete years ago."

She knew the mission I was referring to. The plan had actually been her idea, and it worked.

Seizing her silence, I explained further. "Our boats in Jaffa are only about a day's distance if we hustle. Caesarea is about four days from here. Since they left yesterday, even if they push through the night with the fastest chariots, they still won't reach it before we get to Jaffa. Once they set sail, they'll have to pass Jaffa, where we'll intercede, stopping them, and getting the tablet."

"There are two problems with your plan, Rivka. One, I don't have any row boats and have no idea where I could get them. Do they even make them in this century?" she questioned. "Two, if we somehow magically get them, they'd still see us coming. Either by the sun or the moon, they'd know."

"Doing this in the daytime is obviously out of the question. And as for the moon," I got up and walked to the left of the room to the small window that was in the corner. Pulling the drape aside, my suspicion was confirmed. "See, it's just a crescent. If we do this in the next few days—which we have to because Birsha's leaving—then the moon and its lack of light will be our friend."

"Fine, but we still don't have row boats," she pointed out.

I smirked. "You leave that to me."

Thana scoffed. "You're saying that you can get us men *and* row boats in time to catch Birsha on open waters?"

"Yes," I affirmed.

I gave her a moment, knowing that she didn't really have any other option than to trust me. She knew it too, but she dragged the silence, reluctant to point out I was right and let me take the lead.

"Alright," she concluded, "get everything in order."

Nodding, I grabbed my cloak, trying to think of my next steps. "I'll be back by morning," I stated before turning and adjusting the material as I opened the door.

"Don't forget..." she called out after me. She didn't need to finish her sentence; I knew what she meant.

Don't forget I have Evander in my evil clutches.

I had to use all my self-control to not just turn around and let her have all my pent-up rage. Instead, rather than turning, I simply lifted my hand and flashed her a thumbs up.

Here's to hoping my plan would work.

—————— ✣ ——————

When sent on missions by the Kidon, tracking had always been something I had enjoyed. The anticipation forming on your brow, having to steady your racing heart when you get close to your target. Some missions were for a better purpose, others for a selfish one. But the thrill of the pursuit always stayed the same.

The same feeling was building in my stomach now as I waited in a darkened alleyway. It was one of the few that didn't already have other inhabitants in it even though it was deep in the lower part of the city. One side of this alley road led onto the main street, while the other was a dead end, the city wall. Even though the darkness of nightfall concealed the steep hills on the

181

other side of this wall, it didn't deter me from stealing a glance over my shoulder, trying to will it into sight. During all this chaos, all this confusion and unknown, the land had remained mostly the same. If I just stared at the hills, blocking everything out around me, I was back home.

Not daring to linger longer, should I miss my target, I turned my attention back on the road waiting for him. Any minute he would walk by, if the women were correct. When I told the women in the market stands who had cast a look of disgust towards the Roman soldiers patrolling that I was looking for the Zealot Order with an important message for revenge, they were more than happy to get me started in the right direction of where to find who I was looking for. Between that and my years of skill, it wasn't too difficult. Besides, even though Gidon said I could send a message through his mother, I didn't think I was ready to face them just yet.

Hearing muffled footsteps, I pulled my scarf closer to my face, pressing my body further against the wall. Almost soundlessly, the group of about ten men walked past me. Looking across my shoulder, I waited until they stopped in front of a doorway only a few feet away, lingering only a moment before they walked in one by one. Throughout the entire time, some men were visibly on guard, but I was better at my job than they were at theirs. He was about to enter the doorway, the last of the group, when I saw my chance.

"Gidon," I susurrated.

Caught off guard, he looked around for the voice, unable to find me.

"Pst!" I called again, beckoning him.

His eyes finally found mine, bewilderment distinctly on his face. He said something inaudible to the men in the building before walking towards me, the door shutting behind him.

"Rivka, what are you doing here? How did you find me?" he whispered, looking around to make sure no one who could be on the street saw us.

"I need to talk to you, and I've got my resources too," I brushed off.

He looked around again. "We can't speak here."

Grabbing my wrist, he took me deeper down the alleyways. We walked for a few minutes, taking turns left and right, before he finally pulled me into a small, obscure courtyard. The entrance was hardly visible if you didn't know what you were looking for, making it seem like the perfect place for a private conversation.

Letting go of my wrist, Gidon walked around the courtyard, seeming to make sure no one was hiding in there. Satisfied, he came back close to me and crossed his arms.

"Go ahead."

I pulled the scarf from around my face, adjusting it against my braided hair. "I'll keep this simple. There are two things I want to talk to you about. One personal, the other business."

He stayed silent, probably either contemplating what I was going to say or if he should even listen to me in the first place. The latter was probably silly, since he went out of his way to make sure we had a confidential place to talk.

Clearing his throat, he spoke. "Personal first."

Waiting a moment, I wanted to choose my words carefully, different sentences forming in my mind. But blunt was always best. "I... I want to see Tamara."

The whistle of the wind moving through the hills could be heard ever so softly. Gidon said nothing for a moment and I could understand his feelings. Truthfully, I'd probably turn me out on my face for even asking if I was in his position.

He stayed silent for what seemed like forever, though it was probably only a couple of minutes. But with each second that passed, it felt like my gut was twisting tighter and tighter. I rarely felt like this, making me almost unsure of what to do next.

"What," I began, doubtful it was a good idea to ask, "what did you tell her about me? About my leaving?"

The question almost seemed to offend him, because as soon as the words were out of my lips, he responded. "I honored my promise to you," he said sharply before softening. "I told her you loved her... very much."

"And? What did she say? Where does she think I am?"

He looked to his right, avoiding eye contact. "She's a smart girl, but her love for you is... unconditional. I told her that something had happened, and you had to find your family right away, not able to waste a moment. That you couldn't take us with you. But, she knew I wasn't telling her everything."

Dumbfounded, I couldn't help but point out one word he had used. "Us?"

His head snapped back, stern dark eyes finding mine. "Yes, *us*. You didn't just leave Tamara that day, if you remember."

My muscles tensed.

"Besides," he pushed past. "I don't think it'd be a good idea for you to see her. As I told you in the market, she's settled with my family, and it would only cause her more pain."

Silent, I knew he was right.

"I know you wouldn't want that," he softened.

"No, you're right," I confirmed. The air became thick.

"Then onto the business," I moved on, not able to take much more of the heartache.

"I'm listening," Gidon said calmly.

"I have something that I know will be as much of a benefit for you as it is for me."

His eyes squinted, unsure. "What are you talking about?"

"A way for you to get rid of a whole bunch of Romans, turncoats, and sympathizers."

"Turncoats?"

"Never mind," I brushed past the remark, now dawning on me that it would be thousands of years until that phrase was used.

Gidon's hesitance was as obvious as the stars in the sky. I could understand his uncertainty. I was, by definition, the very thing he wanted to destroy.

"How?" he asked slowly.

"I know where a lot of them are going to be and that some people are going to attack them. You can join forces with the attackers and your strength will be greater than the Romans and you will overcome them."

"Why would you know something like this? Or a better question, why would you want to share it with me?"

"Because I'm the one who's going to be attacking them."

His eyes widened at my unexpected answer. Before he asked another question, I just decided to explain further. "I found the tablet I was looking for. The only problem is that it's on a ship being guarded by royal soldiers. The docks are being guarded by Romans. In order to get the tablet, I need to get rid of these obstacles."

He scoffed, shaking his head.

I read his mind. "I may not be doing this 'for God and country,' but if you join me, that's what you will be doing."

"Reasons aside," he started, his voice deepening, "how are you even going to go about it? Do you have men? Fighters? What happens when it's all over? Who will get the repercussions? We may be Zealots, but those in my Order still think on how to do things smart, what's best for the people."

"I know that, I'm not just running with guns blazing."

A puzzled look crossed his face, but I ignored it, continuing. "First, yes, I do have men; the pirates that I told you

185

about earlier. Second, if you fight with us, the repercussions will fall on them. They're hunted anyways and that's the deal that Thana and I made. Your men will dress like them, and no one will be the wiser."

He pressed his hand against his mouth and waist, contemplating. I gave him a couple moments to think it all through. I knew I was asking a lot from him and didn't want to rush his decision.

"Why are you doing this?" he finally said.

Confused myself, I answered, "What do you mean? I just tol—"

"No," he stopped me, "why are *you* doing this? You, Rivka? What gain is there for you?"

Letting out a deep breath, I responded, "Because I need that tablet. I can't tell you more information than that. But what I can tell you is that getting it is a matter of life and death."

I paused. "You're just going to have to trust me."

Gidon's dark eyes stared into my own. Finally, he gave a simple nod. "Alright. Let me hear your plan and, if it's a good one, I'll discuss it with the men."

Relieved, I couldn't help but let out a tiny smile. Grabbing Gidon's arm, I gave it a tight squeeze. "Thank you," I said simply before diving into the details.

XIV

DREAMS

"**Z**iyad's trying to get aid for his men," I scoffed, the earpiece in my ear buzzing as their conversation came through.

"What else is new," Thana rolled her eyes. "That filthy pig is not fit to be dirt under our nails."

I chuckled in agreement. She lifted herself off the stone wall she was leaning on, walking over to the small window, and looking out of the side. Only the moonlight lit the street, star pinpoints all over the coal sky. The cackles and howls of the wild dogs carried through the open space, unsettling any who may hear.

Thana pulled out a nut bar from her pocket, gesturing an offering to me, but I shook my head, focused on hearing the words the men were saying. We'd been in this building for days, scoping the area for Ziyad's meeting with the leaders in the area. If he got what he was looking for, it meant a lot of people would die. Men, women, children.

"Are they biting?" Thana asked, taking a piece out of her bar.

I didn't answer, trying to make sure I wasn't missing anything. A few minutes passed when I finally heard what I was searching for. I pulled off my headphones. "They'll sell him the bombs and get three of their top men in the country."

Thana crumpled the wrapper in her hand, sticking it in one of her zipper pockets in her jacket. "It's go time," she whispered, pulling the collar of her jacket closer to her.

I checked my watch, seeing that it was just past midnight. Packing the very few things we brought in the zippers of my own jacket, I made sure there wasn't a trace of us in this *abandoned building. We traveled light, bringing only the minimum for survival. As far as weapons went, we both only carried a handgun with a silencer, a few magazines, and some knives.*

Satisfied, I followed Thana down the crumbling stone steps onto the main floor, gun in hand. Reaching the side door, she put her hand up, signaling for me to wait. Cautiously, she checked it out and gave me the all clear, stepping into the shadowed alleyway. We walked about halfway, her covering my six, as we made our way to the target's home. My ears caught wind of something, making me instinctively crouch down. I waited for a moment, checking if it was merited. After a few seconds, I was about to rise when an unexpected visitor turned the corner, locking its eyes on my own widening ones.

I held my breath, the snarling canine now at eye level, its saliva dripping down its long tooth. The few others behind him followed their leader.

"That dog is going to give away our position," Thana whispered loudly, freezing as she watched its lip curl.

"Because that's my biggest concern right now," I breathed, using my left hand against the stone to keep me still. I could shoot it, but I didn't want to waste my ammo that I'd probably need on these creatures. But it was that or we wouldn't complete our mission at all.

Thana knew this and slowly raised her handgun, finger on the trigger, having only seconds to make the choice.

Voices erupted into the open air, drawing the dog's attention towards the noise. Three men came out of one of the buildings, pushing the dogs out of there with the big sticks they were carrying. Their boldness alone mesmerized me, let alone that the dogs actually listened to them, running off into the bushes. What amazed me even more was the men didn't see Thana and I in the shadows.

We let out a silent sigh and then focused—take out Ziyad and whoever he was meeting with, no matter the cost.

I signaled to Thana for us to separate, her to take the right side of the building and me the left. Nodding, she checked if it was clear and then silently crossed the street, just a hair of dust rising from the ground. Steading my nerves, I did the same. The building had no windows and only one door, thus why we couldn't use sniper rifles and take them out from a distance. But it did make it the perfect place for an ambush. Crouched low, we scanned the street. The men were long gone, and no one remained in sight.

It was time.

We took a breath, counting down from three. Reaching one, I stood, giving the door a hard kick. She entered the room, firing at the men. Coming in behind her for cover, I saw two men already down, blood pooling from their bodies. Unfortunately, Ziyad and four others had responded quick enough, flipping the wood table and taking cover behind it. We could hardly get three steps in before they returned fire, their guns booming, leaving us to find refuge in the small stone partition to the room, each on a different side.

We both crouched down, firing at the terrorists on the other side. I could hear a grunt as another one of our bullets found its mark, sending its target to the ground.

"Three," I recounted to Thana, trying to see if it was Ziyad.

Firing, I caught a glimpse of his green collar, insults slipping off my tongue. A hand reached out of the side of the table, gun gripped tightly, before I shot it, its bearer crying out in pain. Thana and I moved in perfect rhythm, reading each other's mind as repetition and familiarity kicked in. We knew what every facial expression meant, every sign. As always, we were in sync.

Taking cover behind the stone wall, I reloaded. "I'm on my last mag!" I warned Thana, slamming the magazine in.

"Same!" she responded, crouching to reload her own handgun while I covered her, firing shots at the two remaining able-bodied men.

Now ammo'd up, we knew that this would be our last chance.

It was now or never.

Nodding to each other, we left our positions from the wall, firing at the men, as we made our way over to them. About halfway to them, they stopped firing back at us.

"Wait!" one of them yelled in Arabic.

On guard, we slowly proceeded forward. They said nothing else, and we cautiously came around the table. Two men were on their knees, hands in the air, the one I shot in the hand was rocking himself on the floor, holding his mangled, bloody hand. Their guns were on the ground, just a hand reach away from them. I kept my gun trained on them as Thana bent down. Grabbing the guns from the ground, she flung it across the room.

"You can kill me," Ziyad cautioned, "but our comrades will be here in seconds. This was all for nothing. I'll live forever as a shahid."

"Let them come, we're only here for one thing," I mocked in Arabic, before pulling the trigger. The man's eyes tightened as a small click sounded.

I was out of ammo.

Spotting his chance, Ziyad grabbed my leg pulling me down. Thana watched, keeping her gun trained on the other man.

Ziyad gained the upper hand briefly, landing a few solid punches, but I rolled clear just in time and pushed myself back to my feet. Spitting blood from my mouth, I didn't let it deter me. I drove my elbow into his nose, barely seeing the blood trickling out of it before I pulled his head down into my knee.

But he was a spirited fellow, grabbing a handful of dirt and rocks into his hand, blinding me as he threw it into my eyes. It gave him just enough time to stand, landing a blow to my ribs.

Falling to my knee, I dodged his next punch, adrenaline just barely masking the pain.

Finally coming to my aid, Thana kicked him in the groin, sending him down in pain before delivering another kick to the head that knocked him unconscious. I stood, wiping the blood from the corner of my mouth as I gave a nod of thanks to her. She trained her gun to his head, finger hovering over the trigger, then paused. We listened for a moment, something vibrating in the distance. The other man let out a small laugh before Thana silenced him with a smack across the face with the butt of her gun. The two of us shared a look.

We could hear the footsteps and shouting from outside as they stomped eerily closer.

Panting, I shot up from my bed. Beads of sweat rolled off my forehead.

It was my repeating nightmare.

Looking around the room, I realized I was back in Jerusalem, thousands of years before that event even happened. Or was it technically in my past?

Looking to my right, Thana was asleep next to me. I watched her chest slowly rise and fall, maintaining its cadence, but was positive she knew I was awake.

Shuddering, I slowly lowered my head, trying to regulate my breath.

———— ✦ ————

Back on the streets, Thana adjusted her shawl on her head, pushing her dark hair behind it. I watched her, unable to shake off the dream from last night. She didn't notice, her mind on the task at hand.

She hadn't said anything that morning about hearing me, but there was no denying that she knew. My guess was that she was trying not to delve into emotions with me or that she just wrote it off to a PTSD dream.

191

Leaving the inn, she got right down to business. "Let's get some last minute surveillance done. See about any rumors on the street that could help us."

Agreeing, we set to meet back at the Pool of Siloam in about two hours, allowing time to gather supplies and listen around the city unnoticed. Splitting east and west, I headed to the busy marketplace in my portion. By the time I arrived, the plaza was alive with the hustle and bustle of the day. I slipped back into routine, I bought some of our desired commodities and kept my ear to the ground.

Cumin percolated against the base of my nose as I passed a stand. With each few minutes that passed and the further I moved in, the amount of people began to grow. By the end of a half an hour, it was so full in certain areas, I could scarcely make it through.

Pushing through, trying to make it to the stand of dates, my ears picked up on a voice. Almost at once I noticed that most of the people in this portion of the crowd were making their way to hear this orator, their eyes focused in one direction. Curiosity for both me and the good of the mission, I decided to see what it was all about.

Squeezing between people's shoulders, making it about halfway through, my eyes beheld the figure that seemed to captivate their attention. Standing on rocky steps at the entrance of a home at the edge of the square was a man. His vigor as he spoke to the gathering crowd at his feet showed his youth, but the deep lines beside his eyes and the few wisps of gray in his dark hair made him look much older.

Moving through the multitude, closer towards the edge, I wanted to get a better look at this young man. My heart raced as I comprehended the words he was speaking.

He was a follower of Yeshua.

But not just any follower, one in His intimate circle.

His voice boomed with confidence and passion, showing just how deeply the words he was saying meant to himself. He spoke with true belief.

"Yeshua is alive! I have seen him for myself," he proclaimed to the crowd.

A murmur went through the audience, those beside me debating if this man's words were true. I had heard that He was alive, both in this time and my own. The entire religion of Christianity was based on it, making it one of the leading religions in the world. But now there was a man insisting that he had seen Him.

Since coming to this century, I have experienced things that were supernatural, without a doubt. I had met Yeshua and, against my upbringing, my lifestyle, and everything else I thought I believed in, I trusted the words He spoke. And now there was a man I could speak with who is saying to have a similar experience with Him. I listened to his words, his declaration and persistence in telling those listening to him to follow Yeshua as he does. His zeal showed to be genuine as he spoke with people from the crowd, answering their questions and taunts with love.

There was something in his face that tugged at the edges of my memory. I couldn't name it, but I knew—somewhere, somehow—we had met.

The sun's position showed that at least an hour had passed. People came and went, the crowd being more full at times than others, but I hardly noticed. His words were like an arrow of truth piercing my heart. He gave encouragement that Yeshua had given us unconditional forgiveness.

Each time those words left his lips, I couldn't help but think of the predicament I found myself in. It made me want to speak with him. Someone so close to Him must know how He would've responded. Or, at the very least, have a similar response of his own.

The opportunity came moments later as his monologue came to a close. He left the entrance of the home and made his way through the street beside him. Lucky that I had moved closer to that side, I followed him down the street, catching up to him before he disappeared into the crowds of the market.

"You knew Him? Personally?" I called out behind him, grabbing his attention.

Turning, he looked back at me. "Yes, yes I did."

Realizing my rudeness, I apologized. "I just wanted to speak with you about Yeshua and your experiences with Him."

His eyes looked gently at me. "It'd be a pleasure. Let's move out of the middle of the street, we'll get trampled," he said, moving along the edge of the stone wall. "I'm Yohanan."

The name gave me pause, thinking back to my friend and his horrific end. In an odd way, it gave me a sense of peace, of closure. "I'm Rivka."

"You don't mind," he asked, gesturing to his water skin.

"No, please" I insisted, eager to ask my questions.

He brought the refreshment to his lips as my inquiry flowed from my mouth. "You're one of His disciples?" I asked, remembering the term from my own era.

Yohanan wiped the water from the corner of his bearded mouth, lowering the leather canteen. "Disciples? All who follow Him are his disciples."

"But I mean one of His followers in His inner confidence. The twelve."

Sheep bleated in the background as Yohanan chose his words. "Yes, I am part of the twelve."

"I didn't think you'd be so young," I observed honestly. The depictions I had seen in cathedrals and monasteries across the world when on missions usually detailed old men. But this man looked no older than thirty.

He gave a small laugh. "I'm one of the youngest out of His immediate circle, but that doesn't mean all of the others are old."

My lips twitched into a smile. He waited for me to speak again, sensing that I had something I wanted to say. I did, so many things, but I had no idea where to start.

Finally deciding to just dive in headfirst, I spoke.

"I was there," I started. "I mean when He died."

He stared at me, eyes winced, as if trying to place me. Then slowly, he responded, "I remember you. You're the girl who came running with a sword."

"That's where I've seen you," I murmured. "You were the one at His feet when He died."

He nodded, studying me for a moment. "I must ask, while there was a lot going on that day, why did you do that? Who were you aiming for?"

Color rising to my cheeks, I answered him. "I was trying to end His suffering. I know a person can stay alive for days hanging there. They already tortured Him beyond belief, I thought that I could end it all."

Instead of judgment making a declaration on his face, a softness and sorrow were there. His lips pursed for a few moments before he decided to speak. "It was a noble thing you tried. An act of compassion."

Caught off guard by the assessment of my actions, I could hardly muster a nod before feeling compelled to move the subject along. "I had heard rumors that He was resurrected from the dead, but I speak to few people, so I haven't encountered anyone who has experienced this personally. Or, at least, that would admit to it. When speaking, you said that you saw Him when He came back to life," I paused. "Is that the truth?"

A gentle smile was on his lips as his eyes had a light gloss. "Yes, I did. After He appeared to us, my friends and I, He stayed with us for another forty days before returning to be with His Father."

Unsure of what to respond to that, I simply took his information in, thinking of how it must have been during that month. Letting me process for only a couple moments, Yohanan spoke, "Did *you* ever have the chance to speak with Him?"

"Once," I answered, "a little before His death."

He didn't press me, but I felt the need to continue. "Our conversation wasn't long. We spoke briefly about forgiving other people, but in those few words…" I sighed.

"I know the feeling."

I frowned, looking away. "It was appalling how He was forced on that cross."

"Wait, Rivka," Yohanan stopped me. "He went willingly. He went more willingly to that cross than most of us to do the throne of grace."

The thought struck me.

Another question still nagged at my heart. One that had been there ever since seeing Thana again. One that I tried to mildly tackle with Sariel, but it left me wanting.

Clearing my throat, I offered my question, "There was someone that greatly betrayed me, someone I considered a sister. When speaking with Yeshua, He told me she did what she did because of a deep root of hate and that I must be the light and forgive her. After speaking to Him, I decided to forgive her. I thought I had let go, but then I saw her for the first time after everything, and it was so…"

"Distressing?"

I nodded. "Did I not really forgive her in the first place? Or are some things just too big to be truly forgiven?"

Yohanan was silent for a moment. "I can relate to your thinking. For me it may not be a single person, but I understand all the same."

"Not a single person?" I repeated back.

He shook his head. "Like many, the Romans leave a bad taste in our people's mouth, almost all having some form of a horrific experience from them; raiding their homes, taking their daughters, inflicting taxes, killing their brothers," he sighed. "But it's not just Romans, but other kinds of people too. Samaritans, for example."

Trying to remember the history that my father taught me, I could only recollect a few bits and pieces about the long history. In short, the Samaritans and the Jews did not get along and their hatred for one another was almost as great as that of the Romans.

"It was a blinding hatred I had for them," he said lowly. But then, an unusual sound escaped his lips—a laugh. "Once, when a Samaritan village rejected Him, my brother and I told Him to bring fire down from heaven to destroy them all."

"Him? You mean Yeshua?"

He nodded, still laughing. "He actually called us 'Sons of Thunder' because we were so riled up against them."

"Talk about a grudge," I chuckled.

His laughter faded, replaced by a somber, serious expression. "But now, I can't imagine not reaching out to them to share the good news of what my Savior has done for me. Sometimes my old thoughts creep back into my mind, reminding me of why I detested them, but then I remember what He did for me, and I make the choice again to forgive and forgive and forgive."

"Forgiveness is a constant choice," I said more to myself than to him.

"Besides," Yohanan continued, "the grievances we carried out against our Lord are much greater than what any person can do to us. And you saw the cost of that forgiveness. Can we really not do less than what Yeshua expects from us?"

Flashes of images from that day came into my mind. Biting the bottom of my lip, I knew he was right.

"But it broke my heart," I stated sincerely, still tethered to the pain.

"I know," he reassured me kindly. "But tell me, since then has that brought you closer to our Savior?"

"Yes," I started, "I suppose so."

"Then if a broken heart brings you closer to Yeshua, thank Him for a broken heart."

He gave one more example. "My friend Shimon was one of His innermost circle. But on the night of His death, Shimon denied he even knew Yeshua, not once, but three times. It broke His heart. There is only one other betrayal I could think of that is worse than that, but I'll leave that for another time. When Yeshua appeared to Shimon after His death and gave us yet another perfect example, not only forgiving him, but entrusting him to proclaim the good news to all around. Rivka," he paused, looking deep into my eyes, "we must follow His example and forgive when it's hard."

He opened his mouth to say more but then his eye caught another man across the road, his hand gesturing to come to him.

"Rivka, I must go, my companions are waiting for me. But I will pray for you and that you will have the strength to continue to make this difficult decision and the peace to know, no matter her response or the outcome, that it is in His precious hands."

———— ✣ ————

Shortly after parting ways with Yohanan, I met Thana at our agreed meeting point. The road out of the city stretched long before us, a winding trail of dust and worn stone, sunbaked and brittle beneath our feet. We walked in silence. Dry wind stirred the haze along the path, carrying with it the scent of sand, ash, and distance. Thana kept her gaze ahead, her expression closed, clearly unwilling to speak. I didn't press her. My thoughts were wrapped around Yohanan's words, heavy and persistent, like the dust that clung to our feet with every step toward the ship.

Forgiveness was hard.

Forgiveness is hard.

But how could I not extend the same grace that was shown to me?

Once we were about a half day's journey to the ship, Thana decided it was time to solidify the details of the plan. We talked at length, our minds working together like clockwork, muscle memory of the endless number of times we had done this exact thing before.

Making it back on the ship near nightfall, I couldn't help but feel confident in our strategy. Gidon was going to bring enough men to match our own, putting the odds in our favor. That is, if they were good fighters. Even if they weren't, it would still create enough of a distraction for me to be able to slip in, find the tablet, and get out of there before anyone would notice.

The next day, Thana wasted no time. It was filled with instruction and repetition, wanting to make sure her men would execute the battle plan flawlessly. I didn't blame her, as my instructions for Gidon and his men were just as meticulous. Mine and Thana's methods were instinctive, our strategies seamless, familiar and in sync from years of working side by side. On some of those missions, we did work with other units and even different militaries, meaning we knew just how important making sure every detail was ingrained forever in your men. One slip up, just one person not in their place, could prove fatal for not just them, but the entire entourage.

During this time, Thana was still keeping an eye on me, but she knew my capabilities and that it wasn't just my life on the line, allowing me to go anywhere on the ship to prepare for the impending attack. Almost anywhere. Her wary eye that she retained on me did not go undetected.

I watched as she drilled her men. Her sharp yells, strict commands, persistence for perfection. Flickers of my dream pressed into my mind.

Biting my tongue, I willed the memory back into the deepest den of my brain. My eyes squinted as I looked at the sun, centerfold in the sky. In a few hours our battle plan would begin. There was still much to do, and I had to get my head back to the task at hand.

Walking across the deck, I grabbed the scratchy rope that was tied alongside the stairs, making my way below. Determination on my mind, I stood before the cabin room that held my desired items. The creaking door swung back on its hinges, the musky smell of wood and water didn't seem like something I'd get used to. My eyes slowly adjusted to the darkness as I tried to see where Thana had stored the linens for the arrows.

I pivoted some barrels from side to side, checking their contents even though the sheer weight alone should have indicated that there was nothing as light as linen stored in them. The floorboards creaked behind me, but I feigned not to hear them, continuing my task. My heartrate picked up as my finger twitched, eager for the right moment to pick up my knife strapped to my calf. Seconds later, the opportunity presented itself.

Pulling my dagger from its spot on my leg, I grabbed the person's collar, pushing them back as I held the steel blade against their throat.

"Quick," Evander chuckled, holding both hands up in surrender.

I smirked in surprise. "Can't trust any of these filthy pirates," I surmised, putting my blade back. I was surprised that Thana returned the golden object to me when we got back—at all, actually—but I didn't press her.

Thana decided to hold her leverage elsewhere. I had seen Evander since returning, but she didn't give me much time to speak with him, constantly making sure I was doing something that would better the mission. After coming back though, she did loosen the security on Evander, allowing him to roam about the ship, so long as he was helping the men. I could tell it was a struggle on his morality, but it was that or being chained to the mast once again and he managed to tell me that there was no point in being locked up like an animal.

He smiled gently at me, the warmth in his eyes filling the room. "How have you been holding up?"

I sighed. "Best as I can under the circumstances. You?"

He leaned his head from left to right. "About the same."

"Being able to walk around must be nice," I said, trying to make light of a dark situation.

"It does have its benefits," he smiled, making his voice softer. "Including, giving us the chance to escape."

Those words being the last thing I had expected to come from his mouth at this moment, all I could do was stare blankly at him. "What are you talking about?" I finally said.

"We can leave. Never see her or these foul pirates again," he stated, grabbing my shoulders.

"We can't escape," I ran my fingers through my uncovered hair.

"Rivka, she's let her guard down, she allows me to roam freely around the ship. And while you were gone, I gave them no cause to quarrel with me in hopes of your return and an opportunity of escape may appear. I've mastered their routines, their practices. We could leave tonight," he said hopefully.

I wanted to do what he said. He was right; he seemed to be in better health, and we might just get away without her catching us. But there was another issue. Another factor involved that I couldn't live with if I ignored it.

Gidon.

It was already too late to get a message to him to call off the attack.

"We can't, Evander," I whispered. "I'm too deeply involved in this now. Thana would know sooner rather than later if I were to leave. Besides I found half the forces that we are using in the attack and formulated half of the plan."

Even if I did leave, Thana wouldn't rest until she found me. She needed that tablet. We would never know a life of peace. I couldn't do that to Evander, or frankly, myself.

He said nothing, contemplating the words I had just spoken. The wood creaked as I shifted weight onto my other foot. Guilt slowly crept up my spine, the realization that I was keeping Evander in this dangerous situation when he didn't need to be. "But you go, Evander. It'll probably be safer if you just escape. I can cover for you, help you in any way I ca—"

"Are you mad? I'm not leaving without you. We're in this together," he stepped forward, determination in his voice.

Looking up at him, his warmth touched my heart. But then I realized that since we hadn't many opportunities to speak, Evander only knew bits and pieces of what was going to happen in the next few hours and how it came to be.

"How can I help you then?" he asked, almost as if he read my mind at that moment.

Biting my lip, I tried to pick out the right words. I told him the plan, leaving out names at first, just giving him a general idea of what'll happen and what his role in it would be.

As I finished, he nodded, pondering my words.

"There's something else," I added. I rubbed my thumb, trying to focus on my words. "All that information that I got, the extra patrols, extra men for us," I paused. "I ran into Gidon at the market when we first arrived in the city, and he told me. And later, when I came up with the plan, I sought him out to see if he'll help us."

"That's good, the more friends in our corner, the better, right?"

"Yes," I said nervously.

Evander looked confused. "Is there something else?"

All the cards on the table. "In the past, he… he had feelings for me. But I don't reciprocate them in that way."

Evander didn't respond.

My finger was starting to go numb from how tightly I was squeezing it. "I just thought you should know."

He waited a moment, eyes on the ground as he processed the information. Looking up, they softened. "Rivka, how could I blame another man for seeing the wonderful things that I see in you. He'd be a fool if he didn't."

Butterflies flew wildly in my stomach. It made me smitten and unsettled. I needed to change the subject. "Let's see how your wounds are healing."

Evander lingered for a moment, a tenderness in his expression that made it hard to look away. Then, without a word, he pulled off the top of his tunic, turned around, and eased himself onto the barrel with deliberate care, the muscles in his back shifting as he moved.

Unwrapping the bandage as gently as I could, I traced my fingers over his cuts. "They're not inflamed, which is a good sign. In fact, they seem to be healing quite nicely, especially under the circumstances."

He let out a short breath. "I did have an excellent physician."

As gently as I could, I began to run an ointment I had purchased in town over him, praying that it would help. As before, Evander didn't flinch, but from personal experience, I knew just how painful these types of wounds could be and how long they lasted.

Grabbing the new bandages I also had, my hands slowly wrapped his back until tying it securely on his shoulder.

Tightening the last knot, my fingers lingered for a moment, my eyes caught on the long scar on his shoulder. I had seen it before, but it couldn't help but make me wonder what had happened to receive it. As my mind traveled, without warning, Evander's fingers found my own, gently interlocking his hand with mine.

Neither one of us said anything for a moment, consumed in the sound of our racing hearts. Without letting go of my hand, he rose, turning to face me. He looked at me as if there was something worth looking at, deep in my soul.

"You never gave me an answer," he said silverly.

My breath stopped. He was right, I hadn't. Thana's attack had come at the most perfect imperfect timing. Swallowing, I saw that this was about to be the moment I would tell him how I truly feel.

My lips parted, but my ears picked up on footsteps.

Knowing we were about to be interrupted, I sighed.

"Later," I whispered, releasing my fingers from his just as the door snapped open.

Evander and I both watched as Thana entered the room. She paused, sharing a look between the two of us. Finally, she spoke. "C'mon, Rivka, there are things we need to do."

Not looking back, I moved towards the battle that lay ahead.

XV

DEATH

The waves were calm. So calm that our small rowboat glided across them without a whisper. We were miles from port now, no sight of land from any side. The steady breathing of the other nine men onboard was hardly heard, each waiting in still anticipation for what was to come. Thana's men had been promised riches and plunder, Gidon's men promised justification and liberation, and me, well, I was promised my life and Evander's.

I discreetly stuck the tips of my fingers in the water, its warmth a soothing presence. The only thing that was visible on the water, hardly, was Birsha's ship, the small torches illuminating against the black liquid. Thana had extinguished most of the torches from our own ship, stealth being one of our greatest advantages. The timing of the moon's cycle was perfect too. The black clouds in the sky would have been a blessing as well if the man on the moon wasn't already showing his back.

Lifting my hand, I let the water stream down my arm, it gliding off my elbow, wetting just the edge of my rolled up, linen sleeves. It was tranquil—serenity wrapping me snuggly in its cocoon before destruction.

Thana stayed behind on the ship, keeping Evander there as insurance until her ship boarded our target. Frankly, it didn't make sense to me. I was here. The way I had planned this evening's events wouldn't change whether Evander was beside me or not. While Thana may be a traitor, I was not.

I looked at Atticus, appointed leader on our rowboat. The inflammation from his face had gone down significantly from his fight with Evander, only the deep purple and yellowed bruising remained. To some, it might make him look fiercer, the pattern under his eyes making him look like the Grim Reaper. But, to me, he just looked like the man Evander dominated.

Gidon, on the boat behind us, watched intently. He had made it clear when we were discussing our plans that the pirates were only means to an end, a lesser enemy needed to help defeat a greater one. None of the pirates seemed to care, but it was obvious that Gidon wasn't thrilled that they were the ones heading this operation.

The side of our boat scraped against the ship's barnacle-covered hull. It must have not been loud enough, because the soldiers did come and check out what was going on. That or they were just too lazy. Either way, it was a good sign for us.

Atticus motioned to the men the next phase of the plan. We all knew our roles, pirate and Zealot alike, but he was giving us timing. Three men positioned themselves with their back to the ship, hands interlocking in front.

One knife in my right hand and the other between my teeth, I put my foot in one of their hands and began making the climb. The ship wasn't particularly tall, so scaling it wouldn't take long. What was the tricky part was lodging the blade into the wood without making any sounds. The other two men and I tried our best, knowing we had the worst of it because we were first. The three of us were chosen first for the very reason that we were the lightest, meaning that we would need the least amount of force to stick our knives into the wood and hoist ourselves up, making the smallest tinge of noise. With any luck we'd jump onto the ship unnoticed, giving us the chance to have more men on board before we attacked. Unlikely, but what is life without hope?

I was the first to reach the top. Peeking over the railing, I counted their forces, trying to give the men below the best heads up that I could. It was most definitely more than we were expecting, but in my mind, between the Zealots and pirates, we could take them. With one arm, I held onto the blade, keeping my body up while with my other hand I motioned the number to the men. My core was burning, but I pushed the pain away, grasping quietly the edge of the railing and pulling myself over. When Aura had first purchased these sandals for me in Rome, they still needed to be molded to my foot. But by now I had worn them in, making them seamless and noiseless as my feet landed on the wood.

The soldiers didn't notice at first, and one of the other men, a Zealot, was able to do the same. But as the pirate touched down, quiet as he was, a royal guard just happened to turn around at that exact moment. He wasn't able to say a word before the Zealot sliced his jugular, blood spraying as he fell to his knees. The thud of his knees was enough to grab the attention of his comrades, because within seconds everyone on the upper deck had turned.

Oddly, they froze for a moment, stunned as they stared at us. Then, as if snapping out of a trance, they let out their battle cries and charged. At that very moment, our men vaulted onto the deck, their arrival shaking the boards beneath us. The air filled with the scrape of steel and the raw cry of battle, and in a breath the whole upper deck dissolved into full-blown mayhem—writhing bodies, flashing blades, the sharp tang of blood already rising.

A soldier made his way towards me, but was clearly green by the way he was comporting himself: awkward, unsure, frightened. He must be the son of someone important, probably placed on the upper deck for his safety. Some things don't change, no matter what the era. I gave one hard strike into his liver, which earned a stunned look and delayed reaction as he fell to the ground from pain. Common; liver shots were probably the worst place to get hit. Not wanting to kill him, I was going to give him a blow to the head to try knocking him out, but either the punch or fear seemed to have done the trick.

A horn sounded, drawing my attention back up seeing soldiers piling up the steps onto the upper deck and fighting their way to the back of the ship. Then something crashed into the boat, knocking many off their feet. In the nick of time, planks began connecting one ship to the other and the rest of our men began piling on, their screams rumbling in the open space.

Within minutes, a majority of our men were onboard and taking advantage of the royal guard's shock. In the masses, I spotted a patch of dirty blonde hair. Evander fought his way forward, with ease and expertise, coming beside me on the right side of the railing in minutes.

"Better late than never," I teased him, taking my sword from its sheath and pushing forward through the fray. He was holding his own, surprisingly well given the injury. He wasn't fully healed, not by a long shot, but you wouldn't know it from the way he moved.

Thana joined, as well. She made it unmistakable that her sole focus in the mission was finding the tablet, leaving us to deal with the soldiers. I knew she didn't trust me to search for it, even though that had been the plan. But that didn't mean I wouldn't try. If anything, it would be much better if I found it before her. After everything, there is no way that I could take her word and believe that she'll let me live.

Managing to make my way down the stairs, I tried to use every opportunity possible to look for Birsha or where he might be hiding.

And as I thought of the devil's name, he appeared.

Across the ship, near the stern, was Birsha surrounded by royal guards. Most were fighting the pirates that had also managed to make their way down, while two were hoisting him over the side of the railing.

Halfway over, his eyes locked with mine. He lingered for a moment, either because he recognized me or for something else. But the second I moved towards him, he disappeared over the edge, some of his soldiers following.

Coward.

Reaching the railing, I leaned over the side, trying to see how they could escape. Livid, I saw that we had provided them with a way. One of the rowboats had shifted forward from the waves, moving to the perfect spot for him and his soldiers to get away untouched. I had to find a way to get him. For all I knew, he took the tablet with him.

A boom rang through the air, and, out of instinct, I ducked to the ground, covering my head with my hands. Again and again the sound came. My eyes widened—I couldn't believe Thana! I knew she had brought a weapon with her, but the sound was much deeper than a meager handgun. It must be something much bigger and deadlier.

Searching for her across the ship, I needed to see where she was aiming so I'd not be in the way. But, only a few feet away from me, she was hand-to-hand with a royal guard. With a sword in one hand and dagger in the other, she couldn't have fired the weapon. Did someone take it from her?

Then the answer to my question appeared. My mouth hung a little when the true culprit stood before me.

That was no shotgun.

The man was well over six feet tall, nearing seven. His tanned, muscular skin reflected against the warm glow of the fire, his jaw set, yellow teeth clenched. And in his right hand, he gripped his weapon—a bullwhip.

I barely had a second to think how odd it was for a soldier to be using it in battle before he put his leather to work. As the sound rang once again, I found that that wasn't the only damage it could do. The tip had found contact with the forearm of one of Thana's men, slicing it open as the pirate dropped his sword to the ground.

Swallowing, I knew this man would cause more harm than most of the royal guards, if only for his strength and ability to distance himself from his foe.

He needed to be taken out.

Gathering my courage, my gaze darted around the ship, looking for something or someone that could help me. Gidon and Thana were still on the upper deck, Evander in the fray. My eyebrow raised as an idea came, the mast forefront. Sheathing my sword in my leather belt, I began to climb it, just enough to be a person's height off the ground. Satisfied with the level, my feet used the force of the wood to give me a boost as I leapt into the air, my arms coming in contact with the brute's neck and bringing his body to the ground. The man's height was deceiving; he moved faster than I'd expected and was already back on his feet by the time I rolled out of the way.

Snap!

The whip landed beside me. I had just enough speed to avoid him, but the man was quick. He threw it again. My hands tried to grasp the small strand of leather, but it just earned me a sliced palm.

Pulling my sword out, I thought maybe I could lure him to try and take it from my grasp, having the leather wrap around the blade, giving me the chance to cut it. That plan was ill thought out, as once he wrapped it around, he pulled it from my grasp. Clutching my knives, I moved like a flash of lightning, launching them with deadly speed. Only he was faster, twisting and dodging with ruthless precision. Now weaponless and out of options, my last hope was to try and catch it again with my hands again.

He raised his whip, but his hand never made its way down as something else found its target. Dropping to his knees, I could see the golden hilt of my dagger lodged through his head.

Turning back, Evander barely gave me a nod before going back to his fight with two soldiers, now on the other side of the ship.

Relieved, I stood, wrapping my fingers around the hilt and yanking it out of the man's scalp, his body thumping to the ground. I couldn't be more thankful for giving the dagger to Evander before the fight. Bending over, I also took the whip out of the man's tight grasp. That'd happen sometimes, the body going into shock and the nerves tightening.

I lashed the whip forward, pleased with the echo. A sting ran across my cheek, my little training with this weapon evident, but not enough for me not to use it. Swinging it again, the tail slapped against a soldier's leg, bringing him down to his knee just long enough for a pirate to relieve him of his head. It rolled to the ground.

Coughing, I looked around.

At some point, one of the men must've knocked down a lantern, because slowly, the ship was turning into flames. The rims of the sails had already caught fire, illuminating the sky as if the sun. The light brought clarity and chaos to the situation.

Thana was on the steps battling three soldiers, their weight bearing down as she was forced down the steps of the stairs. Running, I cracked the whip into the air, landing snuggly around the middle soldier's neck. Using all my might, I pulled the whip down, bringing the guard to the ground. My dagger made its way through his leather armor, landing in his heart. I tried to pull the whip free, but I only had seconds to see that it was tangled and one of the other soldiers fighting Thana brought his sword down above me. Letting go of the whip, I jumped out of the way, now alongside Thana on the steps. She blocked the soldiers' next blows as I got up and took my place beside her.

It only took us seconds to get into a rhythm. It was built into our brains what we had to do. We had chemistry. We both knew what the other was planning and both of us were able to support each other in it. Our minds may be adversaries, but our bodies were teammates.

But even with our shared effort, the men were strong. Their sheer force was almost enough to completely overcome Thana and me. We backed up the stairs, trying to use the high ground as an advantage, but it wasn't much of one. It wasn't long before the two soldiers pushed us all the way back to the stern of the ship. Our backs scratched against the wood. The sword was slick in my hand from sweat and blood.

I gave Thana a quick look, us both knowing we would have to do something soon or their strength would outlast our endurance. Thana and I were both skilled fighters, between being a soldier in the IDF and assassins in the Kidon, we knew multiple ways for people to meet death. But long-term hand-to-hand combat was definitely not our strength, and it was beginning to show. Assassins required stealth, accuracy, and creativity. War needed power and quick thinking. We mostly had the former.

I shoved the royal guard's sword with my own, knocking him back a couple steps, but his rebound was fast. His hand was extending, when he suddenly stopped. A sword came right through him, his face contorting in anguish. He fell to the side as the same happened to Thana's man. Standing in place of my soldier was Gidon, him pulling his swords out of the soldiers' stomachs.

He raised his eyebrow. "You looked like you needed help."

Before I could thank him, Gidon's eyes widened, his face dropping down to my sword extended next to his stomach. The guard behind him let out a sound, falling to his knees.

"No need to thank me," I smirked.

He tried to hide it, but I could see the small smile playing on his lips.

Turning around, my eyes fell on Evander's shoulders at the stern. The soldiers were closing in on him, but his skill shone through. His years of service in Germania showed in every move he made. Between his strength and technique, he wasn't letting the soldiers have it easy. Expertly, he attacked the soldiers with the two swords in his hand, each soldier armed with only one. Still, everyone could use some help.

I ran through one of the soldiers that was strangling one of Gidon's Zealots, his weight falling on the man before he flipped him off, resuming the fighting. Pressing forward, I tried to find the best path to Evander, but every possible route was crowded with pirates, Zealots, or soldiers. My arms ached from the force of fighting so many men, but I pushed the thought aside. This would all be over within the next hour, giving us a better chance to find the tablet. The smoke and flames were accumulating, making it more difficult in some areas to fight.

I was halfway across the ship when I managed to get another look at Evander. He had killed at least three soldiers, but some more seemed to have taken their place. Evander's strength was weakening, his movements slower, but the fire in his eyes made me believe that he might actually be able to take all those men. If I had learned anything on that pirate ship, it was that Evander was no ordinary man.

War, though, still had its toll.

Evander looked as if he didn't see the soldier that was coming up behind him quick enough, just barely moving before his blade swung forward. He saved his own life but managed to lose one of his swords in the process. One soldier kicked it away before Evander had time to retrieve it. He was barely up before the royal guard from behind body slammed into him, angered that he missed the first time. The other soldiers gave them some space as they fought, each landing blows. Evander managed to rise and landed his blade right into the center of the man's chest. Only when he went to pull it out, it was stuck. He yanked and

213

yanked, trying to break it free before the other soldiers came, but it wouldn't move—it was lodged in the man's bones.

I was still too far, too many fights blocking my way to help him.

"Evander!" I shouted. His eyes lifted just in time, catching the dagger I sent spinning toward him and gaining at least a sliver of defense. The two remaining soldiers bore down on him, going on the offensive, violently swinging their blades. Evander could barely get away, but among their swings, he saw his opening, stabbing one soldier in the eye, sending him screaming to his knees. The remaining soldier saw his advantage.

"Watch out!" The words tore from my throat, utterly useless.

But it was too late. The guard put Evander in a chokehold, his sword reflecting against the fire. Evander tried to elbow him in the stomach, but the man was tougher than he looked. I couldn't see how, but Evander managed to somehow loosen his grip, but not before the man slammed him down. He hit the ground hard, legs snapping out in a precise, last-ditch strike, but the only thing he struck was the soldier's sword, which sliced into his thigh. The soldier pulled out his blade, trying to unleash another attack, but didn't get the chance as Evander's dagger found its way into his chest.

I needed to get over there.

My eyes landed on the rope tied to the mast, and an idea sparked. I cut the rigging and grabbed hold, the rope yanking me up before swinging me across the deck. Rolling down, I landed near him. He had already managed to stand up, seething bloodlust in his eyes. I pressed a hand to Evander's shoulder, but he didn't seem to recognize me, lunging, striking as if I were the enemy.

"Evander, it's me, Rivka!" I cried, fending him off. "You're hurt!"

Seizing a free moment, I ripped some material off the dead soldier and wrapped it as a quick tourniquet around his thigh. Evander was confused at first but realized what was going on once he looked down. Pain twisted his face, and he fell down on one knee. I tied the knot, knowing that this was common in fighting. Adrenaline often masked wounds, and some injuries didn't fully register until later, or until someone drew attention to them.

The gash was deep and long, but thankfully wasn't wide. Blood was still spilling from the opening, Evander's eyes beginning to space slightly. I knew if I didn't get him out of here soon, he'd die from blood loss, if not from something much worse.

Wrapping his arm around my shoulder, we dodged the fighting as I took us towards an opening near the back of the ship. Yes, the fire was worse there, but the fighting seemed to be less, mainly just corpses piled along the floor. Evander did his best to walk beside me, but, like most men, he was heavy, his weight was dragging me down. Mustering my strength, I kicked the partially open door back and dragged us inside.

The room was large for one on a ship and based on the fineries inside, it must be either the captain's room or one of Birsha's special quarters. I hardly noticed all the purple material spread over the bed in the corner of the room and the leather chair beside it.

Helping Evander, I propped his back up against the leg of the bed, looking to his wound. Evander pressed his hand against the opening, but crimson was seeping out in spite of it. His fingers tremored, coated in blood, but the intensity in his eyes kept him steady, even as his body faltered. Knowing it wouldn't last him long, I sped into action. Bending beside him, I ripped the hem of his tunic.

"Hold your hand tight here," I ordered, putting the first swab of cloth against his wound and pushing his hand on top.

With the next strip, I wrapped it securely around his thigh, tying it off, then pulling back into more urgent matters.

Like the rest of the ship, this room was on fire. I had to decide hastily what my next course of action would be, my options few. Do I stay and defend Evander in this room, risking being stuck in a burning ship? Do I continue the mission and look for the tablet? Do I help Evander get to a safer place, abandoning the mission altogether?

The second was unthinkable, the whole point of this mission was to save Evander. Mind set, I knew the only prudent choice would be to get Evander off this boat and somehow make our way to shore, tablet or not.

"We're getting off this ship!" I shouted to him over the growling of the fire and clashing of metal. Energy still coursing through him, he nodded once, fierce and determined, gripping my hand tightly as I pulled him to his feet. We barely had time to turn around before the worst happened.

The timbers off the ceiling came crashing down, lit in the fiery red flames, and, worst of all, blocking the doorway. Out of instinct, I instantaneously pulled my forearm against my face, protecting me from the radiating heat. Evander, springing to action, limped forward and tried to grab a beam that didn't seem as kindled as the rest, only to jump back as he burned his hands. He waved me off that he was fine before I could even go to him, knowing that there was a more pressing issue.

Looking around, I tried to find something that I could use to prop the beams. I opened one of the chests, only to find nothing. Grabbing the chair, I tried to use its legs, but the flaming wood was too heavy. I tried kicking the logs, but they wouldn't budge. My foot pulled back in pain, the edges of my sandals and foot felt like they were being melted off.

"Rivka," Evander yelled, coughing through the acquiring smoke, "there's another chest here!"

He flipped the lid open before grabbing the linens from the bed, trying to put out the fire. Kneeling, I pushed past the jewels and parchment, looking for a golden candlestick or something of that nature, but there was nothing of the kind in here. But when I got to the bottom, my hand brushed against a plain, rough linen, with something hard underneath it. Pulling it aside, I could hardly believe my eyes.

There, in the small, blazing room, was my ticket home. The golden tiles shone against the flames, staring back at me.

The tablet.

With one hand against the cool metal, I looked around the room once more. The tongues of the flame only grew, and Evander's linens had caught on fire. Smoke poured upward, thick and choking, until the ceiling disappeared in a gray haze.

There was no escape.

That is, except for the tablet. I didn't have to die in this room, I just had to say the words and I would be out of here—hopefully.

Temptation began to whisper in my ear, somehow louder than all that was going on around me. Wiping the beads of sweat that trickled down my face with my forearm, the words of the tablet called out to me. All I had to say was, "The one who holds the tale of the future holds the key to the past," and presto, I'd be back.

I hadn't even noticed Evander trying to figure out another way for us to get us out. Only his yell as his hands touched the burning logs once more drew me back to reality. Leaving the tablet, I pulled him back from the doorway, bringing him to the ground in the center of the room.

The flames licked up against the walls, the roaring pounding against my eardrums. Black mushroom clouds of smoke continued to pile against the ceiling, reminding me of an angel of death coming to claim its victims.

We were tasting the inferno of hell.

There was no way of escape, not where we would both survive. There wasn't even a point in yelling, only our enemies were outside, and they'd sooner let us burn in here than save us. I couldn't leave Evander to die in this horrific and excruciating death... at least, not alone.

My choice was made.

The lack of oxygen was beginning to take its toll, my chest rising in arduous breaths. Tears rose to my eyes, panic overwhelmingly making its presence.

Panic and guilt.

We were going to die...

"This is all my fault," I whispered, falling to my knees beside him. I was just so tired. Tired of running, tired of fighting. I had no power here. I had to give up. I looked up at him, my eyes barely meeting his. "I'm so sorry, Evander."

The tears and beads of sweat that I did have felt like they were evaporating from the heat.

Evander lifted his free, blood speckled hand, cupping my face gently. He didn't say anything for a moment, looking around at the crumbling furnace around us. He knew I was right. He knew our lives were about to end. He knew we were going to burn. But instead of keeping his mind at the evil pressing in on all sides, he brought his eyes back to me. His soft, green, tender eyes.

"Rivka, this isn't your fault," he rubbed his thumb against my cheek. "I'd rather die today with the knowledge that I have lived knowing... and loving you."

He tightened his grip slightly as he dropped his head towards mine. I leaned in, not sure if our breaths warmed us or if it was the heat from the fire. He pressed his lips softly on my own, the harsh reality stopping for just a moment as we became one. My hand gripped the hem of his collar, hoping it would somehow keep us tethered here to this earth. Some tears managed to slide down as the salt from them wet our lips, our embrace coming to the truth. If it was mine or Evander's, I couldn't tell.

All I knew for certain was that this was the end. But my, was it a beautiful way to die.

Evander pulled away, placing his forehead on mine, his thumb caressing my bottom lip. My eyes stayed shut for a moment longer as the fire roared around us. Finally, I had the courage to open them, my hand still gripping his shirt collar. Never in my life had I wanted to say so much, but said so little. Felt so much, but stayed so exceedingly silent. This was my last chance.

Placing my other hand on the nape of his neck, I took a deep, smoky breath. "You're worth it all, *ahuvi*."

Short. Almost nothing. But he understood. Our eyes said more than words ever could. He pulled me in, resting my head on his shoulder. I could feel him wince in pain, his other hand still firmly on his wound, but that didn't stop him.

His lips lay softly against my brow as the world around us burned. "See you in the next life, my love."

The flames seemed to envelop us. Only the boards directly around us had not yet caught on fire, unlike the rest of the room. Cracking and snapping wood sounded all over, the heat intensifying. The deep purple linens were shriveling like insects, a charcoal black color taking the place of the royal hue.

Chest tight, I tried to steady my breathing, but the thickening smoke was making it even more difficult. Everything was moving so fast and so slow all at the same time. My eyes darted all across the room, my shoulders shaking. Evander grabbed my shoulder with one hand, noticeably weaker than early, and with the other turned my face one more time to his. He said nothing, his eyes intently on mine. His jaw set, teeth clenched, as he gave my face a small shake. I nodded, lips pursed in an attempt to be brave. Then he kissed my brow as the world around us burned.

XVI

CONSEQUENCES

A piercing clatter ripped through the executioner's howl.

Clank! Clank! Clank!

Was my mind playing tricks on me? I looked around the room before looking back at Evander. He heard it too, his head lifting. Was this death's call? Were the trumpets sounding?

Clank!

"I think…" Evander started.

"It's coming from outside," I susurrated. I had barely got my words out before the beams began to shift. And, within seconds, the door burst open.

Smoke gathered at the door, making its way out of the trapped room, and blocking us from seeing who, or what, had come. The figure moved through the gathering shadows, each step closer. When they finally stood before us, the dim light revealed their face, etched with unmistakable features that sent a jolt through me.

"Thana!" I coughed. A dizzy haze clouded my mind, but I forced it aside, steadying myself against the rising tide of weakness. We had to get out of here and fast.

Thana's eyes fell on Evander's wound before turning her attention back at me.

"Grab his arm!" she yelled, pulling his left hand over her shoulder while I did the same with his right. Evander sucked the smokey air through his teeth, gripping mine and Thana's shoulders.

The heat was unbearable and suffocating, but we pushed forward with everything we had. My legs felt like lead, each step a struggle against the weight of exhaustion and searing pain.

THE ABYSS BETWEEN

Sweat poured down my face, stinging my eyes, mixing with ash and smoke that scraped down my throat like sandpaper. Every breath was a battle.

But the opening was just ahead—we had to make it!

Muscles trembling and lungs on fire, we stumbled toward it, the flames licking at our heels. With the last of our strength, we threw ourselves through the opening, bodies bruised and burning, but alive.

We burst into the open, the cool air hitting us like a miracle. Evander and I doubled over, gasping for breath, dragging in lungfuls of clean air as if it might run out. Each inhale burned, but it was air—real air—and for a moment, that was enough to keep us moving.

Through the fray, Gidon appeared, concern riddled on his face.

"Are you alright," Gidon gripped my arm.

"The tablet," I coughed, barely understandable, let alone audible.

Gidon looked back at the doorway. "It's over, Rivka. Just get yourself and Evander out of here."

"But—"

"That's an order!" he commanded. I lingered only a second before giving a single nod and moving forward near the edge of the ship for safety.

Just minutes after we were out of the room, the ceiling of the room collapsed, bringing down the few soldiers that were still on the upper deck down into the furnace.

We weren't in the clear yet. That room wasn't the only thing burning; fire had begun to creep across the ship, its heat licking at the floor boards and its smoke starting thickening the air. The flames hadn't reached us yet, but they were coming, fast. Thana let go of Evander and moved ahead, searching urgently for a way out before we were trapped.

Seconds later, she found it.

221

Soldiers, Zealots, and pirates alike were fleeing in droves, plunging overboard into the churning sea to escape the relentless blaze engulfing the ship. Only a handful remained: the broken, bloodied, or those already dead. None stayed out of loyalty.

"C'mon," Thana called out, her voice firm as she moved toward the edge of the ship. She had barely taken a few steps when a sharp cracking sound split the air.

"Watch out!" someone screamed, drawing attention to the creaking, flaming mast.

Evander was the first to see it out of everyone. He threw his arms around me, flinging us to the ground and rolling a few feet away. Done just in the nick of time, the mast broke in half, falling down in fiery flames onto the ship.

Evander gripped my shoulder, checking if I was alright. Gasping, I nodded. Helping Evander up, we stood, and I looked around, my eyes landing on the ships deck.

Thana.

She was laying on the ground, part of the mast on her. Evander's eyes locked onto the same sight that had frozen mine. Without a word, we forced our battered bodies to her side.

Groaning, she turned her head to the right of her, most of her consciousness gone. Caught off guard at the severity, I looked at the damage that was caused. The mast had fallen on her arm, shards of wood stabbing into her forearm. She was trapped beneath the column, her limbs tangled in the wreckage, and I had no idea how I was supposed to free her. Removing the hundreds of jagged shards that were poking through would be impossible.

"Maybe we could cut the wood that's attached to her and remove the small shards later," I said to Evander as much as I was saying it to myself.

He didn't get a chance to respond before Gidon appeared. His eyes landed on Thana, going wide as he took in the full extent of the damage. He looked around at the fiery hell we were in. Pulling his sword from his sheath, he positioned it in both hands. My stomach dropped at the realization of what he was planning.

"There's no way to save it?" I pressed, my breath caught in my chest.

"Rivka, if we don't do this, she will die. We all will die," Gidon said, trying to make me see reason. Deep down I knew he was right. We had no time to think of an alternative without something happening to the rest of us too.

I closed my eyes, nodding.

Evander had somehow already managed to fasten a tourniquet around her arm, a task that couldn't have been easy with all the splintered wood in the way. The strip of cloth pulled securely just above her elbow, skin slick with sweat and blood, black makeup smeared underneath her eyes. The wreckage around her was a splintered snarl of shattered beams and debris, forming a crude cage that pinned her down and left almost no room to work.

Task complete, I clasped Evander's arm and helped him up, pulling him away from Thana's body.

Gidon gripped his sword in hand, the short, straight edge shining in the light. The sword's edge gleamed with razor-like precision, as if it had just been sharpened moments before, sharp enough to slice through silk and bone alike with terrifying ease.

He took a breath.

The pain must've been intense, because as soon as it was finished in a single, swift motion, she shot up, screaming. It was only seconds before Gidon was crouched by her side and she crumpled back into unconsciousness from the agony. With care, he pulled her away and tightly wrapped what remained of her arm with the cloth I had given him. Without wasting a moment, he carefully picked her up, motioning with his head for Evander and I to follow him.

My eyes landed on Thana's ship, unsure of when it arrived, but thankful just the same. A mixed crew of Zealots and pirates swarmed its deck, reinforcements ready and waiting, a lifeline if we needed to make a quick escape. Evander limped beside me as we reached the edge of the ship, where a fresh problem faced us.

"Planks!" Gidon yelled to his men across the sea. "Put the planks!"

But the remainder of his crew couldn't hear him over the roar of the flames and the distance of the ship. Someone finally caught on, but he pointed to the water, showing how they had fallen in.

Gidon yelled in frustration.

Timbers fell behind us, the heat of the tongues making us feel like it was burning our eyebrows from our faces. We looked around, trying to find something, anything, that could help us. But there was nothing. Either the flames had already gotten to it or it was just nonexistent.

Our doom was upon us.

"There's only one way out," Gidon yelled, going beside the railing, Evander and I following.

"Beniamin!" Gidon called.

Before I could fully process what was going on, I saw Thana flying through the sky, over the water, and into our ship. It felt as if all the air had been ripped from my lungs, until I saw Beniamin miraculously catching her just in time.

Gidon looked at Evander and me. "Our turn."

Determined, I answered with a single, firm nod.

"Jump!" Gidon grabbed my hand, pulling me with him as he leapt over the railing. My fingers tightened around Evander's as he leapt beside me. It was mere seconds over the edge, but it felt like an eternity until we finally made it in the water.

Instant relief was had the moment I was submerged in the cool sea. The sting of salt bit into the fresh cuts along my arms and back, but I welcomed it. Pain meant I was alive. And beneath the surface, even if just for a moment, it felt like time stopped. It was as if everything that had happened until that moment had been nothing more than a dream, or better said, a nightmare. The thing about water is that it refreshes, it revives, it resets.

Gasping, I breathed in reality once again. Gidon and Evander had already come above the water and were waiting for me. Evander looked spent, the loss of blood taking its toll. He was staying above the water, but I could tell that he was struggling.

"Look out below!" Beniamin called, before throwing something overboard.

A rope fell into the water, the splash wetting my already soaked face.

"Evander, you first," I said, pushing the rope next to him.

"No," he said, catching a mouthful of seawater in the process.

"Now's not the time to be gentlemanly. You're hurt and you've lost too much blood. You won't last long in the water. I'll be right behind you. Go, now," I insisted.

Evander's face clearly was opposed to the idea, but I gave him no time to protest, wrapping the rope around his shoulder. He grimaced, but the men from the ship began to pull him up.

Once overboard, the men threw the rope back to Gidon and I. My fingers locked against it, the wetness acting as a layer of protection against its coarseness. With ease, the men pulled me up, hoisting me overboard within a matter of seconds. Feet on solid footing once again, I looked around.

225

Beniamin had laid Thana on the deck as some of the crew were looking at her new stub. Evander's back was propped up against the edge of the boat. He was holding pressure on his thigh, his bandage soaked red.

Dripping, I knew I had to work fast, or Thana and Evander would die. Looking at Evander's laceration, you'd initially think it wasn't life threatening. But infection was brutal out here, that and sepsis.

These next moments were critical for both of them.

Thana's wound was worse, she'd have to go first.

It wasn't a matter of preference, but facts.

"You, bring me that torch," I pointed to one of the Zealots.

Pulling my jeweled blade out, I held it over the flame, trying to kill any germs I could and get it flaming hot. The next part wouldn't be fun.

By this point, Gidon had made it onto the ship and was caught right in the middle of all the action.

Satisfied with the temperature, I took the blade off the fire.

"What are you doing?" Gidon asked, watching me as I brought the blade closer to Thanas' limb.

"She has to cauterize the cut. If she doesn't do this, she'll bleed out," Evander answered for me, military experience evident.

I looked up at Gidon. "Hold her."

Nudging his head, one of his men came, holding Thana's legs while Gidon held her shoulders. I positioned my left hand at the end of the wrapping, looking back at the two men.

"Three, two, one," I counted before pulling off the bandage and placing the hot blade over the stump. Thana came to, but was delirious. She moved, but the loss of blood had diminished her strength.

Ensuring that every opening was closed, I placed the new bandage around the wound firmly but tender enough that it wouldn't irritate it. Releasing the tourniquet, I motioned for one of Gidon's men to take her below deck where she could rest.

Placing my blade over the flame once again, I looked at Evander. "You're next."

———— ✣ ————

The sunrise trickled in through the small gaps in the linen hanging over the window. My eyes slowly parted, pulling me into the morning.

The journey back had been arduous. By the time we made port in Jaffa, there was no time to linger. The news of the attack could spread at any moment, and we couldn't risk being linked to it. We stayed only long enough for Gidon to gather supplies and secure a donkey. He rigged a makeshift harness to carry Thana, every movement precise and urgent. Whenever I had a moment, I returned to her side, tending to the wound as best I could.

By the second day, a fever had taken hold of her. With each hour that passed, the more worried I became that she wouldn't survive. In normal conditions, she'd need to be in a bed, resting, but we weren't afforded that luxury. I did the best I could with what I had.

Evander also held my concern. He moved with a slight limp, each step marked by a subtle hitch in his stride. After a few days of rest in the cramped quarters of the ship, the worst of the bleeding had stopped. Once we made port, I cleaned the wound thoroughly, sealed it, then wrapped his thigh in clean bandages. It wasn't perfect, but it would hold. The injury still slowed him, but he bore it with quiet resilience. My guess was that even though he was in pain, he was a man—a soldier—and was taking it as such.

The next bump in our trail was our destination. The closest place Gidon said where he had connections was

Jerusalem, but as we recalled from our last visit, it may still be in a lockdown, making it very difficult to enter the city unnoticed. We then changed course to Jericho. While it was an extra day's travel, Gidon insisted that it was best for everyone's safety and health.

Levi, Gidon's Zealot friend in the city, was gracious enough to offer his home to use once again. Remembering me from my last visit, he gave me a warm greeting, insisting on his hospitality.

Now, two days since arriving, Thana's fever had finally broken. I watched as she lay helpless in her bed, wondering what would happen once she woke up. What would happen with us?

The moment I had been waiting for had finally come.

Thana's eyelids fluttered open, slow and hesitant. Her gaze wandered at first, unfocused, before gradually sharpening as she took in the large room.

"Where am I?"

The corner of my lip twitched. "In Jericho."

"How did I get here?" her eyes darted around.

"Gidon, Evander, and I brought you."

"Brought me? Why?"

I let out a breath. "You've been unconscious for days. This was the only choice we had."

"My arm is throbbing," she groaned. She looked down to see what was causing it but froze. What little color she had drained from her face. I followed her dark, almond eyes downward, linen sheets tousled. Apprehensively, she lifted her right hand, moving it towards where her other arm used to be. As she got closer to the stub, she hesitated, pulling her hand back.

"It's alright," I whispered.

Swallowing, she took the encouragement and placed her hand on her upper arm. She held it there for a few moments, covering the stub with her entire palm.

Her eyes stayed focused. "What happened?"

I had prepared on how I should tell her. After everything that had happened up until this point—the betrayal, the blackmail, the lies—I thought that I would relish in this moment of her demise. That I would smugly tell her she got what was coming to her, that she deserved it for everything she had done thus far. But in that moment, when I saw the measures Gidon would have to take to save her life, I only felt pity. Pity and regret. My sole thought was what a horrific thing to happen to her and that if I could spare her any pain, I would. Just because she made wrong choices based on fabrication and deception didn't mean I was going to.

"Gidon saved your life," I began simply, shifting in my chair.

She stayed silent. She looked so small, so defeated. I could only imagine the thoughts that were running through her mind. The changes that this would make on her life.

"What do you remember?" I asked, trying to gauge just how much I needed to explain.

"I…" she began, "I remember being on a ship. It was on fire. We were running, but then everything went dark." She pursed her lips, brows furrowing.

"That's more than I thought you would, especially with head trauma," I assured her.

"Head trauma?"

"We were on the ship," I explained, "just as we were nearing off of it, the mast broke, falling on you. The impact knocked you out and the wood…" I stopped. This was proving more difficult to explain.

"The wood," I quietly croaked, "fell on you, shards going through your arm without release. It was either leave you to die or take a chance and save what we could."

The breeze slightly pushed the linen off the windowsill. We stayed frozen that way for a while, me wanting to make sure she had enough time to process everything. Both Thana and I had been prepared for this sort of circumstance for years. In our line of work, this sort of thing was very likely to happen, or worse. Leadership and trainers taught us how to cope, what we should do in that situation, and even went through simulations and mental stress to ensure that we would be ready. But, when you're in the middle of it and it's real life, it's a totally different ordeal.

Honesty was the best thing that I could do for her. They may not have a name for it in this century, but I knew Thana would go through the stages of grief. The faster she got through them, the quicker she would live a more normal life.

"This is my dominant hand, you know?" She gently worked her hand up her arm.

Is? "Was" would be more accurate.

"I know," I said truthfully, offering as much tenderness as I could muster.

Tears began to wet her eyes, a single drop falling from her face onto her lap. I knew this was a normal response, but seeing Thana so vulnerable after everything that had happened was not something I was expecting. But, then again, everything that had happened up to this point wasn't exactly something I was counting on either.

Still, it made her seem…human.

"I've been so awful," she covered her face with her hand.

"Thana," I put my hand on her shoulder. She didn't look up. Frankly, I didn't think she would, this small resemblance of self-reflection and pure honesty rare. But deep down, she knew the truth. Sometimes it just takes a hard lesson to realize it.

"Just get some rest… *chaverah*."

My breath caught in the back of my throat.

Friend.

The significance over what I said settled clearly. Thana said nothing, but her eyes showed that she grasped it too.

I had forgiven her.

"Why?" she finally asked softly. "I don't understand why."

Biting my lower lip, I tried to think of what to say. Up to now, I had been in multiple experiences and conversations that had led me to this choice: Yohanan, Yeshua, his disciple, and more. And while that had been over the course of months and the conversations long and difficult, the answer was simple.

"I met Yeshua," I uttered. "He forgave me, so now I must do the same."

She said nothing else. Maybe she didn't believe me; maybe she thought I was crazy. It didn't matter. It was the truth.

"Rivka," a voice called out. Gidon stood in the doorway entrance, motioning that he wanted to speak to me.

I nodded before looking back at Thana. Placing my hand on her shoulder, giving it a small squeeze. "Rest," I directed, the corner of my mouth going up. I left the room with her lying back down as she stared where her arm had been.

Out of the room and now out of earshot, I looked at him to speak.

The days of rest in Jericho had done Gidon good. He was exhausted from all that transpired, but he never uttered a word of complaint. He and Evander had spent most of their time in the separate rooms that Levi had given them. When first seeing Evander, Levi was confused, especially being a Zealot sympathizer himself. The fact that it was Gidon asking made the whole situation all that more confusing. Yet, he told Gidon that he must have a good reason for bringing a Roman and allowed him into his home. Gidon still kept his distance from Evander, though, whether he vouched for him or not.

"Are you going to tell her?" he asked, his dark eyes looking into my own.

I closed my eyes, hiding one important secret from her. Whether it was for her sake or mine, I couldn't say. Amid the chaos of the burning ship, after we had fled the room, Gidon had risked everything and plunged back into the inferno. Against all odds, he emerged clutching the tablet, just as the mast groaned and toppled toward Thana.

"It's complicated," I finally concluded, rubbing my hands against my face.

Arms crossed, he leaned against the wall. "I don't know all the details that go with this tablet and this woman. What I do know is that you are a very smart girl. Don't think about everything going on around you. What do you think is the best thing for everyone? What do you think is the best thing for *you*?"

Taking his words to heart, I shook my head. I knew there was only one path out.

"I'll take it," I whispered.

Gidon said nothing for a moment, just studied my face. "The decision is yours," he surmised. Then, he retrieved a cloth bound object, placing it in my grasp. My arms lowered from the weight in my hands and heart.

The tablet.

Gidon gave a nod of respect before leaving me to ponder the matter alone. Our entire journey back from the attack I had wondered what I would do. Ultimately, I decided I would make my decision once Thana woke up—*if* Thana woke up.

Now here we were: Thana awake, and the tablet in my grasp.

I parted my lips and released a slow, steady breath. Gathering my courage, I returned back to the room. Thana was where I had left her, staring down, contemplating her loss. Pity washed over me again, pressing my decision on the matter further. Walking over to the corner of the room, opposite of Thana, I placed the tablet upright on a small table. Only when I turned around did I realize Thana had been watching me. Her gaze flicked between the tablet and me, silent and searching.

"You found it?" she finally spoke.

Tilting my head, I gave her the answer.

"Did," she paused, "did you have it all along?"

"No, it was on the ship that day. In the room you saved me from, actually."

Her face contorted. "Why are you putting it in here?"

"We had a deal, and I gave you my word. I keep my promises."

I didn't only do this to hold to my word. In actuality it was a test. To see if her time in this era had changed her like it changed me. Or, at the very least, give her the opportunity to do the right thing. Was it foolish? Maybe. But sometimes you have to take a chance in hopes of a brighter outcome.

"Someone will bring some food for you," I offered a faint smile. "I'll be in the courtyard if you need anything."

Turning, I started to make my way out, when she called out after me. I looked back at her, her black hair disheveled, hollowed cheeks, and thin, petite figure showing just how small she really was. Not in form, but in reality, in the world.

"I…" she started, giving a quick swallow. "Thank you."

XVII

THE FUTURE

"**Y**our friend must be quite exhausted," Levi exclaimed, placing another date in his mouth as he reclined on his immense pillows.

Gidon looked over the rim of his cup as he drank the liquid inside.

"It was a long journey," I surmised, trying to imagine what Thana would be thinking as we passed into the second day of her being awake.

At the very least, she would most likely be in an exorbitant amount of pain. One of Levi's servants checked on her a couple of times throughout the night, giving her wine in an attempt to give some solace through numbness. But the girl said that the last time she refused it and told her not to bother her anymore. My best guess was that between exhaustion and confusion, she just wanted to be alone.

We were having breakfast, or as they would call it, the morning meal, when Levi began to wonder about her and what had happened in order for her to experience such a fate. Gidon had expertly handled the situation, not giving him the details of our mission, but not necessarily lying either. The three of us conversed about that and other things for hours. Between talk of Levi's business and Gidon's history with the man, it had almost reached noon.

During that time, Evander had kept out of sight. He had mentioned the night before that the less he was seen, the better. He didn't want to anger our host and change our fortunes.

Levi hid it well, but even with Gidon's backing he was nervous about having a Roman in his house. His eyes, however, betrayed the conflict within him, wavering between hospitality and spite Nevertheless, he honored his friend's guest.

"Take a plate to our two guests," Levi waved his hand to his servant. "The girl should be awake by now and the Roman will be famished."

"I can take them," I offered, rising and making my way toward the servant and her full hands. She looked back at her employer, wide-eyed, unsure if she should hand the plates over. Levi waved at her once again, signaling that it was alright. Stoic, she placed them in my hands and excused herself next to Levi.

Walking through the stone hallway, I tapped my toe against Evander's door. I studied the detailed woodwork as I waited for him. From what I had noticed, only the rich seemed to have door partitions, and Levi's were even more extravagant. Intricate carvings and emblems adorned every inch, the kind of craftsmanship I hadn't expected from a Zealot. It caught me off guard; rich, refined, and deeply tied to a cause I'd assumed was born of desperation.

Evander smiled when he saw me, pulling the door past him. "A friendly face."

"I brought food," I lifted the plate, handing it over to him.

"Just what I was looking forward to," he said, brushing his fingers against mine when he grabbed it from me. Observing the other plate in my hand, he added, "Came to join me?"

I shook my head. "Unfortunately not. This is for Thana."

"Ahh," he scrunched his nose.

"If you want company, you can come eat there," I offered, feeling some sympathy for his solitude. Even if it was self-imposed, it was for self-preservation. Being an outcast, or better said, the enemy, he didn't want to make an already somewhat uncomfortable situation worse.

"I'll let you have some time to check on her, I'll come in a little bit," he turned the corner of his mouth upward.

Giving a quick nod, I made my way to her room as Evander shut his door. Arriving in front of Thana's door, I gave it a quick rap. Waiting only momentarily for her response, I was left in silence. I could understand. Sleep was probably the only refuge she had.

As quietly as I could, I pushed the large wood open.

"Thana?" I called out.

She wasn't in her bed, and from the looks of it, she wasn't anywhere else in the room.

A piece of cloth laid bundled on the bed in Thana's place. On top of the neatly folded clothing was a piece of papyrus. Putting the plate down on the side of the bed, I looked at the burnt amber material. Picking it up, I recognized the Hebrew lettering. It was from Thana. I sucked in a breath as I read her words, realization flooding over me.

"Remember me the way we were and all the things we did."

My finger glided over her signature.

Head snapping up, I looked to the small table. Walking over to it, I picked up the tablet. It had been lying flat on the table instead of upright, but it was still here. Closing my eyes tight, I held my breath. The facts of the situation were covering me in the dismaying truth.

Thana was gone.

I stayed in that position for minutes, just trying to wrap my head around the situation. Then, another thought came. Opening my eyes, I studied the tablet. Did Thana actually make it home? Or would the tablet take her somewhere else? It wasn't exactly a science. Or better said, it wasn't a science that I understood.

But did it matter? She had left.

The gold gave a slight tap against the wood as I set it down, coming to terms with what had happened. Biting my lip, I looked back to her shawl and note. Levi's wife had brought it to

Thana to keep her warm during the cool nights, and to cheer her up. The material was an expensive blue, silver thread elaborately embroidered throughout.

I went to grab the cloth to return it to its mistress, but my eyes widened at the weight of it. Thana hadn't only left behind her clothing. It made me cautious. Looking around, making sure no one else was near the room or could see, I slowly pulled back the soft material. In a glorious revelation, her gift stared back at me.

Her pistol and flashlight.

Picking up the handgun, I weighed it in my hand. I pulled out the magazine—eight bullets stared back at me. With a sharp click, I slammed it back into place, the metal-on-metal snap echoing briefly. Then, with a controlled exhale, I set it down on the table, the weight of it landing with a dull thud. A whirlwind of thoughts ran across my mind.

Thana and I would never be the same.

We may have reconciled, forgave, but—if I ever saw her again—the consequences of what she'd done would still be there, lingering between us. It would hang over us like a storm cloud. Unspoken, yet impossible to ignore. I had forgiven her..., but I knew I'd never forget.

Covering the trinkets back up, I sat on the edge of the bed.

A shadow was cast in the room. Evander, arms crossed, was leaning in the doorway. Looking up, I watched him as he walked over towards me. He grimaced as he lowered himself beside me. Tenderly, he pulled my hand into his, interlocking our fingers.

"She left," I whispered to him. "Thana must have snuck out during the night," I explained so he wouldn't question it.

Out of the corner of my eye I could see him nodding. My thoughts drifted back to Yohanan's words. I had forgiven my enemy, and Evander and Gidon had done the same.

A smirk tugged at my lips as my mind wandered back to that fateful encounter.

Truth was, they hadn't done much when they first saw each other. On the ship, as we prepared to board the rowboats, I caught a brief glance exchanged between them, but no interaction. Then, as the ship was sinking, both were consumed by survival, focused solely on doing whatever it took to stay alive. It wasn't until we were off the ship and heading toward Jericho did they actually intentionally speak.

Up until that point, Gidon mostly directed his questions and directions to me. But as soon as we left the hustle and bustle of the port city and were on the dusty, rocky road did the tension finally reach its height. Based on my observations, Gidon would have been fine with not uttering a single word to Evander the entire length of the journey. It was up to Evander to pacify or worsen the situation.

Gidon was a few feet ahead of Evander and I, leading the donkey that carried Thana. That's when I heard it. Evander. A deep, long sigh. Barely having time to turn and look at him to check if he was alright, did I register what was about to happen.

"Gidon," he called out from behind, stopping in the middle of the road. Gidon ignored him, or hadn't heard him, as pulled the donkey forward.

"Gidon!" Evander repeated, firmer.

He stopped, but didn't turn around. My body tensed. Slowly, he moved, looking back to face his enemy. Evander walked towards him. You could hardly notice the limp as he walked with such intention, such direction.

Now face-to-face, they stared at one another, eyes locked, neither willing to break the silence or make the first move. The air between them felt heavy, almost electric, charged with unspoken tension and anticipation. I couldn't tell what Evander's goal was. Was his expression edged with anger, or something else entirely? The uncertainty hung over the moment, making it feel fragile and raw.

Neither said anything for a moment, their chests heaving with slow, measured breaths. My body was taut, ready if I had to somehow intervene in whatever was about to happen. Gidon's chin was raised, eyeing a challenge. But instead of accepting it, Evander did the opposite. Slowly, he extended his arm, veins standing out as he held it steady, waiting for Gidon to meet him halfway. Suspicion flickered across Gidon's face, wondering what Evander was up to. His swarthy figure remained firm, gaze on Evander's outstretched arm. The tension hung heavy in the air as I waited to see what the two enemies would do next.

Gidon lowered his head, his arm gripping Evander's tightly. Evander returned the hold with equal strength, their muscles flexing under the strain.

"Thank you," Evander said simply, as men often do. But Gidon knew all of what he meant, giving him a single nod.

Reconciled.

They may never be the best of friends, but at least it was over. Complete.

And now, here I was in my own similar situation. Yes, the life I once knew with her was gone. Never coming back. But now, there was…peace.

"Rivka," Evander said, "Gidon said he wished to speak with us."

Taking another moment to value this peace, I closed my eyes, contemplating and savoring. After a moment passed, my eyes reluctantly opened. Rising slowly, I trailed behind Evander, our footsteps muted as we slipped out of the bedroom and navigated the shadowed corridors winding through the house. We entered a small room bathed in the warm glow of noon sunlight filtering through two narrow rectangular windows. In the center stood a low table, surrounded by piles of cushions. Gidon was already seated at the head, waiting.

"Your plan is to return to Rome?" Gidon questioned, looking back at Evander and me as we approached and took seats along the side of the table.

"Yes," we said in unison and then shared a look.

Ignoring our synchronization, he continued, "Levi has offered his home to you both until you make your return back to Rome."

"Thank you, Gidon. I know he does this out of friendship for you," I stated.

His lip twitched, his dark tunic emphasizing his bronze features. "And Thana? What do you wish to do with her?"

"She's gone," I said truthfully. "Must have escaped in the middle of the night."

Gidon opened his mouth to say more, but I cut him off, not wanting to give answers that I couldn't or didn't have. "What about you? Where will you go? Back to Jerusalem?" I asked, leaning my palms on the table.

"No, not yet. I have," he paused, looking at Evander, "some business to attend elsewhere."

I laughed to myself. Old habits die hard. He was undoubtedly going to meet some Zealot comrades, probably out in the hills or one of the smaller towns on the skirts of the border.

"The longer you both stay, the more difficult it will be for Levi and his family. That being said," he turned again to Evander, "try not to stay too long... Roman."

Here, that word was an insult. But as Gidon said it, an ever so tiny smile played on the corner of his lips.

In good humor, Evander responded in kind. "As you say... Zealot."

Gidon rose, and Evander and I followed his cue. He began to make his way out of the room before he stopped in front of me. Not fully turning to face me, he leaned his head down slightly closer to mine.

"I'd say goodbye," he added, "but I'm sure I'll be seeing you both in the near future."

Giving a small chuckle, I raised my eyebrow, looking at Evander who was hiding the little grin on his face with his hand.

"I wouldn't be surprised."

———— ✤ ————

The fading light drew my attention to the horizon, where the sun cast orange streaks across the dark, rippling water. The hair on my arms rose as a breeze whirled around me, making my hands cross tight against my chest. Then, a familiar hand settled on my shoulder, giving a light squeeze, followed by both hands resting gently on my upper arms. I leaned back into his chest, letting out a soft, contented sigh.

We had left Jericho over a week ago, making our way to Caesarea to board a ship back to Rome. We had barely brought anything with us, having lost most of our belongings when encountering Thana. But there was one important thing that we did bring.

I rested my right hand on the leather satchel strapped around my waist, fingers brushing its worn fabric, while my other hand reached out to grasp Evander's. His presence was as cathartic for me as I believed mine was for him.

A needed peace.

During the voyage we had spoken a lot over the things that had happened. While he understood that Thana was now gone and had been in charge, he mentioned how he felt uneasy about the pirate's lingering power.

"Evil never really dies," he said to me.

Honestly, I wasn't sure if the pirate threat would stop now that she was gone. Had she even started their gang in the first place or just used it as a way to seize control and power? In any case, they must have a multitude of forces if they were able to hinder our aid from our surprise first attack, as Evander suspected. Evander, still vexed by their gain of power, did not lighten his resolve to try and stop them as a threat. Whether that was the soldier in him or the man, I wasn't sure. It was probably both as they worked hand-in-hand—I admired him for it. We had hardly made it two days into our voyage before he composed another plan for their retribution, a light behind his eyes as he did it. Even if he didn't admit it, I knew he missed his military life. His tenacity and passion through each fight and drive as he formulated strategies was as clear as the sun. Evander may have enjoyed his rest while back home in Rome, but this was what he lived for.

I thought that staying away from my own time would be the end of life as I knew it. The life of war, plans, and espionage. Turns out that the first century has more things in common with my own than I originally thought.

Pulling my hand from Evander's, I placed it on my covered object, mind wandering on what was going to happen next.

"What do you plan to do with it?" Evander asked, his eyes studying my bag that held the secret. More secrets than he could ever know.

I traced the handle with my index finger, the roughness contrasting against my skin. Evander thought its only purpose was used to satisfy Thana's greed. Her leaving it behind had left him perplexed, leaving me to explain. The only account I could tell was that she saw the error of her ways, decided that she wanted nothing to do with it and left. That was probably untrue as she left no indication that she left the tablet willingly. It was just by chance that it had stayed behind with me. Or maybe it would never leave this time.

There were so many questions in connection with this tablet. Too many for the mind to comprehend. It was so complex, in function and its effects.

When I had first found it after coming to this time, I was unsure of what the right course of action was. Originally, I had wanted to go home. Yes, because it was my time, but for the main goal of revenge. But even when I found it, I knew that revenge shouldn't eat away at my heart and that something else should fill the void instead. Seeing Thana made me rethink my decision. But now that it was all said and done...

In my line of work, and in life, really, I always wanted options. Options meant there was always a way out. Always an escape. But life isn't about escaping it, it's about living it—the good, the bad, and the beautiful.

Nestling my head against Evander's chest, another thought crept into my mind. One the old Rivka would think, and I couldn't help but wonder if she was right.

"Sometimes," I began, weighing in on Evander's thoughts, "I wonder if all of this happened because I wasn't strong enough. Maybe I was too soft... too weak to do what needed to be done. And maybe, in the end, it was all for nothing."

He pulled me off his chest, his green eyes looking deeply into my own dark ones. "Rivka, love can never be wasted because it doesn't rely on reciprocity. Having a soft heart in a cruel world is not weakness, it's courage and strength. I'm so proud of you because of it."

A glisten covering my eyes, I wrapped my arms around his waist, pouring every ounce of love I had into the embrace. His words steadied me, giving me the confidence to face what came next. We were miles from the coast now, the port nowhere in sight. The water stretched dark and endless, its shadow revealing the sea's profound depth. This was as good a place as any for what needed to be done. Pulling the strap from my satchel over and off my head, I lifted the flap and pulled out what I was searching for.

The wrapping was simple. Burlap wrapped twice to hide any reflection the gold treasure might reflect. Multiple thin, leather straps fastened reliably around it, ensuring that the contents wouldn't slip from the shroud. Every detail of the wrapping was intentional.

My fingers found their way to each of the six knots I had tied, making sure they were secure and the only thing to release the bonds would be something sharp. Satisfied with my work, I let out a shaky breath.

I didn't want to escape life anymore.

Here is where I felt alive. It's where I found purpose.

My eyes held tight against one another; some strands of my hair whipped against my face. My lashes batted steadily, fingers gripping it in my right hand. Staring at its plain covering, I dangled it over the edge.

This was the right choice.

Steadily, the color in my fingers began to return as they unlatched their firm grip. My eyes followed as the object fell into the depths. A small white blush circled around it as the sea swallowed it, soon to be forever lost.

I muttered inaudibly to myself.

Evander raised an eyebrow. "Come again?"

"I just said 'funny.' I thought that doing that would give me a greater sense of loss."

"If not loss, what do you feel?"

I let out a breath. "Relief."

His eyes stared intently into my own. Rome wasn't built in a day, and neither are the relationships in life. Trials, tribulations, love, loss, and chaos come. And yet, even in the middle of my chaos, there was him.

Evander tucked the strands that were still flying around my face behind my ear, his hand lingering as his palm cupped my face. Limber, my hands wrapped around his waist again, my head laying against his chest. Closing my eyes, I took him in, cinnamon and frankincense filling the air. His heart beat steadily against my ear. It was like a slow melody playing. This was our song—our hearts intertwined, beating as one.

EPILOGUE

The Mediterranean Sea, 15th Century

The blistering sun beat wildly against the two men's tan skin. Three weeks they had been out at sea, trying to bring in enough fish to feed not only their families, but their village as well. Too long had the people in their town suffered under the circumstances of the war their leaders had put them through. As with all wars, poverty came for the common people.

Poverty and death.

Like many in the country who were not called to serve, these men had to make their own way to provide for those around them. Fish was one of the few ways to do that. So here the two men rocked, only five creatures in a barrel, nets cast in the water.

Santiago, the younger of the two, lay down in the small, free corner of their tiny boat, straw hat covering his face and thick, black hair. Hector could hear his snores over the water and was positive that it was scaring the fish away. Grunting, he twisted the net tighter between his hands and fingers, wanting to make sure he felt even the smallest tug.

As the minutes passed, Hector's eyes bat slowly, sleep trying to take him as her victim as well. He wrestled with his will for what seemed like hours before he gave in, letting his opponent win.

But the moment he willfully rested his eyes, it happened.

His hands were yanked in front of him so hard that it almost pulled him overboard. Startled, and now wide awake, he instinctively pulled back against it.

"Santiago!" the balding man called out, struggling as he pulled his net from the sea.

Alarmed, his companion sat up immediately, still dazed. His eyes slowly focused on Hector's shining head before realizing what was going on. He grabbed the net and the two of them heaved it up; the wet, rough rope grating against their calloused hands. Minutes later, the net was in the boat, fish flopping all around. The men grinned, slapping each other on the back at their success.

They had hit the mother lode.

But, between the silver scales wiggling around, something else caught Hector's attention. Bending over, he shoved the fish aside, eyes landing on the true prize.

In the mix of dozens of fish, a golden treasure stared back at him. A gasp escaped Hector's lips, pulling Santiago's attention to the unusual object.

"*Santa Maria,*" he gestured across his chest and forehead, making the sign of the cross.

Hector's fingers grasped the precious metal, wiping the remains of the water off of it.

"How is there not a single barnacle on it, huh?" Santiago asked, looking over his companion's shoulder.

"It must have not been dropped there long ago. Maybe it was supposed to be sent as aid for the war?" he guessed. "Look! There… there seems to be some markings on it."

"What's it say, *amigo*? What's it say!" Santiago shook his shoulders in anticipation.

Hector hardly noticed, still in awe of his newfound treasure. "I don't know," he rubbed the golden thing, trying to remove the few layers of hardened dirt that were stuffed in the creases.

"Use a blade," Santiago suggested, removing his small dagger from its sheath in his belt.

Hector waved it away. "I do not want to damage it."

Trying with his fingernails, he thought that might do the trick, but after several minutes with no success Santiago pried it from his hands. Carefully, he used his knife and was able to remove most of it. Santiago, illiterate, returned it back to Hector, hoping he would shed some light.

Hector shook his head. "It is not a language that I understand. It looks... very old. Maybe it's just a design."

"But its condition—the material looks wonderful!"

The older man shrugged, not sure what more there was to say on the matter. He placed it on his lap, both staring at the oddity some more. "We must take this to Padre Alejandro. He will know what to do with it," Hector grabbed his handkerchief from his neck, sweat stains pressed into the brown fabric, and wrapped his treasure carefully.

Santiago licked the corners of his mouth. "Yes, of course, of course. The Padre will know what's best."

But as he said one thing with his mouth, the lust in his eyes said another. Hector watched him as his black eyes stared deep on the covered object, a corner of the wrapped golden tablet glistening in the dazzling sun.

More by Sara Gherasim

THE HOLY RELICS SERIES

The Abditory

The Abyss Between

Servina, The Friendly Dog